The Other Woman

HILDRED BILLINGS

BARACHOU
PRESS

BARACHOU PRESS

The Other Woman

Copyright: Hildred Billings
Published: 20th June, 2021
Publisher: Barachou Press

This is a work of fiction. Any and all similarities to any characters, settings, or situations are purely coincidental.

Contents

CHAPTER 1

Do you know how I got here?

It wasn't by pussy-footing around. Nor did I ever stand for the slanderous lies that often spread about me. We're talking back in college when the queen dingus of my sorority decided that *I* had stolen her boyfriend and ostracized me for the rest of my senior year. Which is preposterous. How could I, a dyed-in-the-wool lesbian, steal some dumbass's boyfriend?

Utterly preposterous. Even if I wanted her ugly boyfriend, I would have made a much grander show of it.

Because that's how I operate. Nothing about me is understated or discreet. From my days of running the junior pageant circuits to clawing my way up through internships I, Evelyn Sharpe, have never once held back when I've decided I want something.

For fuck's sake, my birth name isn't *Sharpe*. I changed it when I graduated college. Dragged my ass down to the city hall to file the name change with determination burning in my eyes. Had nothing to do with a so-called "faulty" relationship with my parents, and everything to do with my bland birth name. Who would you rather hire? An everyday woman with the last name that's like "Smith" (but not) or Evelyn Sharpe, someone whose name sounds like it's as likely to stab you in the eye as my six-inch heels?

Don't get me wrong. I'm not a supporter of weaponized feminism, as I see it called on social media. I'm quite honest about my reasons for the hobbling heels, the plunging necklines, the just-too-short pencil skirts, and weekly blowouts that accompany my perfume of the season. I know what people, especially men, see when they walk into my office.

They see a woman named Evelyn Sharpe. End story.

Oh, don't give me that look. Think of me what you will, but keep it to yourself. I've dealt with judgments like yours since I was old enough to realize that I would always be at some stupid disadvantage because of the crack between my legs. Figuring out I was gay in high school? God. He could've killed me right there in the lunchroom when I finally realized that the reason I always stared at Jenny Papadopoulos wasn't because I wanted to *be* her, but because I wanted to be *inside of her.*

Isn't it stupid? I can't help that I was born a lesbian, two checkboxes that advertise *knock this chick down a peg!* Uppity woman. Man-hating dyke. Depending on what people first see when they decide to hate me, I've heard it all. You can't shock me. Not then. Not now.

I can help a few things, though. Besides changing my name, I was discerning about my college and major. I only took on part-time jobs that served my résumé the best and got me interviews with the biggest industries that rented office space in my region. I may not have chosen where I was born and where I grew up, but I used what privilege I had to get the hell out of Dodge and follow my fate.

This is how I got cocky. After so much academic and professional success, I thought that would translate to my love life.

Not so fast!

You're going to hear me admit something that I very rarely tell anyone. Not sure why I'm telling you. Is it because you're a stranger? Some voyeur giggling at my misdeeds and along for the damned ride?

It doesn't matter. Because the one thing I absolutely *fail* at is picking decent romantic partners.

Do you see my word choice there? Decent. Not *good.* Not *great.* Not *soulmate* level of excellent choices. Just decent!

This is my curse. This is why I suffer now.

Because, if you haven't heard, I've recently suffered a fantastically messy breakup that I, the queen of planning ahead and checking every fucking detail down to the fraction of a percent and shade of color, saw coming.

Sera. My Sera. The gorgeous, sensual, vixen of a woman who came into my life and seduced me in only a week. The one I've been with for seven years and lived with for five. The one who tacitly agreed to marry me in the foreseeable future. We were going to move to New York City after my transfer went through. She would be my wild, genius artist and I would be the office manager who brought in the insurance and 401k.

My Sera. The one I had sex with at least twice a week for years. Sometimes less, often more. The one who shared my mutual desire for some of the shadier sides of sex. If I suggested exhibitionism, she was the one looking up local sex clubs that hosted orgy nights at least once a month. Whips and chains? She signed us up for an online BDSM safety class! The one time I expressed a desire to "have sex on the beach" she booked us a trip to Hawaii for our annual vacation out of the Lower 48. We absolutely did have sex on the beach, and it was amazing. I didn't know you could come that hard while outside!

That Sera. My heart and soul. My other half. The reason I looked forward to going home.

That. Bitch. *Cheated on me!*

Look at me! It's been three months since we broke up over it, and I'm still fucking mad. Mad like the Dickens. Mad like I'm going to flip some goddamn tables and punch out my high-rise office window!

Most of all, I rage at myself.

How could I be so stupid? So blind? Tell me, how does a woman who is so meticulous about her public-facing life screw up something as simple as *don't live with trash?* Was I really so in love? I don't remember falling in love as "normal" people do. Not like in the movies, where everything is hearts, roses, and *I think she loves me.* My sex and romantic life have always been as practical as my professional life. I met someone who I was compatible with, although I didn't think Sera was my type when we first exchanged hellos at a mutual friend's party. We moved in when it made financial sense to do so. We talked at length about what we saw for our future – New York City, friends, retirement. Sure, we had spontaneity! I never knew where we would travel for fun or what we should do when we got there. That was always more Sera's wheelhouse. She was the explorer. The wanderer!

I suppose I loved her. Damnit.

Except what pisses me off the most is the disrespect. I gave that woman seven years of my life. Some of the best years of my life! I'm old enough to have worked my way up to account manager at a national corporate insurance company. Fucking exciting, isn't it! Yet it's what I do. It's what I'm good at. I know how to wiggle into my business attire and convince men old enough to be my father that they should buy our insurance for their Fortune 500s. Never had to sleep with anyone to do it, either, but God knows there have been offers!

I make good money. I'll be a millionaire in another ten years if I'm not stupid with my funds. My calendar is balanced to the point that I can take off with only a week's notice. Raymond, my personal assistant, knows more about my schedule than I do, anyway. The man knows what it means to create meticulous spreadsheets he uploads to our private cloud. Sera used to have access to it. That's how she hid her affairs from me for so long.

I don't know how many women there were, exactly. It's not like we live in a big hub for Sapphic dating. Yet Sera always had a way with the ladies. She's charismatic and romantic to a fault. She's got that whole effortless butch thing going. Motorbikes, denim jackets, cool attitude... damnit, she had it all, and she knew how to use it, too. People used to look at us having dinner together, me in my secondhand Chanel and Sera in her torn jeans, and think we were mismatched sisters. What they didn't know was that I was rather attracted to that "wild" side of her that didn't take things too seriously while still being a responsible adult. If Sera said she would take care of something, she did it without complaining. She was a damn fine cook, too. Nobody would look at that woman and think *housewife material* but she once confided to me that she wouldn't mind being the house minder while I was out earning bread.

All the easier to cheat on me, the lying bitch!

Sure, I don't know how many women there were, but I know who the last one was.

Suspicions had long irked me leading up to our breakup. At first, I told myself I was simply paranoid. Sera had always been flirtatious with other women – including the waitresses, drivers, and secretaries we encountered daily – but it never threatened my image of our relationship. Didn't I like how outgoing she was? That she wasn't afraid to be herself after moving in with me?

Yet about one year ago, I began to suspect... something. She was often out to lunch. Would forget when she was meeting me at work so we could go out to dinner, or spaced out important dates. On the last birthday I celebrated with her around, the woman who was usually so thoughtful and planned so much completely phoned it in, as if she had forgotten to the last minute. Her eyes were always glued to her phone. When I asked what was so funny, she'd say it was Twitter memes. Except I knew those chuckles. That was the same laughter whenever she thought *I* was funny.

She changed the password to her phone. Sometimes I used her phone when mine was in another room or the battery was dead, but one day, I couldn't get in, and Sera refused to tell me the new password.

Perhaps I was paranoid, but it was justified in the end, wasn't it? That's why I'll never feel bad about hiring a private investigator to follow Sera around for a week. Within two days, I received photos of my *darling* girlfriend canoodling with a redhead she had met a month before. By Friday, there were compromising reports that the two had gone out for a drive and *parked* in an isolated place.

Parked.

Parked! Like teenagers!

I'll never forget what it felt like looking at the pictures of Sera on top of some other woman in the back of our car. Was it shock? Sadness? No. Just utter betrayal.

I bought that car. It was all my money. Some things should be *sacred*.

While that was plenty enough evidence to break up with her, I held on to it for another week, biding my time and making my plans. As soon as I broke up with Sera, I'd want her out of *my* condo. We may not have been legally married, but I wanted my ducks in a row as if I were preparing for divorce. Once I decided there was no coming back from her infidelity, I was merciless. I cut her off from every bank account but whatever was in her name only. I packed up a few of her things when she was out with that tart so she wouldn't waste my time when I dumped her. I had my lawyer look things over so I wouldn't be surprised. One never knows when a vindictive ex will get petty and spiteful.

Like me!

I never anticipated catching her in the act in our own home, though. The whole time, I foolishly assumed that she was smart enough to keep her affairs away from the condo. What kind of idiot brings the other woman home? To *our* bed?

Sera. That's who!

I came home early the day I planned to tell Sera that I knew about the other women and that it was over. I wanted to shower and change my clothes, after all. Feel refreshed for the big moment. Maybe wear some lingerie so she *knew* what she had given up the moment her mouth and hands ended up on some other woman.

Do you know what I found, though? Can you imagine what I discovered when I entered my home that fine Friday and saw the trail of clothes leading down the hallway into *our* bedroom?

Sera must have heard me come home, though, because by the time I burst into the bedroom, she had thrown a blanket over her sidepiece and attempted to hide her in the closet! Right out of a fucking sitcom!

I will say, though, it saved me a lot of explanations later. With that scene right before my eyes, nobody would ever say I was in the wrong for dumping her and telling her to get the *fuck* out of my house right there!

Things may have been crazier than that, though. My shoe may have ended up on the back of Sera's head when she turned around to latch the closet door.

I've calmed down since then, though. I swear.

Four months. That was four months ago, friend. I've been to therapy. Yoga classes. Online guided meditations. I took a short sabbatical from work to spend a week in the Caribbean and to completely de-Sera *my* condo. Pitifully, she attempted to get back with me. You should have seen the bouquets that showed up at my door! Never mind her getting a brand-new phone number because she knew I blocked the old one. This was the same woman who stood outside my place of work to try to "apologize." I never bothered to hear her out. Why the hell would I? She cheated. It's over. I can put up with certain shit in a relationship, but we all have our boundaries. Our breaking points! *That one was mine!*

No one lays a violent hand on me. No one steals from me. No one fucking *cheats on me* and thinks our relationship is surviving that. I don't have time for infidelity. Threesomes are one thing. You want to participate in a fucking orgy, Sera? Let's talk it over! Hell, *hell,* I might be swayed to try an open relationship if we're on the same page and discuss it at length. But I will never, ever condone cheating. I'd rather be single, thank you!

No. No. I'm fine. I simply get worked up when I have to tell someone what's happened in my life recently.

I'm ready, though. To get back on the horse. To date! I've been on a couple dates. I'm not counting the drunken rebound I indulged in the Caribbean. For fuck's sake, I barely remember it. Since coming back from my sabbatical, though, I've been on the dating apps and saw what's out there. A couple cute girls have been fun at dinner, and one wasn't so bad in bed, but there was no *spark* there. Unfortunately, I think it's me. I can't get back to dating or moving forward with my personal life until I've perfectly extracted my revenge on the woman who stole seen of my best fucking years.

Hey. When I say *fucking* years, you know what I mean. To think, I wasted all those orgasms on someone who didn't truly appreciate them.

Bastard.

I have a plan, though. A little thing that, with some luck, I'll embrace. Once it's over, that's it. I'm officially moving on from Sera and the redheaded tart who happened to be in the wrong place at the *right* time.

Come with me. I have a meeting to attend down the hall. You'll want to see this.

CHAPTER 2

Evelyn

Today, I'm meeting with Oscar Birch, the representative of Aspen Plastics. The only reason I know so much about the regional plastic conglomerate is because I have to – if I want to convince Birch to buy corporate insurance from *my* company, then I'll wow him with my knowledge of Aspen's history, all the way down to the founder's mission to bring plastic to...

Yes, I sound like a capitalistic shill. Welcome to *my* industry.

I had to fight my coworker for this account. You see, I have a "friendly" rivalry with Quintin. Ideally, any account we don't score for ourselves out in the wild goes to whoever has the lighter load. Accounts equal money. It also equals cover letter space, so you can see why Quintin and I always want to make sure we're one step ahead of the other. We also care about the *quality* of our accounts, because if our company ever decides to downsize or the owners go their separate ways and take one of us with them... duh, we want to be the person who survives!

That only happens if you can vouch for your necessity for the company's future.

Aspen Plastics isn't a *big* account. Sure, it will bring in a few million every billing period, but I have way bigger accounts. The kind that put billions into advertising, bringing you quirky, funny mascots every American recognizes to some degree. When they buy insurance, they don't fuck around. For every billion that goes into advertising, at least two go into covering their asses.

No, the reason I had to take Quintin out to lunch a week ago and butter him up for the kill was because I technically have two more accounts than he does right now. The overall value of our accounts is about the same, but as I said earlier, it doesn't look good if one of us lags behind the other. When Aspen Plastics announced they were shopping around, we naturally jumped at it, but the understanding was that Quintin would do the courting and signing.

Oh, I have my reasons, though. I need to be at this meeting. Even if the account eventually goes to my rival, at least I'll have this moment.

At least I'll have this upcoming weekend to enact my master plan.

There's my boss right now. Peter Gray holds multiple titles, including Head of Accounts, which means Quintin and I report to him. Technically, Peter has accounts that he's held on to as he moved up the ranks because he has fantastic relationships with those companies, but the general idea is that he assigns the accounts and oversees our performance.

You know, when he doesn't do all the other shit he's supposed to do around here.

"They're here." Peter moves out of the way so I can approach the double doors to our main conference room. He doesn't look at me, probably because he's a few inches taller – easily, one of the tallest men I've ever met – and at any moment he might be staring down my cleavage. It stopped bothering me a long time ago, but the man is so devoted to his wife that he had the gall to tell me that Sera was probably bad news. He "had a feeling," which he expressed to me when we were half-drunk at the last Christmas Party.

I mean, he wasn't wrong...

"Everything ready to go?" Peter's phone is soon in his front pocket. "I'm counting on you, Sharpe. By me, I mean *my* boss who is breathing down my neck about expanding our repertoire."

"A plastics company is exactly what we need," I say with my most dashing smile. Peter allows a slight nod. Not because he approves of my tactics, but because they get results. That includes my outfits, the hair, and the seductive smiles that have won us more accounts over the years than

Quintin can ever claim. I keep telling him to grow a pair of tits, but it's not hitting him. "Let's do this."

Peter opens the doors for me. "Your confidence is infectious, as usual." We step inside. "One of these days, you'll tell me your secrets."

"You simply have to know what you want, Pete." What I don't tell him is that what I *want* isn't this account. Oh, no. What I want has nothing to do with Aspen Plastics or Oscar Birch, who is already sitting on one side of the conference table, overlooking printouts my assistant Raymond has graciously brought him.

What I want? *What I want?*

I want the cosmos to know that I'm watching it. I know its game. It can't pull the wool over my eyes and make me think that my shitty ex-girlfriend can cheat on me without consequences.

Oh, don't worry. I'm not about to do anything illegal. As my mother once said about her first husband, *"No dirtbag is worth going to jail over, Evie."* Nor do I plan on sabotaging this account. It so happens that Oscar Birch has brought a *very* interesting person with him. Someone I instantly lock eyes with as soon as I enter, my Emmy-winning smile knocking them off balance in their swivel chair.

Allow me to paint a picture.

A woman as fair as the celebrated Hollywood actresses of old graces the world with a heart-shaped face and two doe-like hazel eyes that instantly look down at a tablet she's propped up on the table. Her clothing isn't anything to write home about, but she's at least someone who knows how to dress for her body type. These pear-shaped girls, God bless them, always try their best – but it takes a woman who has expert fashion tastes or at least knows someone who does to get it right in the corporate office setting. The sleeveless cowlick sweater accents her chest without emphasizing its size. Dare I say it? She's paired it well with a full brown skirt that cuts off at her knees. I can't see any farther without crawling beneath the table, though. I don't need to.

Why do I care so much about the assistant Oscar Birch has brought with him today? During any other meeting, the PAs and secretaries blend into the background. They take notes. Return calls. Briefly remind their employers of this figure and that request from *their* bosses. The best assistants, be they male or female, know how important it is to remain meek and quiet while business is conducted. As long as their jobs aren't threatened by a potentially bad deal, they don't give a shit if things go south in these meetings. Much like Raymond's job is to ensure the folders are prepared and we all have beverages at our disposal. The company needs to succeed so they can keep their jobs, but how we go about it doesn't concern them.

Normally, I don't give a shit who comes with the entourage as long as they mind their manners and do their jobs. I might note a fashionable blouse or interesting hair color, but I rarely remember these people after the meeting is over and I'm making phone calls.

Today? All I see is her.

I knew she was coming. That's why I'm here, and Quintin isn't. This woman, with her freckles and white sweater, doesn't look at me twice as she sets up the Bluetooth keyboard for her tablet, but she's the reason I put on my most eye-catching office wear and acquired my weekly blowout one day early.

She must see me. She must leave this meeting thinking of nobody but *me*.

God knows I've spent many nights lying in my bed, remembering that head of red bobbing up and down in the backseat of *my* car. The only reason I haven't traded that hunk of junk in is because I desired the daily reminder of what I wanted to do.

There she is. Keira Lawson. According to my detective, that's her name, anyway.

"Good morning, everyone. Mr. Birch." I stand behind my chair, careful to not let my folder cover the entirety of my cleavage. My body is always slightly facing the left, where Keira continues to ignore me in favor of her notetaking. Oh, but I know she's noticed me. We locked eyes when I entered. She doesn't recognize me. I would have seen a sign on that fair face of hers.

But I? I recognize her. I'll never forget that frizzy red hair with the full bangs on the right side of her face and the sharp, winter-toned bows she ties around the bulk of its length.

Was that what Sera found so appealing? You don't see many redheads in this corner of the map. Especially redheads who sport the freckles, the greenish eyes, and the kind of body type that Sera once called "sculpted from God," knowing full well that *I* am not pear-shaped. Sera loved thighs, though. She always said that what I lacked in ass and thigh was more than made up for in my bust, and I believed her.

I loathe the image of my lean ex humping away between these thighs sitting at my conference table, but I cling to it, because soon...

Soon, I will be the one smothering Oscar Birch's personal assistant with my own body. The other woman who contributed to the worst breakup of my life?

She will be mine. Even if only for a night.

CHAPTER 3

T his morning has been a disaster. A complete and utter failure on my incompetent part.

I can't blame it on staying up too late once again, losing myself in the video games that have consoled me for most of my life. For once, I set a timer to go off right at ten so I wouldn't get in bed any later than eleven. I had to be up at six for this morning's meeting at Symmetry Insurance, and boy was I *up* at six.

Showered. Hair brushed. Dressed in the outfit I picked out the night before.

No, this whole morning is a disaster because Mr. Birch has, once again, put me in a crazy compromising position.

I did everything right. I picked up his coffee the way he likes it from his favorite corner café, which I had to go ten minutes out of the way to get before presenting it to him in our office. As soon as we were in the back of the company car, however, he announced that he had found yet another "lovely young man" looking for a hardworking wife.

Mr. Birch is a decent man. A good boss. He has never asked more of me than is reasonable, which is a feat when you consider the man has such seniority in Aspen Plastics that he often forgets how important his job is. When he's not scampering off to play golf with most of his industry buddies, he's watching TV in his office or taking private calls while I work at my desk. He doesn't care what I wear as long as it's professional. Not once has he leered at me, made an untoward comment, or said anything ill about his wife. This is the same man who tells me exactly what to buy her for her birthday or their anniversary if he can't go get it for himself. Other assistants are usually tasked with picking something out. Something "they think a woman would like."

Where Mr. Birch fails as someone in my life is his meddlesome nature. It starts innocently enough. He asks you about your family. Are you married? Do you have any kids? Stuff that would be illegal to ask in an interview, but is free game once you have a nameplate on your desk. Woe be me, I was single and childless. At thirty, no less. In Mr. Birch's world, this is one of the highest crimes a woman can commit. Especially "women as nice as you, Keira."

Honestly, I think he hired me because of my name. It's Gaelic, much like most of my genes, if you can't tell by looking at me. Mr. Birch comes from an old Irish family that arrived in America before, as he always says with a chuckle, "it was cool." He's lived in that insular world for so long that he's still of the outdated mindset that every woman must be married to a nice boy by the age of thirty, or she won't have enough time to fulfill her destiny as a homemaker.

Yeah, it's sexist! But you can forget it during a normal workday. It's when he races up to you at lunch and insists you come with him that you find out he's set you up on a blind date with his wife's best friend's nephew, who happens to be named *Kieran*.

I'm sure this is breaking some law, but I can't bring myself to report him or quit. The pay is too good, and the workload too reasonable. Not to mention the benefits. When I needed some time off three months ago, it was approved without a second glance. Hell, I don't think Mr. Birch realized I was missing until my substitute showed up from the temp agency.

So I put up with it. For now. Like when we were in the car on the way to Symmetry Insurance and Mr. Birch insisted that I hear him out about a family friend's grandson who was coming to America for grad school. Did I want to meet Sean now or later? The boy was going to be busy soon, don't I know!

Sometimes... I humor him. Because a part of me hates myself so much that I'm still in the closet and like to fool the important people in my life that I'm straight.

I don't know what's wrong with me. Maybe it's because I don't have any family left. I'm always too busy trying to secure my future to have any real friends who are there for me. Never have I let my luck wash through my fingers. I'm grateful for everything I call mine and have achieved in my life. Most of it was completely on my own. My life may not be glamorous, and I'm never gonna have more than a few dollars to my name, but I'm doing okay. I'm grateful, I swear!

But I still have those voices in my head, you know. They tell me that I lost everything because I like women. Therefore, to be happy in any relationship means I'm two seconds away from ruining my life.

The only reason I'm sitting up straight in this conference room chair is because I powered through an energy drink while in the car. Mr. Birch is only now finishing the coffee I went out of my way to procure. A man named Raymond has offered us more caffeine or water to get us through this meeting, but I'm so focused on setting up my notetaking that I accidentally grunt at him like he's some commoner and I'm the Princess of Administrative Tasks.

I suck in my breath when the door opens. A nervous habit I picked up as a child.

"Good morning, everyone. Mr. Birch."

My movements slow as I attach my tablet to its Bluetooth keyboard. An action I've done half a million times at this point in my career, but something about that voice I now hear has completely distracted me from my task.

Of course it's a woman who has walked through the door. Right there in my date book is the name *Evelyn Sharpe - SYMMETRY INSURANCE.* She's the accounts person Mr. Birch will be discussing potential business with today, and I am to not let a single word go unrecorded while they hash out details and future deals. The usual. Completely mundane. The whole reason I put on my résumé that I have a certificate in transcription and can type 140wpm if I'm in the zone. All true, of course.

But I'm not used to a woman stealing my breath away as much as Ms. Sharpe has…

It must be her. Who else would confidently walk into this room at the appointed time? Certainly not Raymond, who stands in the corner with his hands clasped before his stomach. Apparently, Symmetry does not transcribe their own meetings. Not like Aspen Plastics expects of Mr. Birch, who is so old school that he remains amazed that I don't have to do everything on a portable typewriter.

Ms. Sharpe, though…

I'm used to powerful women who command their corners of the world. Even when I first started my job a few years ago, they were everywhere – especially if you knew where to look. Don't ask me if the number of women in positions of power has gone up in the years since. I'm too busy staring at the tablet and my flying fingers when I'm not turning down another blind date with one of Mr. Birch's friend's cousin's sons. I couldn't tell you what style these women usually have these days. How can I, when I spend more time in front of my mirror than theirs? Besides, the femme office types aren't really *my* type. Purely from an aesthetic perspective, I don't usually go for the ball-busting office queen who wants to raise in the ranks faster than her nails dry.

Yet here I am. Staring at this representative of all womanhood.

Is it wrong if I'm instantly drawn to her chest, of all places? I can't help it. Ms. Sharpe is wearing a finely-fitted blouse as red as the blush now touching my cheeks. Can you honestly tell me that you're not staring at her cleavage, too? First, you're beguiled by the sinfully red hue that contrasts with her dark hair and the rigid countenance she carries herself with. Then you realize that's a simple teardrop necklace that hangs from her throat.

The slight twinkle of the stone reminds you that there are breasts in that blouse, and you're not leering at Ms. Sharpe like she's a hot piece of meat on display in the shop.

I'm salivating. A little.

"I'm Evelyn Sharpe." She extends her hand, tipped in bright red nails, at Mr. Birch. He stands, checking the buttons on his jacket before exchanging a handshake. From the flinch on his face, he did not anticipate Ms. Sharpe to have such a firm handshake. "It's a pleasure to meet you, Mr. Birch. And this is?"

She's looking right at me – and I'm looking right back at her.

My mouth is slightly agape.

It's those eyes! You know, I never notice the color of someone's eyes. Why would I, when they're so far away and my vision isn't exactly known for being the best around? Yet I can't help but see that fine glow in Ms. Sharpe's dark brown eyes. No, don't you see? They're not the kind of *dark* that sucks in all the light from the room. They're not black holes! Instead, don't you think they look like two tiger's eyes ready to pounce and devour the world.

She's looking right at me! What do I do?

"I, uh…"

"This is my assistant, Ms. Keira Lawson." That's it. That's my introduction. No handshakes. Nothing more than a polite nod and a little smile before Mr. Birch and Ms. Sharpe sit back down again. "It's a pleasure to finally put a face to the voice on the phone, Evelyn." That's my boss for you. Every woman, except those technically about him at work, is referred to by their first names. He thinks it makes him more *approachable*. "I'm looking forward to what you've put together for my company."

Shit! I was supposed to type all of this!

"Are you all right?" Ms. Sharpe asks me. To my horror, my fingers are on my temple and my eyes glaze over as they attempt to focus on the tablet screen. A cursor flashes. Before Mr. Birch can say anything, my fingers fly over the keys. It takes a few seconds for me to realize that nothing is appearing on the screen because the Bluetooth isn't properly set up.

What the hell is wrong with me!

"I'm fine. Allergies have my brain fuzzy, Ms. Sharpe. That's all." I refuse to look her in the eye – my own might wander back to her cleavage. "My medicine will kick in at any moment. Please, continue the meeting."

"Keira is one of the best assistants in town," Mr. Birch oh-so-helpfully interrupts. "I trust that she has everything under control."

"Of course. Ah, here's Peter right now."

Another man enters. Thankfully, his additional presence distracts me from Ms. Sharpe's appearance and back on my own work. As soon as I put on my reading glasses I can adjust my vision so she's not in my purview – but I still hear her voice, and I smell her misty perfume.

Damnit.

Auto-pilot engaged. Note the important words being said by all parties and fill in as logic dictates. This is mostly in my shorthand, anyway. If Mr. Birch has a problem with my final product, he's not afraid to jog my memory with promises to give me overtime. Which I should take, come to think of it. I couldn't only use the extra money. I could also use the extra distraction from my personal life.

All I can figure is that Ms. Sharpe is pinging my radar for the most insidious reasons. The same reasons that make me consider going out with Mr. Birch's wife's nephew or whoever.

You see… I shouldn't be telling you this, but I've recently been through a pretty bad breakup and could use the rebound, I guess.

Man, it isn't like me to share these kinds of details with a stranger, but concentrating on my notetaking isn't distracting me enough. I've gotta get it off my chest.

A few months ago, I was seeing this girl. Well, a woman, of course, but I'm still calling ladies my own age "girl" like this is high school and we're having a wholesome slumber party. Though, if you looked at my ex, you might not be inclined to call her "girl." It's not a knock against her at all. If you haven't guessed by now, I usually have a type and, well, Sera was it.

Cool. Effortlessly *suave.* We met at a bar where I had gone to blow off some steam at the end of a long week. One of the loneliest dives in the city which isn't exclusively "gay," but the only guys who wander in there are either lost or hanging out with one of their female friends. Sera was there with one of her guy friends. Playing pool in the back room while I sat at the bar having a beer and scrolling through my phone. I never go – er, went – to that place in the hopes of some cute boyish girl picking me up and making me hers, but there she was, catching my eye through the opened door that separated the front of the bar from the billiards room.

When her friend left, she approached me, asking if I wanted to play a round with her. She must have known that I have never in my life played pool. I didn't know the rules! But Sera was more than eager to correct my stance and put her hands on my waist as I stumbled my way through a full game. She creamed me, of course.

Er, maybe I shouldn't put it that way. Because we ended up making out in the bathroom. Then doing more. In the bathroom.

Sigh. I should have known it would be a messy relationship, but I'm always so hungry for female validation that the mere thought of some *hottie* with a belt buckle and a denim jacket offering to teach me how to play pool is enough to make me spread my legs in the ladies' room!

I was stupider for thinking that getting her number was some sort of win. Her becoming my girlfriend, fooling around with me at home whenever I got off work early, taking me out of town for dinner and hotel rooms... it was a flight of fancy I've rarely experienced before. When Sera looks at you like *that,* you don't think twice. You get in her car, you park in the middle of nowhere, and you have sex in the backseat. Multiple times.

On multiple occasions.

It was never meant to be. I should have known that from the beginning, and it's why I'm still kicking myself in the ass now. Whirlwind romances don't happen to me. In-real-life romance novels don't spontaneously manifest for Keira Lawson, one of the lamest lesbians to ever huff moth balls in the metaphorical closet. If someone is putting on the moves and sneaking me around under the guise of *romance,* she probably has a fucking girlfriend she lives with and won't tell me about!

Okay. Phew. Sorry about that. Except I'm not sorry if you suddenly have a sour opinion about me now. I didn't know. I swear it. As much as I loathe cheaters, I'm more in love with someone crashing into my life and promising me the moon and the stars if I move my hips *just* the right way. That's why I overlooked the obvious, like why she was always texting someone her whereabouts, why I could never go over to her place, and why she could never go out on the weekends. I made a million excuses in my head and bought hook, line and sinker every lie she told me. Because I wanted it to be real. Sera had quickly become the love of my life, and for three months, she completely consumed my thoughts – and my soul.

Then the most horrendous thing happened. The most embarrassing moment that will haunt me 'til this day. I don't want to talk about it now. I've got to concentrate on my work, or Mr. Birch will bother me for the whole afternoon.

"I will certainly forward this information to my superiors at Aspen Plastics," Mr. Birch diplomatically says toward the end of the meeting. It's the first time I look up from my typing in well over fifteen minutes. These meetings? They never last very long, but let me tell you, it's not easy to purposely avoid a woman in the same meeting. Especially if the reason you're avoiding her gaze is because she makes you tingle in ways your ex used to, and you have no idea what to do with that information.

It's the need for a rebound, isn't it? Four months since Sera humiliated me and I had to grow a spine hard enough to dump her pathetic ass. Right now, every woman is starting to look good enough to eat.

Don't get me wrong. You've seen Ms. Sharpe. She's as hot as the summer and probably as likely to burn me.

"Ms. Lawson, was it?" Evelyn taps a binder against the table. Mr. Birch has said his goodbyes to her and is now speaking to her superior, Peter. "That's some diligent typing there. You know, I see quite a few assistants come through this office. I don't think I've ever seen one as talented as you, though. Not even Raymond is as astute as you in a meeting."

On one hand, I love that she's paying attention to me. I mean, look at her. Someone as important as her doesn't need to focus on *me* for more than a minute of her day. Come to think of it, does anyone go out of their way to talk to me during one of Mr. Birch's meetings? Sometimes. Usually, they're middle-aged and male. You get used to it working this gig for more than a year.

On the other... why? Why is Ms. Sharpe approaching me on the other side of the table while I pack up my tablet and keyboard? There I go. Always assuming people have ulterior motives. Can you blame me, though?

"I'm doing my job, Ms. Sharpe." I zip up my tablet's case and place it in my bag. Her eyes are always on me, analyzing every movement with the slightest hint of curiosity. "Mr. Birch likes it when the notes are neat and ready to read by the beginning of the next day, so I attempt to provide."

"As per your job description, of course."

"Why?" I ask. "Are you looking to hire a new assistant?"

Luckily for me, she picks up on my trite joke. "No," Ms. Sharpe says with a chuckle. "Raymond may not come off as good as you, but he has his uses. Guess you could say my interest is always piqued by the women who come through those doors. Don't know if you've noticed, but I work in a sausage factory." Her shoulder motions toward Mr. Birch and Mr. Peter Gray. Not so far away is Raymond, who offers them both fresh coffee from the other room. Mr. Birch declines. Thank God, too. He's had enough caffeine for the day.

"My office doesn't look much different," I confide.

"Isn't that how it goes now?" Only now have I noticed that Ms. Sharpe's lips are a fine red as well. She doesn't plump them up like other women do. Besides, I was so distracted by those worldly eyes that I can't *think* about her lips. Do you know what lips are for? Kissing.

Kissing, and getting into trouble with women who are already taken.

"Don't let it get you down." Oh, she's still talking to me? No, I don't have a problem with this. After all, Ms. Sharpe will go down as a heart-fluttering highlight of my day. But as much as I'd love to fantasize about her, I still feel shitty about my breakup. It may have been four months ago, but it's still too fresh. The shit I endured that last day of my relationship...

No amount of looking at Ms. Sharpe's cleavage or gazing into her eyes is going to help me overcome something I should talk about with a therapist.

"Tell you what." Much to my amazement, Ms. Sharpe grabs one of her cards from a holder on the side of the room and hands it to me. *Evelyn Sharpe – Accounts Manager* is emblazoned in gold on a black background. The cardstock is thick and pricey. Indeed, this a woman who knows her worth. "That's my personal phone number on the back of this card. Why don't we go out and get drinks tomorrow?"

"Tomorrow?"

"Yes. Friday. Unless you're busy?"

"N... no." I shake my head. "I simply don't understand the sudden invitation, Ms. Sharpe."

"Oh, *please.* Call me Evelyn. Or Evie. People I like call me Evie. So far, I like you."

Can I help but cock my head? Because I must be hallucinating this. Never before has one of Mr. Birch's female business associates come out and asked me to drinks. Not that I get a romantic vibe from this enigmatic woman. Still, how often does something like this happen?

"So very kind of you." I gingerly place the black business card into my bag, snug between the tablet and its keyboard. "I don't know what to say."

"Say yes, Ms. Lawson."

I absentmindedly tuck some of my escaping hair behind my ear. When I look back up at Evelyn, she's still tracking my movements. Self-conscious thoughts return to my mind. I better say something before I lose all nerve to respond. "Sure. Tomorrow evening. Do you have a place in mind?"

"Hm. How about I call you later? Give me your number."

The terse way she tells, not asks, has me rustling for a pen and paper. Unlike Evelyn, I don't have any fancy business cards – definitely none that are featured on expensive card stock. Yet before I can finally fish a pen out of the bottom of my bag, Evelyn has her phone out, expectantly awaiting my number from my very own lips.

Once I tell her, she places her phone back on the conference table and crosses her arms. All that does is make her chest *more* obvious.

"I look forward to it, Keira." A devilish smile makes me forget where I am for a moment. Am I really in the conference room of a corporate insurance company? Is this really one of the most beautiful women I've ever seen standing in front of me, hip cocked to the side as she invites me out for *drinks* tomorrow? Don't get me wrong. I'm under no illusion that she has any romantic intentions for me, but I can't help but imagine us sitting in a quiet, sophisticated lounge while she tells me all about her life climbing the corporate ladder. As I always do, I will sit there hanging on her every word, wondering when she'll get around to kissing me.

Shit. She's trying to ask me a question.

"Huh? I'm sorry. Excuse me. It's these allergies," I say. "I can't tell which way is up, which way's down, and..."

"I was asking if it's okay to call you by your first name. Keira. That's it, yes?"

"Ah... ah, yes. Of course. Call me whatever you like." Great. I'm stammering. I always do this when a pretty person takes an interest in me. You should have seen what a half-drunk mess I was when Sera first approached me in that bar!

"It's Gaelic, isn't it? I once had a friend who was named Ciara, but it was pronounced like See-air-ah."

"Yes. My parents were quite phonetic with the spelling. I like the name Sierra, though."

We stand in silence for a few more seconds. I pull my bag strap up my arm, unsure what to say to Ms. Sharpe – I mean, Evelyn. At any moment, my boss *or* her boss might overhear me say something that could get me fired. Nothing vulgar, you know. Could be totally innocuous.

Could be the end of my career!

With another tap of the binder against the table, Evelyn walks away, chin hanging over her shoulder. "I'll let you know, Keira. I'm looking forward to getting to know you better."

I swallow something hard. Possibly my pride. At least, though, for a moment...

I forget all about Sera, and that's the greatest thing that's happened to me in four months.

CHAPTER 4

Evelyn

D id you see that? I barely had to work for it. Put on a nice outfit, bat my eyelashes, treat her like the princess she probably thinks she is...

Voila. I have a date with my ex's mistress tomorrow night.

Suppose I should feel sorry for her. This won't be a normal finger and linger, after all. While I'm not out to break poor Keira's heart, I am absolutely out for someone's blood.

Wouldn't it be nice if a certain someone saw us out tomorrow?

I've considered it, of course. As I sit here late in the evening, in the condo Keira has already seen at least once, I contemplate inviting her out to Sera's favorite bar. That grungy dive on the far side of town, where the bartenders are crass and the drinks so watered down that you might as well be handing over seven bucks for piss-stained water. Sera took me there enough times for me to know it's not my scene, but if I want her to see Keira and me together, I know how to play my cards.

That won't be the deal on the first date, however. Part of this is for my own precious ego. Sleeping with Keira should be easy enough. Once I've done the deed, I'll reassess.

Oh, please. You really think I have a solid interest in her? She's pretty. I'll give you that. It's not every day you see women with hair that orangish-red and a penchant for body-hugging skirts. I'm sure she'll be an entertaining lay. What energy she dared to exude was submissive enough that she'll probably squeak for the whole half hour I rock her world. To be fair, I'll enjoy it, too. It's been a while since I was completely on top for once. Sera was so weird about that. She didn't mind it if I occasionally smothered her with my body and made her come with nothing but the thrust of my hips, but it was like a mathematical equation in the grand spectrum of our love life – every time I did it, she had to make up for it two-fold.

I'm telling you the truth when I say that woman had a complex!

Tell me, where should I take Ms. Keira Lawson for our fateful date tomorrow night? There's an array of fine drinking establishments in this city, from the tiny, secluded lounges at the top of business buildings to the tourist-attracting bright lights of neighborhood landmarks. Either one is fine with me. Crowds don't bother me. If I have to raise my voice to be heard, that's fine, but I get the feeling that Keira likes things more lowkey. She's not concerned with how many people see her out and about. Her name isn't Sera, for fuck's sake.

Hmm. You know what? Sitting here by the window, staring at the buildings surrounding my own, isn't helping me decide. Someone's energy is polluting my plans. It's time to put on my robe and draw a bath. While the hot water fills the tub and the bubbles come to life beneath my fingertips, I'll apply my face mask and coil my hair on top of my head. Once I'm submerged in the near-scalding heat that evaporates all stress and worries from my aging muscles, I shall lean my head back, close my eyes, and allow the tranquil sounds of classical music from my phone fill my ear.

Lighthouse Lounge! That's the one. It's perfect. Low-key but high-end. A fancy enough place that Keira will feel like the luckiest girl in the city, but also well-known enough that there will be plenty of people there to act as cover should she get shy. Although I know Ms. Lawson's predilections skew female, she may be reticent about it. In the closet? That would be interesting.

I'm not, however. In the closet, that is. Everyone at work knew about Sera, and *everyone knew when we broke up.*

I should have brought my bag of pretzels in here. I hate it when the crunchy bits fall into my bath, but they make a perfect relaxation snack…

Pretzels. Keira. I wonder if she can bend into a pretzel. Wouldn't that be something?

My fingers drum along the edge of the bath. One foot pokes through the bubbles. With a dramatic sigh, I open my eyes and peel the mask off my face. I can't be content with simply *seducing* Ms. Keira and considering that revenge well-extracted. I want her to know what she did to me. She must know what part she played in breaking my busted heart.

Once I'm out of the bath and back in my robe, I turn the classical music playlist off and look up Keira's number in the recent additions to my address book.

What does it mean if it takes three whole rings for her to answer? I don't have that kind of ingrained patience.

"Hello?"

Her reticence implies she doesn't know who this is. Her weakened tone means she has less of a spine than I anticipated earlier today. *Hmph.* What to do with this information? Is this girl so milquetoast that she's not worth the thrill of a vengeful lay? Perhaps I'm wasting my time, after all.

"Good evening, Keira." I lay across my bed, hand in my hair. "I hope I'm not disturbing you tonight. This is Evelyn Sharpe. From the meeting at Symmetry Insurance today?"

A gasp tickles the phone. "Evelyn. Yes. Hello! I... I didn't think you would actually call."

"I'm not bothering you, am I?"

"No. Not at all. I'm relaxing at home."

"Do you live alone?"

Perhaps that's an inappropriate question where you come from, but in my Evie-centered world, I want to get straight to the point. If it turns Keira off, so be it. This is all part of the plan – to implant into her pretty mind that I might like to be alone with her.

"Yes. I do."

"That's quite the feat in a city like this one." From across the room, I study my reflection in my floor-length mirror. I wear nothing aside from my robe, and its only function is to keep the chill off my skin. Otherwise,

I'm quite inclined to go nude in my own home. Especially on warm nights like tonight. "You must be doing quite well for yourself if you have an apartment in the city. No roommates at all?"

"I mean, it's a studio, and I live on the edge of the city."

"A commute? Even more admirable. Anyway, I shouldn't pry into your personal life like that. I'm calling to let you know where we're meeting for drinks tomorrow night. Lighthouse Lounge. Do you know it? It's right above that Starbucks across from city hall."

"I've heard of it. Mr. Birch has mentioned it a time or two, but I've never been."

"Oh, you'll like it. A lovely place for the working professional. Let's gather there at seven. Drinks will be on me. They have some food there, but not much. I'd grab something after work if I were you."

"Okay! I usually get tacos from this truck across the street from my office. They've got the best fish tacos in town. Have you ever tried them?"

"Fish tacos. From a truck?"

"You know, the food trucks around downtown."

"Yes, I'm familiar with the concept. I don't think I've ever partaken, though." I trust the food trucks to be as clean as the boiler room in my building. I've been there exactly once, and I hope to *god* I never go again. "You might be interested in the lounge's beer on tap selection, then. I hear beer goes great with fish tacos."

"Thank you for informing me, Ms. Sharpe. I shall see you tomorrow."

"Did you forget to call me Evelyn?" I sweetly ask. "Or Evie. I'd love it if you called me Evie."

"Evie." Keira tests my name with her tongue. "It suits you, yeah?"

"Both suit me, but trust me when I say I like to leave 'Evelyn' behind in the office at the end of a long day. As you shall see tomorrow. Have a good night, Keira."

I hang up before she has the chance to say goodbye. That's how I play. Keep them guessing. Keep them wanting more.

There's much to guess and want on my end as well. Eventually, I pull myself off my bed and wander toward my closet, where I throw open the door and step inside.

This has always been mostly my domain, from the racks of shoes to the meticulously divided work outfits and evening dresses. Once upon a time – say, four months ago – there was a section in the front corner that housed a few worn jackets, plaid shirts, and a single suit that I insisted on buying my stubborn ex.

It's all gone now. Only the empty hangers remain.

I stare at that emptiness before turning back to my work wear. There won't be any time to come home and change for my date with Keira. Whatever I wear to the office will be what she sees me in as soon as she arrives at the Lighthouse Lounge.

Impressions are everything. Why do you think I wore the outfit most guaranteed to make her want me today? It's only right that I pick something out that will make her want to jump my bones tomorrow.

I love it when a plan all comes together.

CHAPTER 5

Keira

When you have no idea what to expect from a stranger's impromptu invitation to drinks, you also don't know what the hell to wear.

So here I am. Standing in front of my closet, bra and panties on my body and not much else.

Honestly, I'm thinking about changing the underwear. It's the same set I wore to work today, and nothing says *I feel really sexy* like carrying over the same sweaty undies you wore in the office all day.

Come on, don't get me wrong! I don't *think* I'm getting laid tonight. That would be preposterous. Odds are, Evelyn Sharpe wants to pick my brain about something completely unrelated to who I am as a woman. Been there before. Back when I first started executive assisting around the city, several women came out of the woodwork and offered me drinks, dinners, and memberships. A lot of powerful women kinda get off on taking people like me "under their wing." Mentorships, I guess. I'm sure most of them only have the best of intentions, but the ones I was roped into became more about blowing a woman's ego instead of helping me in any meaningful way. Evelyn will probably be much the same.

So why am I having drinks with her?

Because she's hot.

Do I need a reason beyond that? Evelyn tripped my loneliness like I have nothing else to live for right now. It's been so long since *any* woman paid positive attention to me. It doesn't have to be sexual. I just need...

I need attention!

Bam! I slide my closet door closed, only to realize I still need to pick out a suitable outfit for the Lighthouse Lounge. Instead, I tap my forehead against the closet door. What am I doing? Why am I doing it? This is only going to be a repeat of all the other women who took minute interest in me, only to forget all about my needs and dreams two weeks later. Or, maybe, Evelyn's interest in me *is* sexual. Yet what good does that do me? The last thing I need is to get involved with someone like her. I'm still so embarrassed over what happened with Sera that I can't tell if what I need is a hot, one-night fling or someone sweet and tender over the long term. Guess that's one of those things about me. I've been such a doormat my whole adult life that I'm easily taken advantage of – I swear it's something I'm working on.

It gets harder, though, whenever someone like Sera shows up and shakes my foundation.

Slowly, I roll the door open again. On one side are my work outfits. On the other is a mishmash of casual dresses and the fancier stuff I get out whenever there's a wedding or charity function my boss is dragging me to as his plus one because his wife can't make it. Another thing that excited me when I first started this gig. Then I realized it was merely another way Mr. Birch found *unwanted* attention for me.

It exists, you know.

What in the world do I wear! Shit!

I grab the first dress that bridges casual and formal. Technically, it's a cocktail dress, but it's something I got for ten dollars at the thrift store. Quite the find, really. Sometimes, you really score at shops that don't understand what's come through their doors. I'd usually get a dress like this from the department store for about a hundred and fifty bucks, but this number had no visual issues *and* the fabric is so soft and stretchy that I almost didn't believe the tag. Good, though. Lately, anything I eat, be it a cookie or a salad, makes my waistline expand. It's to the point I have an appointment lined up for the doctor because I'm convinced I have some kind of food sensitivity that's rearing its ugly head now that I'm hitting thirty.

The dress glides over my head and shimmies down my body. The major downside to this stretchy fabric is that I have to be careful about it bunching up around my thighs and right beneath my butt. When it's all right, though, I look pretty damn good! It's only my hair that gives me grief now. The makeup I wore to work will hold for another few hours and doesn't clash with the dress. Thank God. I don't have time to put on a whole new face.

Hair up? Hair down? Up might be too formal. Down might be too casual. I still can't tell what Evelyn expects from me. Naturally, I expect a busy woman like her to show up directly after leaving the office. She'll be in another one of those skirts and blouses with wavy hair loose on her shoulders, and I'll die inside. Impossible, isn't it? Nothing I wear will compare to how effortlessly she puts herself together. Evelyn Sharpe is a slightly older woman who has it all figured out. At my age, she was already working for Symmetry Insurance and moving up their ranks. Me? I've floundered from one gig to the next. Mr. Birch is the one I've work longest for, but that doesn't say much when your longest tenure before Aspen Plastics is eight months.

If I don't pull myself together...

Breathe in, Keira. Breathe in, then breathe out!

The air is more humid than it was when I got off work. Small droplets splash against my frizzing hair. Damnit. I took such careful attention on my way out the door, yet here I am, placing my hand on my scalp and hustling across the street to get to the Starbucks near city hall.

Except I'm stopping in for an Americano. I'm rushing inside and making a beeline for the staircase by the Starbucks' side entrance. Good thing I wore flats with this dress! Because I'm five minutes late, and my feet must fly.

The Lighthouse Lounge is easy to see from the street down below, but the bottom half of the floor-to-ceiling windows are frosted and most of the

top is stenciled with the red letters spelling out *LIGHTHOUSE.* It's a peek
into the upper-middle-class after-work hangout without compromising
anyone's privacy. There are plenty of tables by those windows, but nobody
will recognize your hairpiece or the glint of your watch as you sit down to
either scroll through your phone with a glass of wine in hand, or converse
with a coworker about who has first dibs on Nancy from staffing. The few
times I've been here were a hodgepodge of experiences, from awkward
pseudo-dates to debriefings from a sweat-inducing meeting down the
street. Every time, I grabbed my usual drink of a cosmo to settle my mood
without looking like I'm about to get sloshed.

I might need to get drunk tonight, though. Because, as I've feared,
Evelyn is already here ahead of me.

She's sitting at the near-end of the bar, legs crossed and elbow pressed
decadently against the oaken counter. Nothing about Evelyn Sharpe
should surprise me after what I witnessed in her office, yet one of the first
things I notice is the Old Fashioned sitting half-consumed beside her. The
part of her that isn't focused on the phone in her lap is taking careful stock
of the lounge – who is here, what are they doing, and how does it affect
her? I'm familiar with that level of alertness in not only women but
businesspeople in general. Evelyn is an outgoing woman who always
searches for new opportunities to network. It's a wonder that she waited for
me to get here and didn't automatically ditch our meetup to talk to
someone far more interesting. Evelyn Sharpe... she never lets an
opportunity pass her by.

Is that why I'm more nervous than ever to approach her?

"H... hi." My cross-body chain wants to strangle my chest. No matter
how much I adjust it, however, I'm still convinced that I will lose my
breath at any second.

Can't be because this woman is so effervescent that I'm convinced I've
stumbled into a church and am beholding a statue of some saintly figure.

Not sure what she's the saint *of* since, you know, I've never been in a cathedral in my life...

"Hi," I repeat.

"Good evening." Evelyn picks up her drink and motions to the stool next to hers. "Have a seat. Looks like the end of a long week."

I don't know if that's a question or a statement. Either way, I smooth out my skirt and help myself to the stool that brings me *so close* to Evelyn's smooth legs. No tights or hosiery. Interesting. She wasn't wearing any the other day, either. It's almost *like* she wants me staring at her skin in either envy or...

No, I dare not believe it. I've gotten into trouble with my lust before, and tonight really isn't a good night to start another tiff. Pissing off someone like Ms. Sharpe could land me in a temp agency.

"It has been a long week," I confide, right when the bartender notices me. "A cosmo, please. With a lime wedge."

"A cosmo? I appreciate it." Evelyn's eyes travel up and down my body. Is she checking me out? Or judging me? Where does one end and the other begin? "It will be as red as that ravishing dress of yours. What is it? Yves St. Laurent?"

"This? Oh, no. I think it might be Calvin Klein."

"Ah. Nothing wrong with that." My drink arrives before Evelyn can finish her thought. "Cheers to the weekend."

We clink our glasses together, a giggle not far from my lips. This is really happening. I'm having drinks in an upscale lounge with Evelyn Sharpe, one of the more enigmatic feminine minds in this city. Maybe she can't change my professional destiny, but this is an opportunity I now don't regret taking.

"Stop me if you've heard this before," Evelyn says, "but is your favorite color red, by chance?"

"Huh? Oh, no." Where has my breath gone? Everything I inhale is lost in my lungs. Isn't it supposed to come back through my nose? Or am I misremembering how my own biology works? "This is an accident." Is it too much, though? The hair? The dress? The drink? The only thing that isn't all red is my bag, which is gold with turquoise beads around the perimeter. Another cheap but flashy thing I picked up from the thrift store. I swear I don't get *everything* from the thrift store! I'm simply good at picking out lightly-used items I can wear a lot for the next few years. "I'm usually never this coordinated."

Evelyn shrugs out of her half-jacket. This whole time, I thought it was part of her ensemble – a little white jacket that fits over a simple black dress. When her shoulders emerge and she rearranges her hair, though, I realize that what she packs beneath is meant to draw my eye to her breasts again. Yet she's so effortless and so confident that I must be imagining things. A woman who isn't afraid to show skin after work must know what she's doing, right? Any semblance of flirting or seduction is completely in my head.

I'm desperate. Clearly, she smells it on me.

"You're right where you need to be," Evelyn says with a friendly smile. She twirls her glass upon the counter, finger rubbing the rim and reminding me that I'm not the only woman in the room who has a drink. Right. I should probably try mine, especially after our small toast. "I find that my fellow women are much too critical of themselves. It's natural, though, when we have such competitive careers in a cutthroat, male-dominated world. That's why we ladies have to stick together. You ask me, there isn't enough feminine camaraderie in this town. It's every woman for herself. Everyone pushing one another out of the way to get the occasional attention of a man who has wage power in the industry. Doesn't matter if you're in corporate insurance like me or selling plastics like your company. Hmph. Plastics." She sips the last of her drink, tipping back her head and exposing the white of her throat. That may be the palest part of her body. Paler than my own throat, and I was often teased for being a pasty ginger in high school. "Do we really need more plastics in this world, Keira?" Great.

Now I'm bewitched by the way she says my name. The hard K and the soft *ah*. Like I'm not fantasizing enough about her. "I've been trying to cut down on single-use plastic in my life."

"Honestly, same." Aside from my first sip, I've done nothing but move the lime slice around the rim of my glass, as if imitating the woman I both want to be and want to experience as if she's a thrill ride at an amusement park. "Don't tell my boss, though." If I force this laughter any harder, I'm going to bray like a donkey. "It's a job, though. Beggars can't be choosers in this economy. I've got student loans to pay."

"Tuition wasn't *as* high when I went to college, but it still took me ten years to pay it off. Spent that whole time working my ass off, too, so I was far from lazy. I empathize. The younger the interns in my office get, the more I feel sorry for them. Look at you, though. You beat out every other person fighting for your position. I bet there were hundreds of qualified people applying. You should be proud to have made it as far as you have. I would be."

"Thanks." What else do I say to that? It's not that I don't know what I've managed to accomplish so far in my life. It's, you know... when you compare yourself to someone like Evelyn, it's hard to not feel like I'm on the wrong career path. What am I to do after another few years go by and I'm still an *assistant*. While there's nothing wrong with what I do, really, the fact is that I can't support myself forever with a job like that. There are few opportunities to make more money. Or at least enough money to save up for retirement. Most assistants I know either move laterally while they're still young and get on a proper career track, or they get married to supplement their income.

Yours truly isn't getting married anytime soon. Moving laterally is the best thing to plan for, but...

"What did you major in?" Evelyn asks. "You strike me as someone who went for a business degree. Grad school?"

"No. I went straight into the workforce after my BA. Economics."

"Hm. That so? Interesting choice for someone who ended up an administrative assistant."

"Out of everything I was interested in, it was the one with the most income potential. Everyone made a big deal that I should think about money above my own personal interests."

"If money wasn't an issue, what would you have majored in?"

I hate this question, if only because it reminds me of how much happier I could have been studying things that interested me. Instead, I did the "right" thing and followed the money – all the fat good it's done me. Still, when I say, "History," I sourly remind myself that my parents would have shaken their heads to hear that word come out of my mouth.

"History is quite the important subject. If we didn't have history majors, we wouldn't know how we're prone to repeating our mistakes over and over. I often think we need a few history majors in the office to correct how often we chase the wrong clients based on previous experience. And, you know, English majors. To correct our terrible English."

Although I know it's a joke, I can't help but stare at the bartop as if she's offended me. "What did you major in, Ms. Sharpe?"

"Oh, nothing exciting. Like you, I focused on marketability. If I could go back knowing what I know now, though, I would tell myself to do something 'fun' for a minor. Turns out minoring in political science doesn't get you far in the business world. I would have been better off doing art history at that point. Same difference. Saner studies."

Silence marks the passing seconds. Evelyn isn't perturbed, however. She orders another Old Fashioned and sparkling water to go with it. Her foot twirls in the air as she plays with the tip of her black hair. I'm the one acting awkward, here.

"If I may ask..." I begin. "Why did you ask me out for drinks? You don't know me. Why could you possibly *want* to get to know me?"

Evelyn chuckles. "Oh, darling," she says with such flirtatious affection, "I want to get to know every interesting woman in the city. I'm a quick judge of character. Doesn't take me long to know if someone is worth my time. The moment I saw you sitting in that office," she leans forward, her cleavage so pronounced that there's literally no way to look directly at her without gazing at it, "I wondered *who* is that enchanting young woman sitting next to someone as uninteresting as Oscar Birch? I thought I knew almost everyone in this city. Anyone worth knowing, anyway. This isn't New York, where there's always someone new to strike a conversation with. Nor are we Podunk, Indiana. Still, I make it my business to know who is who out here. One never knows when it will come in handy. Or when I might make a new... friend."

I think this is it. The moment I realize that Evelyn Sharpe has ulterior motives for inviting me out here.

What to do? If I'm wrong, then I embarrass myself in such an unfathomable way that my name might be tarnished in this town. As much as I think this woman next to me is the hottest thing to walk into my life since I sat in *another* bar, it's rather unnerving to have her leer at me like that. Is it the power imbalance? The fact that there's *no way* she wants me as badly as I want her? Because Evelyn Sharpe is looking better with every passing second. It's not only the sexy dress or the casual way she leans against the bartop. Her shining confidence lures me in more than anything else.

So easy to imagine her on top of me. Maybe that's why I'm shifting on my stool and thinking about ordering another drink. Whether she wants me or rejects me, I'm gonna need it.

CHAPTER 6

Evelyn

She's already wrapped around my finger. This sweet, sensual goddess who doesn't know what she does to a woman.

Before, I convinced myself that the only reason I wanted to bed Ms. Keira Lawson is because her naked ass has already been in my bed. Hell, in the backseat of my car who knows how many times! Thanks to my horny ex, it's possible that Keira has used some of my sex toys. There's a thought that completely destroyed me only two weeks ago. Now, though, as I look at this voluptuous pixie sitting next to me, sipping her red cosmo through red lips, I think *this isn't going to be so bad.*

Indeed, Keira isn't my usual type. Somewhere out in this city – hopefully, crying into her denim jacket and slugging back another beer – is Sera, the tomboy-turned-butch who has been my usual go-to for most of my life. When I have a choice, anyway. It's not about the aesthetics to *other* people, either. I'm not attempting to hide behind a woman whom many mistake for a young man. Who cares what other people think! It's not my fault if I've always fallen in love with more masculine women who are assertive in their style and mannerisms. You should know by now that I'm someone who *loves* self-assuredness. Own who you are and don't back down. The aesthetic of clean lines, short hair, and casual clothing is simply a bonus.

Keira, however, is checking off some boxes that I didn't know I possessed.

If I analyze this situation from a purely scientific perspective, I see what Sera was into. Like me, Sera has her usual type – and I'm her *usual* type. So is Keira, by extension. We're both curvier women even with our different body types. Femme. Tasteful choices in wardrobe and unafraid to let our hair fly free. It's clear that Keira has a lower budget to work with than I do, but she's nothing less than put together and professional. Like I said the other day, she knows how to dress with what she has.

Those little lips and the freckles on her cheekbones are eye-catching, aren't they? Don't tell me you glance at her and think she's anything less than compelling to watch. From the way she sips her drink to how she folds her arms on the counter... there are things I could do with that body and frame that would be quite thrilling on any other night.

Yet I'm here on a mission, aren't I? This is to soothe my battered, bruised ego. This is the woman I caught with my beloved ex. For all I know, Keira knows exactly who I am.

I don't think she does, though. If Keira is aware that I'm Sera's ex, then she's a fantastic actress who should be ahead of me in my own company. The average woman that I know – college educated, articulate, and mature in demeanor – couldn't hold back her disdain or shock upon meeting me. Even if she could refrain during a meeting in the name of professionalism, by this point tonight, she'd be accusing me of ruining her relationship with Sera or profusely apologizing. Keira seems nervous, but it has nothing to do with *our* invisible history.

Hm. She's into me, isn't she? I knew it.

While this makes seducing her easier, I almost feel bad for her. Almost. After all, she slept with a woman who was in a relationship with someone else. She doesn't know who I am? Fine. Doesn't change those other facts.

I'm still going to sleep with her. Don't worry. This is for my ego, first and foremost.

But now I might enjoy it for other reasons. Will I completely forget about Sera while I make love to this rose-colored beauty? Will Keira bring her own sexuality to the table and remind me how great it is to fuck someone else for once? God, it's been so long. The other women I've touched since the breakup were simply... functional. They served a purpose. I proved to myself that I still have that seductive side of me. I'm still *desirable.*

Great! Let's put it to use.

"What do you know about me?" I ask the woman gazing at the collection of liquors and spirits on the wall before us. Golden light illuminates the labels while white Christmas lights direct the eye toward the top shelf, where a whole paycheck can be blown in a night. I'm discerning with my drinks, but I don't think a "top shelf" splurge is necessary on a Friday night. Not unless I'm celebrating something truly monumental. "You must know something good about me if you agreed to drinks with a female stranger. Could it be that I offer you something you're after, Ms. Lawson?"

She forces her latest sip down. There it goes, tumbling down that long, pale throat, her jawline as mesmerizing as the springy tendril of hair bouncing against her ear. "I honestly don't know much about you." Keira isn't looking at me. Is she gazing at anything but the memories of a recent relationship? "I mean, I know your name and what you do. Obviously. I had to know that when I put together a profile for Mr. Birch a few weeks ago. *Long* before your first formal phone call with him."

"Much appreciated. Whatever nice things you said about me must have convinced him to look my way."

"To be honest, it was a profile of everyone in your office. Mostly your boss and your coworker. We were under the impression he would be representing the account."

"As it happens, he was unable to make it and graciously handed the pass off to me. I'm lucky that the only real competition in my office is how many accounts we collect. There are a few occasions when gender is considered for a particular account, depending on the nature of the company we're courting, but it's rare these days."

"Yeah. I was under that impression." Keira clears her throat. Honestly, I can only pose on this stool for so much longer. Might be time for me to slowly turn toward the counter and give the left side of my body a well-deserved break from such rigorous stretching. Even if it means hiding my cleavage for a few more minutes.

"But you hadn't heard of me before your work?"

"I had seen your name here and there, but it wasn't something I was completely cognizant of until a few weeks ago, no." Keira's finger wraps around that spiral of red hair. "I'm sorry. Should I have heard of you before then? We're not in the same industry."

"Oh, sweetheart. It's not like that. I was merely curious."

"Why? Had you heard of me?" Her tone is incredulous, as if such a thing is impossible. In truth? I doubt I would have ever known Keira's name or face if it weren't for Sera's infidelities. A shame, too. A shame that this was how we had to meet, now that I'm sitting so close to Keira that I can smell her perfume. It's different from the one she wore the other day. It's... muskier.

Similar to Sera's. Both nostalgic and infuriating.

"I didn't know your name until recently, no," I say, "but I knew your face. You have a unique look in this neighborhood. Even my coworker said something about you when we found out Aspen Plastics was interested in becoming clients. Think he mentioned that you were popular among the guys who meet up for drinks every other week. Everyone knows Oscar Birch's assistant is the only redheaded gal for miles who can turn heads like you do."

"I'm not sure what I think about that," she says.

"Why's that? Not interested in their attentions? You could do way worse, but if one of them hits on you, I suggest playing a little hard to get. Make them work for it."

"I'm not interested in their 'attentions,' suppose you can say. I'm not like that."

"Oh?" I feign surprise. Don't want her thinking that it was why I asked her out tonight, after all.

"You knew that though, didn't you?" Finally, Keira faces me. Her hand is still on her drink, and her posture slumps forward, but having those glassy eyes look right into mine sends a small chill down my spine. "Forgive me if I'm not reading the room correctly, but I got that vibe from you, too. Especially after sitting here talking to you for a while."

"Huh? Vibe?"

"That's you're gay. Or at least into women to some extent."

"Ah. Perhaps."

"Sorry for calling you out like that. I thought that's why I was here."

"Because I want to hit on you?"

Air snaps through Keira's flaring nostrils. She's cute with her eyes wide and blush on her cheeks. You know, I can think of a few other places that could use a little reddening. We already have her hair, that face, and the dress on her back. I wonder... how red can her ass get when I've been smacking it for a few minutes?

"It's hard to tell," she says, never breaking eye contact. "You're an attractive woman. You came on pretty strong, short of sexual harassment. Here we are, two relative strangers having a drink in a classy lounge while you sit there with your chest hanging out of your dress. I changed clothes for this, too. As soon as I got home and put something in my stomach, it was all about looking attractive. I had to be prepared for you to flirt with me. Assuming that's why I'm here..."

I indulge in a hearty quaff of my drink. "Yes, well. I was inclined to ask you for drinks before you left because you intrigue me, Keira. What about it?"

"Indeed. What about it?"

Something about the snap in her voice implies she'd rather I cut to the chase. She's calling me out for the perv I am, but she's still more submissive than me. A real pillow princess, I bet.

That's fine. I can work with that. Especially when all the cards are now on the table.

"Fine. You want to know what it's about?" I drop all pretense that this is a friendly thing between potential gal-pals. Hmph. "There's a hotel across the street. Right over there. Very nice place with thick walls. Could probably get a good deal, not that I'd ask a girl to go Dutch on the first night. Except I know for a fact we could turn down the lights, fling back the covers, and go at it until dawn." I shrug as if her rejecting me would hardly sting. "You could see what's actually under this dress you keep staring at."

That blush intensifies on Keira's heart-shaped face. Eventually, she flags down the bartender and says, "I'd like to pay my tab, please."

Lucky me, she's in no hurry to leave my side.

CHAPTER 7

Keira

T hat same dreadful feeling from before lingers now. It says, *"Aren't you making a mistake?"*

Been there. Done that. Wish I could say I got the hat and T-shirt, but all the resulting breakup got me was a broken heart and a few chips against my ego. Yet I can't stop myself from following Evelyn out of the bar and across the street. There's an old city hotel that has been remodeled a few times over the decades. Since I've moved here, I've seen the sign on the side of the building go from a dull blue to a vibrant red, and the spackled green awnings transform into an inviting hot pink. Once, it was the kind of hotel that attracted the less than favorable people who liked to get into trouble. Two remodels and a new owner later, it's now the chosen hotspot for anyone who likes to frequent the Lighthouse Lounge. Tourists, business trips, and hot one-night stands on a weekend night.

So what if I was right? Evelyn wasn't fucking around when she invited me out for drinks, and she didn't mince words when she invited me up for sex. I'm grateful. I don't want to play games or constantly question her motives. Who wants to guess if they're going crazy while a hot woman dotes on them? Not me. Better for Evelyn to outright say she wants to do me. That way I can cross the street with the knowledge that, for at least a few seconds, I had complete control over the situation.

Dread. Lots of it.

Come on, don't get me wrong. I probably won't regret tonight. Evelyn is so sexy that I'm about to combust when she steps into the lobby and asks the front-desk clerk if there are any non-smoking rooms available on the "quiet" side of the hotel. He takes one look at me before glancing back at Evelyn. He does a good job of not raising his eyebrows when he asks if we want one bed or two. Of course, we only need one. We probably won't stay in it the whole night, but we'll make the most of it. For at least an hour. Probably.

"How about I have a bottle of wine sent up to the room?" Evelyn says in the elevator, where she checks her hair in the mirror. Is it rude if I outright check out her ass now? Because it's not bad to look at in that tight black dress.

"I really shouldn't drink more," I say.

"No worries. Thought it might help with the nerves."

"I'm not nervous."

A small smirk reflects in the mirror. "You have more anxious energy in your skin than you do freckles. Relax, Keira." There's my name again, purred against the back of her throat. "We're here to have some fun. Unless you've changed your mind."

"No." Yet I can't look her in the eye when she turns toward me. What can I do? I can't tell her the truth. Not, *"I'm looking forward to fucking you, Ms. Sharpe, it's just you're the first person since my ex and she kinda fucked me up."* I don't want kid gloves. Nor do I want her pity. God, what if saying something turns her off? Lots of women don't want to be the rebound. Especially since there's no question that this is meant to be a one-night stand.

I should make the most of it, shouldn't I?

"If you don't want to wait..." Evelyn is closer to me once we reach our floor. "That's fine. We don't have to turn on the lights in the room."

I'm the first to step out of the elevator, leaving her half-bent. Hair obscures her face as her eyes follow me out of the elevator. Before I worry I'm off on the wrong floor, Evelyn slams her hand against the door to keep it from closing.

"5H," she purrs. "At the far end of the wall. To your left, there."

She's not bothering to hide it now. That lascivious look in her eyes. This woman is undressing me where I stand, and she's already seen my goods.

Guess she likes what she's seen.

I beat her to the door, but she's the one with a key. Evelyn slowly approaches, her cavalier demeanor keeping me at bay while I tuck back my hair and clutch my purse close to my body. She slides the keycard into the lock and jerks on the handle with such precision that my ankles buckle. Damnit, I'm wearing flats, too. Except Evelyn doesn't seem to notice. She's pushing open the hotel room door and inviting me inside with a hook of her finger.

Only one light comes on, and it's the back corner lamp by the window. I slip off my shoes while Evelyn removes her jacket and hangs it up on the back of the door.

Her hand slides up the outer edge of my thigh, shivers commanding my body to press against the wall while Evelyn pushes up against me.

"You must know what I was thinking when you walked into *my* office." My hair fills her fist. Other lovers would have pulled it from the moment they realized I'm putty in their embrace. Yet Evelyn merely traces the outline of my ear and exposes the side of my neck. My hands press against the wall, bracing myself for her impact.

Everything is felt through my clothes. Her body. The cold wall. The dim light on my skin. Evelyn toys with my sleeves before urging my arms above my head. As she wraps her arms around me and presses her mouth against my throat, I lean back my head and meet her shoulder.

"I absolutely had to know." My blood is pounding in my ears and my knees are digging into the wall. Yet I hear every word she says. "What do you taste like, Keira? Are your cherry-red lips as sweet as the fruit? Can I get drunk on your pussy?"

Between her stalwart body and the wall before me, I'm not going anywhere. Good thing, because I'm melting. From my ankles to my shoulders, every bone in my body collapses upon the one beneath it. A soft moan escapes my lips. Is it because Evelyn has kissed my throat? Or do I respond to her hand going between my legs?

My hands open against the wall. Knuckles buckle. Evelyn's hips sweetly thrust against my ass, and suddenly all I can think about it is her getting drunk on my body.

"Uh huh." Her teeth are on her lips, and her humor hits my flesh. "I knew you were a squeaker. I hope you make more noise when I'm on top of you, though. Nothing gets me off harder than knowing you've been sent to St. Peter."

It takes me too long to understand the reference. That's how far gone my mind already is. I've simultaneously forgotten women like Sera while only thinking of how this might fuck me up, too. Yet I want it, don't I? Evelyn Sharpe, with her intoxicating perfume and the slight movement of her hips. I don't know what to expect.

"Do you want to surrender your body to me?" Evelyn grabs my breasts when she asks that. If you look at me now, all you behold is the closing of my eyes and the opening of my mouth. My tongue grazes the wall. My thighs part open, enough to invite her between them. She wants to get drunk down there? So happens I want to crush her head with my thighs.

I want to do a lot of things. That's probably why I can't get a word out of my throat.

This is how I am. Some would call it submissive. I've been told that I'm both a "delight" to play with and that I'm "infuriatingly quiet." In the end, I like having the control taken away. Like I can explain it, though. When I know someone well enough, I can be more vocal in the bedroom, but it takes a while to get there. It's not that I'm shy. You have to understand, the fantasies in my head and the way I am in bed aren't so different. Even in my fantasies, I'm not aggressive. I mean, I'll tell you that I like you and would like to go to the hotel with you, but only if you invite me first. Like Evelyn. Who must have read me like a book when she saw me walk into the lounge. Really. It's not like I tried to hide it. Look at my dress. I turned some heads when I walked in there. I'm definitely turning one head now as Evelyn hikes up the skirt and grabs my bare thighs.

"Jeeeesus." She licks the tip of my ear. "You are one fine woman, Keira. I knew you were packing something hot beneath your clothes, but I wasn't prepared for this."

"Weren't you, though?" I'm still squeaking like a horny chipmunk. Great. Nothing kills the mood more than that. "I saw the way you were looking at me."

"In the lounge? Or in the conference room?"

"B..." My word is interrupted when she smacks her hand against my thigh, grabbing on tight and squeezing with all her might. "Both!"

With a satisfied groan in her throat, Evelyn backs away, leaving me pressed against the wall and my breath still stalled in my lungs.

"This dress teases me more than that lilt in your voice." Evelyn doesn't ask permission when she pulls my dress farther up my torso. My arms lock against the wall. Eventually, I spread my hands apart and hold my breath so my whole dress can ascend over my head and land on the floor. "There. Temptation gone."

I turn around. Because I do it on my own? Because Evelyn urges me with a single touch? I don't know. All there is to know is that my back is now against the wall, and Evelyn is stepping between my legs and bringing a kiss to my lips.

I meet her halfway. It's the polite thing to do.

You never know how someone kisses until you taste them for yourself. While I'm definitely the type to fall into a hypnotic trance and keep kissing until I can't anymore, Evelyn is more methodical. Every kiss means something. She doesn't put her lips on mine unless she has a damn good reason, like clamping down on my tongue or moaning into my mouth. Her tongue isn't anywhere long enough to punch me in the back of the throat, but the intent is there. She wants to feast. Indulging in my body is about more than satisfying some sexual urge. The force of her mouth, the spring of her lips, and the taste of her tongue are more exquisite than I have any right to describe beyond...

I want her. I want more.

This is the moment I have a single regret. It's when I realize that the sex will be amazing. She'll find things to do to my body that nobody else has ever done, and she'll make me come so hard that her name is the only one on the tip of my tongue for the rest of my life. Like a succubus, she'll drain me of my energy and leave me to die in bed.

And I'll always think of it. I'll always miss it.

I'll always want more.

I'll regret tonight, not because of anything Evelyn did, but because I'm so *bad* at one-night stands. As soon as someone is sexually compatible with me, I yearn to lock them down and ensure it's my ass they're pounding for the foreseeable future. It's why I couldn't let Sera go at the first scent of trouble. Honestly, I had no business getting her number after we fooled around in the bar bathroom, but she made me so hot and understood me on such a deeply sexual level that my fear of missing her overtook all sense and reason.

Here I am again. Ready to make the same mistakes.

"I can't wait." Evelyn's hair brushes against my cheek. It's a ruse to distract me from her fingers slipping into my underwear. The lace easily gives way. Of course it does. It's almost like I picked a lingerie set that doesn't prohibit getting busy at a moment's notice. "I need to know what you feel like on the other end of my hand."

My eyes won't open. The only parts of my body cooperating are my legs, which open wide enough to accept Evelyn's hand between them. My chest pushes up and my scalp touches the wall the moment her finger is in my slit. Truly, this isn't a woman who wastes her seconds. Even though we have this room for the whole night, she's going right for my clit.

Or so I think.

To be fair, she does touch it. I gasp, pelvis thrusting forward to catch her finger. Instead of feeling it on my clit now, though, I've caught it somewhere else. Namely, inside of me.

"Do you like it, Keira?" I'm so overwhelmed by my own fixations and her actions that I barely understand her. Her finger is fucking me so easily that I almost mutter for another. Wouldn't it be nice if I could get an orgasm out of the way right now? I won't have a single inhibition after that. Hell, I've been known to go from zero to sixty. If you can get inside me, get me off, *and* I'm still wanting more, all bets are off. Bring out the toys and test your mettle with the rest of my body. Make it hot. "How does it feel to have me inside of you already? We've only been in here ten minutes."

My grip on her shoulder falters. I can't concentrate on holding on *and* talking at the same time. "It's how I like it," I whisper.

"I thought so. Don't be afraid to tell me what you want, though. Only know that I'm expecting some attention later, too."

"Wouldn't dream of hogging it all to myself." My eyes squeeze shut again. I can't stand having them open as two fingers dance within me.

"Your body has swallowed me right up." She kisses me, but her lips are better off on my cheek or throat. Instead, they spend most of their time up against my ear, where her tongue probes whatever it can find. My thighs instinctively crush her hand. Evelyn doesn't relent. Good. I'm not trying to push her out. I'm trying to keep her in there for as long as I can. "You want to get on the bed, don't you?"

"Make me come first."

"If I do, then you have to do whatever I want."

"Yes. Okay." A groan grasps my throat as her fingers pick up speed. "Whatever you want."

She has me. Evelyn knows it. Not only is my pleasure hers to command, but she can make me do whatever she wants. I'm such a sorry slut that all she has to do is crack the metaphorical whip that sends me down to my knees. I'll spread open whatever she wants and stick my tongue anyplace she desires.

"I think I want you saying my name." Evelyn's new position isn't as romantic, but it gives her wrist the leeway it needs to slam her fingers deeper inside of me. "When you come. Say my name."

It doesn't take much longer. I'm so exposed to her and so deep in my own head that it's a miracle I'm not already writhing on the floor and grunting ancient tongues. Her fingertips graze my G-spot at this angle, yet here I am, wiggling against the wall and attempting to remember her name.

"I'm coming." Her lips touch mine, but not for long. Evelyn simply wants to be closer to my face when the moment arrives. "Ev..." It's hitting me now. Every pleasure pattern in my body is awakening. "Evelyn..."

My orgasm may be weaker than usual, but it's not her fault. Besides, who is to say that it wasn't worth it? My thighs squeeze against Evelyn's hand, refusing to release her from my core even though my climax is subsiding. Slowly, my eyes open. There she is, the queen of my cunt.

Evelyn Sharpe.

"Good girl," she says with a wicked smile that lulls my pleasure out of me. For now.

Her wet fingers abandon my thighs, but they have not forsaken me. One by one, Evelyn's digits walk along my stomach, leaving a trail of my own orgasm on my skin. She playfully tugs on my navel and offers me a kiss.

My legs are shaking so hard, though, that she misses my lips and hits my forehead.

"Let's get you on that bed, huh?" Evelyn pulls me away from the wall. "I'm afraid you're going to fall and hit your head. That's not the kind of excitement I'm after tonight."

With my hand in hers, I follow her to the main bedroom as if drunk on sleep. Every time my bare feet stumble, Evelyn turns around and steadies me, that sweet visage reminding me that I'm in good hands. Although everything about this "relationship" is quite sudden and unexpected, nothing Evelyn has done is untoward or unfavorable. If anything, I've been one step ahead of her this whole time.

This is why I don't feign surprise when she stands at the foot of the king-sized bed and gestures for me to get on it.

I crawl forward on my hands and knees. The mattress absorbs my weight as if I'm sinking into oblivion with a huntress right on my heels.

"You don't need these." Evelyn grabs the elastic of my underwear and pulls them down over my ass. Whatever heat I harbored in my flesh is now gone. All I feel is the air reminding me of what happened a few minutes ago. Is it instinct or desperation that leads to me splaying my knees wider so Evelyn can see what she's done to me already? When my underwear lands on the pillow in front of me, I tuck the bed covers between my fingers and brace myself for the touch of her fingers against my ass.

Soon, it races up my back and unsnaps my bra. My breasts are barely supported as my nipples desperately search for stimulation. I can hardly believe it, yet should I be so surprised? This is how it goes.

Especially when someone as enigmatic as Evelyn Sharpe wants me.

She presses the small of my pelvis. Almost immediately I fall over onto the bed, rolling over and losing my bra. I'm completely naked. My legs are spread, knees cocked into the air. It's just me, Evelyn, and this hotel room with the supposedly great soundproofing.

I know what I am. I know what I've done. Somehow, this doesn't quite feel like the penance I deserve.

Yet I'll take it, because at the end of the day, I'm nothing if not predictable.

CHAPTER 8

Evelyn

I'm entranced by what I see before me. As pride becomes my greatest sin of the evening, I behold the mess I've already created in this private hotel room.

Did I think that Keira would be so easily seduced? Of course. Anyone who goes to bed with someone like Sera is *easy* to seduce. Hello? Have you met me? I'm not pretending to be any better here, although in this situation I'm definitely the seducer.

There is a surprise, though. I didn't think Keira would be so *hot.* Granted, she's an absolute doll in her own right, but you heard me earlier. She's usually not my type. While I can appreciate a curvy beauty with her own sass and sex appeal, I didn't anticipate slobbering all over the girl as soon as her dress came off. I was going to play it slower, you know. Beguile her with my wit and charm. Maybe take off some of my clothes to ensure she liked what she saw. Cajole her over to the bed and start *making love,* or whatever asinine thing you want to call plain old fucking.

I didn't anticipate fingering her against the wall. I don't know what came over me.

Besides lust, I suppose.

Now here she is. Look at her. Naked as God made her and waiting for me to consume her. She lightly touches herself between the legs while staring at the back of her eyelids. Would it be too bad if I let her keep going? There's something mystical about the way a woman pleasures herself when she's waiting for more to happen. After all, isn't part of this seduction about my battered and bruised ego? I've already fucked the girl who ruined my relationship. Now I'm just playing with her.

Having my own fill, if it were.

"Had I known a tigress like you was prowling my city..." I pull down the zipper of my dress and shrug out of the sleeves. Keira's eyes open in time to see me shimmy out of my dress and step out of the pile of fabric around my feet. My strapless bra barely contains anything now that I don't have a whole dress to support its futile efforts. Might as well take it off, too. It's plenty warm in this hotel room. I don't mind getting naked with a sexy woman who looks bold enough to say my name while she climaxes.

That *was* wonderful, wasn't it? I'll be thinking about it for the rest of my life. Specifically, when I think about what my shitty ex did to me.

Hmph. If there's one thing I can guarantee tonight, it's giving Keira some of the best sex of her life. Changes in plans are happening. If there's one way I can bring balance to the universe, it's by imprinting myself onto Keira's mind. I want to be the one she fantasizes about when she's alone in her bed with only a vibrator to keep her company. When she thinks back on the great lays of her life, I'll be in the top three. She'll hardly remember our mutual ex.

With any luck, I can extend the same consideration to her. This body I'm gazing down on is one of the finest I've ever beheld, after all.

"I mentioned I wanted to get drunk on your pussy, right?" I crawl onto the bed, in between her legs. Keira holds her breath as my knees hook beneath her thighs and prop her open. My preferred penetrative position when I'm on top, not that I've got anything on me tonight. Oh, well. Depending on how this goes, I might play with her for a few more dates. I'll up the ante and turn her into a venerable sex goddess. She's about to hit thirty. I remember being that age.

Wasn't that around the time I met Sera?

"You've already shown me how much you like it when someone touches your little clit." I dig my fingers into her thighs. Keira, who has propped herself up on her elbows, throws back her head and groans as I lean into her. "I can only imagine how crazy you get when it's my tongue doing the work. What do you say, hm?" I'm already lowering my face to her stomach when I say that. "Should I get roaring drunk on your body?"

"Yes," Keira whispers. I barely hear her. "Please."

"Say my name when you ask."

"Evelyn." She's already on fire when I kiss her thighs. The scent of her arousal hits me right in the face. Every woman takes getting used to, but there's such a heavy musk to her body that I can hardly hold back my tongue from her slit. "Can I still call you Evie?"

"If it rolls off the tongue better." Speaking of tongues, that's mine exploring her mound. I'll spare you the carpets and drapes comments and leave it up to your imagination. After all, you can't see a damn thing. My face is in the way. "Feel free to get into it. In fact, I insist."

Why, yes, that's my whole face now in her pussy. She's as soft and as exquisite as I imagined upon undressing her.

All the better for me to get into it, too. After all, I do love eating pussy. If there are a pair of squeezable thighs on either side of it, all the better. Who am I to deny a little cushion as I bury my tongue in a woman's body and purse my lips around her clit? It swells in my mouth and tastes as sweet as candy. I can lick Keira's lollipop all night at this rate. I'm already at the center, too. Don't ask me how many licks it's taking. We both know the answer.

Just one.

Her voice peals above me, loud enough for me to enjoy while still too quiet for her to be really letting loose. Perhaps it takes her a while to open up – emotionally, that is. Physically, Keira can't get much more open. I better make short work of her if I don't want her straining these pretty legs of hers.

Isn't she *lovely?*

Well, I'm assuming. I can't see her right now. All I "see" is the hairs in my face when I bother to open my eyes. Keira's curves prevent me from beholding anything but soft skin when I glance up from my new abode. Fine. I work better when my eyes are closed, anyway.

Let me concentrate on what's before me. I want to feel every ounce of her pleasure on my face.

Because it's mine now, isn't it? It all belongs to me. *Evelyn Sharpe.* No one in this town fucks this woman like I do. No one stays in the back of her mind forever like *I* do. If I have one goal tonight, it's to ensure Keira thinks of me every time she's with someone else. Not for my own vanity, mind you, but because I insist on it. My ex can't have *everything.* She doesn't get cake and wolf it down like a barbarian, too. Sometimes, *I* get to leave my mark. Me. The woman who spent seven years with one person only to have it blow up in my face.

Is there no such thing as loyalty anymore?

Time to take a breath and remind myself that this is also sex for my pleasure. After all, I've told you that I enjoy going down on a good girl. If I erase Keira's name and face from my memory and only treat her like a hot one-night stand who amuses me more than I can convey, then I truly come out on top. Her sweetness overrides my bitter memories, anyway. The heat of her thighs and the salt of her sweat remind me of what it means to be a sexual human. Already, this is the best lay of my rebound term. I think I can successfully call this the end of my bouncing back from a toxic relationship. After tonight? I'll be ready to properly date again. The world will have to ready itself for Evelyn Sharpe's Hot Girl Summer.

As soon as I get this girl coming all over my face, though.

I'm not dragging this out any longer. I want my tongue deep inside of her and my breath so controlled that I don't have to pull back and interrupt the flow. The tension in her muscles only turns me on more. Whatever my tongue can taste is allowed into my mouth. Hot and wet. That's how I like it, and that's what Keira serves up when I pay extra attention to her swollen clit.

Here it comes. Here *she* comes.

That voice cracks like thunder before I feel anything new. Then it's nothing but trembling thighs and Keira's hot pussy burning my lips. I'll drink her up and not spill a drop. Her back may arch and her hands may clasp her chest, but I'm the one in total control. She's not going anywhere. Nor am I.

Fuck me for being human, though. As much as I'd like to stay down here, I need to breathe. My lips are bruised and my back aches from staying in this position for too long. Air. A good stretch. That's what I need.

And... to see that beautiful, freckled face when I sit up and admire my handiwork.

"That was fun." I urge her hand away from one of her breasts. Peaked nipples for my wet lips? Yes, please. "Give me a minute and I'll do it again."

Keira is all mine. I could do whatever I want to her. It's almost a shame that we're not in my bedroom, with my boundless imagination dictating every moment we share. You know why we're not there, though? Why we're in this moderately decorated hotel room with the thick walls? Because Keira knows what my home looks like. She's been there before. The last thing I want is to play my hand too early. Oh, I don't care if she finds out about my relationship with Sera. I only care that we hook up at least once. Knowing what I do about Keira so far, she'll run away at the first sniff of the truth.

I'm a little selfish, anyway. Spending time with Keira has been fun. Sometimes, I push away thoughts of my ex. This is a standard hookup at the end of the day. Her. Me. This bed we're covering with our bodies.

"Do you like to eat a well-rounded meal in the bedroom, too?" I sweetly ask the woman making those hungry doe-eyes at me. "Don't suppose you'll mind if I get some dessert when you've rested up. Don't worry. You don't have to move. I know what I'm doing."

I trail my fingers down her stomach before straddling it. Experience tells me it's easier to ride a girl's face when the wall is before me, but I want to memorize every inch of Keira's body. You never know when it might come in handy.

Balancing my thighs on her face isn't the easiest thing in the world, though. Not without my headboard to keep me upright. But I'm not about to give up. As soon as Keira's mouth touches my pussy, I'm leaning forward, hands digging into the bed as I gaze upon the smooth stomach and the pleasant patch of hair now smothered with my own kisses.

Should I be surprised that Keira is more than competent with her tongue? No, suppose not. She's still in bed with me, after all. She wouldn't be here if I wasn't already grinding my hips against her.

For every moment I remember why I'm here, I suffer another where I'm completely blissed out. This is, after all, sex! Why the hell shouldn't I get into it? Why don't I deserve to cut loose and enjoy myself! I don't know how many times I came home from a long day at work and treated myself to a buzz on the vibrator or called up my ex to tell her to get her ass home to fuck me. I mean, that's the kind of relationship we had for a long time. It was mutual, too. Do you know how many times I got texts on my way out the door after a long evening? *"Where are you, babe?? Cum see me soon..."* She always thought she was so clever, spelling "come" like that.

I fell for it every time. I've fallen for many of the universe's tricks. That's why I'm in this hotel room right now. On my dime, no less!

Is it worth it? Am I having my mind blown? Jury's still out. Am I enjoying myself?

Ask the hearty moan coming out of my throat.

My original goal was to brace myself against Keira's legs and count the freckles on her body. Maybe have a nice orgasm before calling it a night. Instead, here I am, slamming my thighs against her face in the desperate bid to get her tongue in there deeper. This is already a league above the other rebound sex I've had since the breakup! I swear it's not only the thrill of fucking my ex's side piece!

"Shit!" My nails dig into Keira's flesh, and she doesn't flinch. That's what happens when I finally come, though, my body rolling in excitement and my toes curling in the air. I ride out every last millisecond I feel. My brain works overtime to produce enough oxytocin to make me see stars in every corner of this dim room.

I don't immediately roll off Keira or hop off her face. I'd much rather drag my thighs down her torso, rub my fingers into her legs, and tease her with my hair as it drops from my head and against her face. The large breath I feel – and hear – her take tells me I've done a mighty good job tonight. This is a woman who has had some good sex, too, and I should take some credit for that.

"Whoo, boy." I lay beside Keira, whose hefty chest rises and falls. Everything is warm, wet, and *ready.* No wonder certain women have gravitated to her. "That was quite the ride. Hope you liked it as much as I did."

My attempts to keep my tone light aren't sinking in. Either that or Ms. Lawson is so lost in her own post-orgasmic world that she doesn't realize I'm still there. Is she thinking about me, at least? Or does someone else occupy her mind right now?

Come on. Don't do this to me, Keira. Fuel my ego more, if you please.

"That was..." Another heavy breath racks Keira's voluptuous body. "Pretty damn good. Sorry. I'm sort of in outer space right now."

"Has it been a while since a woman rode your face like that?"

"Honestly? I don't think anyone has ever done something like that before."

"Really, now. Surprised you went along with it. It's not always for the faint of heart."

"I liked it, though." Keira rolls over, hair twirled around her finger. "I really liked the part where I didn't think about anything at all. It was... pussy. Forever."

"That's what I hoped to deliver. Excuse me, though." With a soft push of my arm, I'm off the bed, not one to offer any cuddling after a hookup. "I need to step into the bathroom."

As soon as the door is closed and the fan is on, I lock the handle and turn on the faucet. I don't look at my reflection as I wash my hands and take a deep breath. No, my breath isn't as impressive as Keira's was a moment ago. This is simply me vainly attempting to reground myself as I go over what I've done.

This was what I wanted, isn't it? Me. That woman my ex cheated with. The bragging rights to say that I slammed my body on her and got my fill of her body.

So why don't I feel better?

CHAPTER 9

M y Italian soda isn't as creamy as I like. Most of the flavoring has gone straight to the bottom of the plastic cup, and no matter how many times I stir the ice with my straw, sucking more liquid into my mouth tastes like bitter fake raspberry flavoring.

The whipped cream is good, though, but that's why I wish there were more!

"Oof." Laura, my closest friend around here, comments when I plunge my straw back down to the bottom of my cup. I mash ice along the way. "Date last night that bad?"

"Huh?" Don't mind me. Jimmying my straw around a plastic cup and smashing ice together along the way. It's cathartic. The more I do it, the more I can pretend I have no anxiety.

Laura grabs my cup and sets it back down at our table. "You've been messing with that thing for the past five minutes. If you don't like it that much, go ask them to make it again."

Sure, it's warm out here, but I'm pretty sure that heat on my face is me blushing at such a suggestion. "I could never do that. Come on, Lor, I've worked in food service before. I know how bullshit of a job it is. As long as it's drinkable, I can deal with it."

"You also spent five bucks, so it stands to reason that you should get what you want."

She has a point, but I can't concede right now. Laura has always been blunter than me, anyway. It's one of the reasons we're friends. When I first moved to the city to start my "illustrious" career, I worked at a juice place in the outdoor mall that fills with tourists every summer. Across the cobbled walkway was one of those trendy youth clothing shops filled with employees who look prettier and act cooler than you. That's how I met Laura. She'd come over every other day on her break to order a smoothie, but we didn't have a conversation until I happened to look up one afternoon and see a belligerent customer giving her grief in her shop's doorway. When she came over for her usual, I comped her smoothie and she teared up in relief. Not only was that the day I realized that those "bitchy" employees at the trendy shop are putting on an act, but they don't get to work there by being Mary Sunshines, either.

Laura has always been a phone call away ever since. My first real friend since moving here a few years ago – hell, one of the only real friends I've ever had. I'm approaching my thirties and it still surprises me to this day.

"You're right." I lick some whipped cream off my straw. "I'm still not going to go up there and complain, though. Working at a juice place for so long means I don't have it in me."

"Want me to do it for you?" Laura motions for the plastic cup to appear in her hand. I shake my head, clutching my subpar Italian soda to my chest. "Fine. Just stop smashing your straw into your ice, please."

I take a pathetic sip. Laura waits the customary three seconds for the liquid to go down my throat before saying, "So, what happened last night, again? You and some hotshot business lady in town?"

No choice but to nod. There's no lying to Laura. She can read me like a book at this point in our friendship, although I'm still working on seeing her the same way. "I had this feeling, you know," I say. "That she had some sexy ulterior motive for asking me out for drinks so suddenly. Just the two of us. I was pretty sure she was gay. I won't lie. It's why I went."

"Then you ended up at that historical hotel across from the city hall..."

"It was a lot of fun for the first hour."

"More than one hour, huh?" Even behind a pair of thick sunglasses, those fuzzy black eyebrows bounce up and down Laura's forehead. "When is the cosmos going to make me gayer? I keep hearing these stories about ladies who go all night long, but does my physiology get with the program and hook me up with a girl who gets my motor going for once? No. That's all right. I've made my peace with five-minute men. Some of them really get a lot done in five minutes."

I shrug. It doesn't bother me when Laura goes on about the guys she dates, but I don't relate to them at all. Although I had a couple of boyfriends when I was younger, the most we ever did was fool around enough for me to realize I don't care for men. Sometimes I encourage Laura to talk about it so I can reassess my attractions. I mean, you never know! Maybe I'll wake up bi tomorrow. It hasn't happened yet, but I've heard of crazier things changing the older you get. Laura is over here hoping she wakes up bi one day, too. We're on opposite ends of the Kinsey Scale right now.

"As I said, the first hour was good. Then it got a little weird."

"Ooh, did she want you to leave, but you weren't getting that vibe?"

"I... don't know, honestly." It's hard to explain what happened to Evelyn after she came back out of the bathroom. Takeout was ordered alongside the TV turning on. Stupid me thought we might hang out on the bed even if we didn't have any more sex; instead, Evelyn helped herself to a Danish and decaf coffee from across the street. She had ordered me an iced tea and a muffin, but I didn't have the appetite. A part of me was so disappointed. In Evelyn, sure, but in myself as well. How could I be so stupid and think this would end any other way? It certainly wasn't the first time I awkwardly hung around after a hookup. "She never expressly kicked me out. I kinda left after another hour. She was watching the news while I put my clothes on in the bathroom and told her I should get home. She didn't promise to call, either. I think that was it." I sigh. "It's like I *knew* it was a friendly hookup. Come on, she has to do that to girls all the time, right? Maybe I'm naïve, but at this point in my life, I'd like at least some canoodling before it's time to split. Based on some of the stories you've told me about your exes, Evie wasn't that much different from a lot of the guys you've seen in hotels."

"Men, women, at the end of the day there are only so many differences." Laura holds out her hands in mock disappointment. "Sounds like this Evie is really awesome at seducing and bedding a girl, but needs more manners after the fact. Hey, you're probably weirded out by the experience because we're used to hearing about men and their post-nut clarities, but women get it too! Just ask me! I've slept with people *purely* because I'm horny, and once it's gone, I'm like, 'Fuck you, Laura, why did you do that? Now you gotta go to the clinic because you fucked someone in a dingy club bathroom.'"

I giggle. "Guess that does make me feel better. It definitely was not a grungy club bathroom. Jeez." Now I'm for sure blushing. Doesn't take much! "Definitely not my style. I'll leave those adventures to you."

"Don't make it sound like you're not having adventures of your own," Laura says. "This Evie lady sounds like a fine tiger. Is she a cougar? I never asked how old she is."

"She can't be more than ten years older than me. Besides, I'm almost thirty. Does that still make her a cougar if I'm not a co-ed anymore?"

"Depends. Have a cougar fetish?"

I laugh so hard that some of my whipped cream goes right up my nose. Once I've regained my composure, I say, "No! Believe it or not, every lesbian does not go through a lifelong phase of wanting to sleep with someone old enough to be their mother. It's more like eighty percent of us."

"But you're not in the eighty."

"If you couldn't guess from my hot bod of recessive genes, I don't like being super mainstream."

"Uh huh. She sounds like a player. Asked you out for the express purpose of sleeping with you, and when you put out, she didn't have a reason to stick around. Which is fine, of course, since it doesn't sound like you were expecting her to be your girlfriend."

"You don't have to dress me down quite like that."

"Am I wrong?"

My straw presses against the bottom of my cup. I'm careful to not rattle the ice too much. "No. I knew what I was getting into. Ah... I dunno. I didn't know what to expect outside of some hot sex for a while. The abruptness with which it ended is what caught me off guard. I know it happens especially when dating guys, but I've never experienced something like that before."

Every time Lauren chuckles at my lesbian naivete, I have half a mind to jam my straw back into the ice. "You want to know what I really think?"

"Do I get a choice? Sometimes you go for it without consulting me."

"I think she was cheating. She's got a honey waiting for her at home and she can't fool around too late. She also can't commit beyond one hookup. Maybe if you were truly exceptional in her mind, but if she's careful, she still wouldn't risk it."

"Please. Don't joke about that."

"I'm 100% serious! It checks all the boxes, girl. Look, she wants to bang, but your date is short and she cuts right to the chase. Takes you to a *conveniently* located hotel that she knows for a fact has good insulation between rooms. Not only is she cheating, but this is a habit of hers. She knows the safest places to go and the most effective way to get a girl's clothes off. What? Don't look at me like that. I won't judge as long as you didn't know. Not your fault if you're not used to dealing with..." Her face falls. "Oh. Right."

I no longer have the appetite for my treat in a cup. "Yeah. Right. Thanks for forgetting about Sera. Because I sure can't."

"Aw, honey. I'm sorry. I forgot that's why you two broke up."

My arms fold on the table. The cool spring breeze makes me wish I had brought a thicker sweater with me. What was supposed to be a fun

Saturday getting lunch with my bestie has now turned into a sucker punch to my gut. "It's still kinda fresh, you know? I admit it did go through my mind when we were on the way to the hotel, but I thought it was paranoia after what happened with Sera. Finding out she was a cheater and I was her mistress really fucked me up. I didn't think I would date again for a long while, then Evelyn... well, she was so hot! Came right on to me, too! Like Sera, now that I think about it."

"I'm sorry."

"Maybe it's because Evelyn is really femme. She didn't necessarily remind me of Sera. I didn't put those pieces together until we were at the hotel and she gave me those come-hither eyes in the elevator. Sera used to do the same thing..."

"You know what? I'm full of shit, hon. I'm sure Evelyn wasn't cheating on nobody by taking you to bed last night. She's a player. Probably perpetually single. Maybe she's got a book full of numbers that you're in now, but she's nothing like Sera. You've gotta believe."

"Why?" I ask. "Because I still have nightmares about what happened in Sera's place?" Shudders consume me. I hold my sweater closer to my body, but it's not enough to keep out the internal chill freezing my bones. "Literally the first time she ever took me to her house after dating for two months. I should have known something was off from the very beginning. She told me she had a prissy roommate who was always home, but once I saw the condo, I knew it was *way* too homey. That wasn't a couple of friends settling in for a while. That was a couple, Lauren. She attempted to fuck me in her marital bed."

"Whoa, she was married?"

"No!" My outburst attracts the attention of a barista walking by with a wet rag in her hand. "You get what I mean, though. She was in a committed long-term relationship. I probably would have figured it out after that day, but Sera's girlfriend came home..."

"Please. You don't have to tell me the story again. No need for you to relive that."

Except I already am. I'm back in that big master bedroom, with its built-in bookshelves, king-sized bed, and a vanity befitting a princess. From the moment I stepped in it, I didn't believe it was Sera's room at all. She swore to me it was. Didn't matter that I had never seen her wear the makeup I saw on the vanity or wear tights like I saw draped over the back of a chair. There were faded, square-shaped spaces on the wall, suggesting that pictures had been removed. God, I was so stupid. How could I proceed to take off my clothes as usual? Because the bed looked comfortable?

No. Because I had fallen in love with Sera and wanted everything to be true. I couldn't let myself think that I had literally gotten into bed with someone who was already taken – that I was so *foolish* to not see the signs earlier. My own ignorance didn't matter. Whoever unfortunately came home early that day led to me having a blanket over my head and my half-naked body shoved out the door while fighting exploded behind me.

That wasn't the last I saw Sera. She came crawling to my apartment the next day, begging my forgiveness and offering to explain. She claimed that the relationship had been long over and that her ex was only angry about having me there in "her" house, but I didn't buy it. That was the day I grew a spine and told Sera to fuck off.

Laura is the reason I got through the worst of that experience. She popped me a bag of popcorn, poured me some cheap wine, and stayed up with me all night while we streamed *Scrubs* on TV. One of many occasions I've wished my best friend was at least a bit gay. If I could be with Laura and not have to worry about anyone else...

As my mom used to say, you can shit in one hand and wish in the other and see which one fills up first.

"It doesn't matter," I say with a sigh of finality. "I'm never seeing her again. She's probably already forgotten about me. Best that I sit my ass down right here and not think about her, either." I hold out my half-drunk Italian soda for a toast. "All I need is my bestie today."

Laura is quick to raise her to-go coffee cup. "Here's to a couple of chicks looking out for one another!"

As our cups smack together, she laughs. I, on the other hand, attempt to hold every unleashing wince in my body.

CHAPTER 10

Evelyn

It's Monday morning and I'm back at work. Goodness, where does the time go?

If you're still here, that means there is more story to tell. Not sure what I think about that. From the moment I realized there was a pair of eyes over my shoulder, I assumed this was about my petty revenge against my ex. Fine. I didn't mind if someone came along for the ride. The more witnesses, the better. Humiliating Sera – somehow – and feeling better in my own body and mind was all that mattered. Now it's Monday morning, though, and after a blessed weekend of quiet on my behalf...

You're still here. Why?

I'll overlook it for now. There is work to do, and I don't want to explain to my boss why I feel like someone's watching me. He's thus far completely ambivalent. As long as I do my work and don't create a stir, I'm his number one woman in the office. That's all I have to focus on. That, and forgetting Keira Lawson.

Damnit. That's why you're still here. Because I haven't stopped thinking about Keira since Friday night.

Granted, it's difficult for me to put such a stunning lay so quickly out of mind, regardless of my reasons for sleeping with her. Difficulties accumulate, however. We're talking about a woman who looks as good with her clothes off as they do on. How readily she put that whole body to work when we were in bed... oomph. Don't mind me, I'm merely wondering when I'm ever going to ride a face like that again.

It would be ridiculous for me to reach out to her for a second date, right? Utterly preposterous. Anyone else, and I might. Except this is Keira we're talking about. The only reason she was on my radar was because she happened to be Sera's sidepiece at the end of our relationship.

Getting into bed with Keira again would only be bad news. If I ever go back to therapy, I'd be chastised from here to next Tuesday. Even if Keira knew nothing about me at the time of dating Sera, it doesn't matter. She would only ever remind me of how angry I am.

Anger. And lust. For those hips, if I'm being quite honest.

"Evelyn." Peter pops into my office, startling me. Great. My thoughts had wandered back to being between those thighs, my face completely covered in liquid heat and the sweat of a woman who is about to come. I really do need to properly get back in the saddle, don't I? Ugh. "Quick pow-wow about Aspen Plastics."

Peter must be the last man on Earth who says "pow-wow" unironically. Never mind. I'm still in no position to passive-aggressively jibe him for outdated terminology. I'll let it slip sometime today that I'm 1/8 Onondaga on my mother's side.

"What about Aspen?" One leg swings over the other as I lean back in my chair. No skirt today. It's pure pants city below the belt, so don't think Peter is getting a free show or that I flash my panties to get an up around here. "Did Oscar Birch call? Have they already decided?"

"No," Peter helps his butt to the edge of my desk, "but I heard a birdie at dinner with my wife last night. Actually, that birdie was Thomas Royal, from Trenton Solutions."

How excellent. Trenton is our #1 competitor in the world of corporate insurance. They're more than happy to pick up clients who are no longer happy with us and have been known to snipe companies that we're courting. It stands to no surprise, though, that Aspen Plastics might be hearing from them as well. If I were in their position, I'd do the same thing.

Which means this isn't necessarily good news.

"What did he say? Keep in mind he loves to yank your chain, Pete."

"I'm well aware, but he had no reservations mentioning the great meeting he had with Aspen on Friday. They also heard back from them as early as Saturday afternoon.

"Saturday? You have to be shitting me." Also, I had no idea that Aspen were meeting with Trenton the same day I hooked up with Keira. She certainly did not let that slip while we were having drinks. "If they weren't offering to sign the dotted line right there, though, then I'm sure we still have a shot. I gave a helluva presentation, and you know it."

"Of course you did. I was there." Peter clears his throat. "You're one of our best account managers."

I furrow my brows. "I'm one of the only two here, Pete. Is this your way of saying I'm the second best one?"

"Not at all. You and Quintin bring unique things to the table."

"But...?"

He sighs. Here it comes. "But I'm wondering if Quintin would have been the better fit for this pitch. He was the one I originally picked, you know. Aspen is rather known for its 'good ol' boys' membership. While Birch took a liking to you, he's still old school. I mean," Peter chuckles, "you saw his assistant. He likes them young, pretty, and put together."

"The fact she types quickly and accurately has nothing to do with her shining credentials, I'm sure."

"Do you personally know her?"

I study Peter's face and carefully select my answer. "Just because I'm not an assistant doesn't mean I'm not familiar with the group of them around here. Lots of overlap with the Women in Business League. I may have met Ms. Lawson before that day, although we were far from acquaintances until this past week."

"She's not the matter here. It's Oscar Birch." Another labored sigh. If Peter keeps at it, he'll pass out, and I'll have to laugh. "I want you to call his office by tomorrow and have a pleasant follow-up. Invite him out to lunch, you and him. I'll sit back and call off Quintin from trying to get into bed with him instead."

"Quintin wants you to take me off the account, huh?"

"That's all you got from that?"

"Nooo, what I got was that you want me to use my feminine wiles and eminent sex appeal to sway him to the side of Symmetry Insurance. It wouldn't be the first time. Nor the second! Hell, sometimes Quintin gets booted off an account and I'm brought in because all the boys in the opposing club are lecherous fools who like the idea of an account manager with big tits and flirtatious sass.

Peter slips off my desk. "Let it go on record that I never said that, Ev."

"You heavily implied it and let me fill in the blanks. Good thing I went to college and exceeded in critical thinking, yes?"

"Don't come on to the man, of course," Peter says while on his way to my door. "He's married with kids. A traditional Irishman without having been born there. Er, you already read up on him."

"That's the real reason his assistant looks the way she does. Probably nepotism that got her the spot."

"Right. Get on it, Ev."

Peter leaves my office, but the door is ajar. I'm in no hurry to close it, though. My thoughts are wholly reserved for the words now bouncing around my head.

Lunch with Oscar Birch? To sway him away from Trenton Solutions? Interesting.

Although I have other work I was supposed to complete today, this issue with Aspen Plastics is now my number one priority. First, I need to figure out which day works best for me, which requires calling in the office assistant to go over my schedule for the week. Oh, and if Birch comes back with a *different* day, then I'll have to work around that, too. Where the hell is a good place to go for lunch? It would have to be somewhere between our offices. Preferably closer to Aspen's so nobody on that side feels put out. Also, I'll need a compelling pitch. A follow-up that I didn't have when we spoke last week.

Then I'll need a good reason for not having it last week!

This is the rub of this job. You put more effort into *getting* clients than you do keeping them. Once in a while, a current client wants something more from you and you start bending over backward to make them happy, but for the most part, they're happy to buy their insurance and go on their merry way. It's only when a client has an unexpected growth that they start rethinking. "Luckily," the economy has been dumpy enough that it's never been a big issue.

I know what you're thinking. There's one possibility that I haven't explored in the past five minutes. Surely, you were thinking it from the moment my boss said, *"Call up Aspen Plastics and arrange a lunch later this week."*

I should reach out to Keira. Flatter her, flirt with her, and remind her of the great night we shared.

Hm. I'd rather not. The less she's involved in this, the better. For one thing, involving her would only make her feel used. I'm not *that* petty about her right now. If she had been a bitch from the word go, I might feel high and mighty dragging her out to dinner with her boss and me, but that doesn't serve me anything but trouble. I'm better off forgetting she ever existed. If I only have to deal with Oscar until the deal is sealed? Excellent.

I'll miss gazing at those lovely lips and grabbable hips, but it's for the best. For her sake, and mine.

Or so I think until ten minutes later when Quintin appears in my doorway.

"If you're thinking of asking me out for drinks on a Monday night," I sweetly say, "I'm a bit busy. Trying to arrange lunch with Oscar Birch."

He leans his arm against my doorway. "As much as I'd love to rib you about that, Sharpe, you've got bigger fish to fry in this office."

"What are you talking about?"

"You've got a guest hanging outside the front door. Raymond won't let her in, but I couldn't refrain from telling you all about it."

I jerk up in my seat. "Who the hell is it? Friend or foe?"

"You've got that many burnt bridges in this town?" Quintin laughs. "Oh, man. I can't wait to see your face when you walk..."

There's Raymond, popping up behind Quintin and not waiting for him to get out of the way. "Ms. Sharpe," Raymond hisses through his teeth. "You've got a situation outside the waiting room."

That's it. I'm up and out of my seat. Neither of these fools will tell me what's going on in *my* own office, and if I want to get anything taken care of, I'll have to see to it myself."

After pushing past both men blocking my doorway, I smooth my blouse and ensure it's properly tucked into my pants before marching into the waiting room and encountering a receptionist who immediately gives me a pitiful look.

"I tried to keep her out, Ms. Sharpe," Emily whispers. "All I could do is have her wait outside the door. Do you want me to call security?"

A familiar figure looms beyond our frosted doors. "No, it's fine." Time to put on my façade. The one that declares to everyone around me that it's cool, I'm fine. Nothing about this bothers me in the *slightest*.

"Ms. Sharpe?"

Clearing my throat, I march forward, aware that everyone in my small office is watching me as I open the doors and confront my embarrassment of an ex.

"What are you doing here?" I snap at Sera, who is pacing back and forth in front of the doors of SYMMETRY INSURANCE. "Don't you know I have a perfectly good voicemail if you want to pick something up from the house? I don't need you causing a stir in my office!"

Yes, I made sure the doors were closed and that nobody was in the hallway before I said that. I may also be luring Sera away from the office and farther down the hall. No, not the direction of the restrooms, which will only make things worse. Instead, we're by the supply closet. The one the janitors use at night, so hopefully nobody will bother us.

I rather wish someone would bother us. I want this sad sack of misery *away* from me.

I can't even be pleased that Sera looks like a mess. Absolutely, her demeanor has always been a bit "wrinkled," and I'll be stupid to try to convince you it never attracted me. But Sera is definitely not the debonair she was only a few months ago when she was seducing women like Keira into *our* bed. How long has it been since she washed her hair? Changed her underwear? Fuck it, not my problem!

Are those bags beneath her eyes? Why is her hair sticking up like that? Jesus, someone force a breath mint down her gullet.

"I'm *so* sorry for showing up like this, Evie." Right. She still thinks she gets to call me *Evie*. Like we're close. Or she signs my paychecks. "I really needed to talk to you face to face. You never return my calls. Don't tell me I can leave a voicemail when you've blocked my damn number."

"Gee, why would you ever have that impression? Because I was tired of your drunken calls at 2 a.m.?"

She pinches both sides of her head and squeezes her eyes shut. A small part of me feels terrible that the woman I used to love looks like this. A year ago, I would have my arms around her, soothing her soul and asking what *the hell* is going on. Who died? Was she fired from work? Even then, Sera's response to such things was to usually have a drink at the bar and watch TV until bedtime. Maybe she'd tell me about it. Maybe she'd get on with life and wait to tell me until she was enacting a plan that almost always came to fruition. Sera used to be like that. Once she put her mind to something, she accomplished it and didn't let setbacks settle into her skin as I do sometimes.

"I'm so sorry, Evie. About everything. All of it. I'm sorry about what happened a few months ago, and I'm sorry about the others..."

Why is she doing this to me? Fuck me, I don't know the names of any of the other women she's slept with while with me, and I don't want to know. It's weird enough that she admitted to it while we were in the middle of our breakup. Which was *months ago.* This is supposed to be over! Why the hell is she here bothering me in the middle of the afternoon at work?

"You're embarrassing us both right now. Tell me why you're here. I don't need your pathetic apologies. I've heard enough of them already."

She swallows a shallow sob before responding. She's got ten seconds to say something before I turn around and go back into the office. "I'm seriously sorry. I don't know why I'm here. I... I had to see you, okay? I've spent the whole weekend thinking about what I need in my life, and it's *you,* babe! I've been such a fucking mess these past few months! Absolutely nobody compares to you. You're like... the light in my soul that keeps trying to go out. I don't know what I would do without you for another day. *Please* Evie. Can we put all of this behind us and move on? I'll be everything you ever needed of me. I'll quit my job and become a housewife for you. Cook you dinner every night and wash the car every weekend. I'll rub your feet when you get home and..."

Is she seriously doing this? Is this the hell I've deserved? Lord, what did I do to enact your wrath? I can't pretend for two seconds that I'm grateful to have been with someone I loved for several years. Not when this is the outcome!

"Would you stop? Seriously. You really thought you coming to my place of work and rambling your ass off was going to accomplish something? I almost can't believe you. Actually, I can. You've done some embarrassing shit long before this moment, but this takes the cake. Jesus, Sera!" Am I losing my cool? Of course I am! I was in the middle of planning my next great attack at work, and here comes the bane of my existence. We've been broken up for months, and she's *still* pulling this shit. Do I need a restraining order? Or would she finally get the hint if I told her to fuck off forever?

Probably not. She can be a little dense.

"It's over, dumbass." With one hand on my hip and the other shaking in her face, I feel like my Aunt Rose giving her own dimwitted daughter what-for. Nobody in the family is more like my grandmother than Aunt Rose. Put them together, and every family dinner is alive with dressing down my cousin Trista while everyone politely ignores the big gay skeleton in my closet. Bless Cousin Trista for taking the hits in my stead, though. "What the hell did you think was going to happen by coming here today? That I would feel sorry enough for you that I'd take you back? Sheesh, what does that say about me? About you? Don't you get it? It's *over*. You didn't just cheat on me once. It was a whole pattern of disgusting behavior on your behalf. That's all you're going to be to me from now on, Sera." I turn around. "A cheater. God help you if your future girlfriend finds out, but it probably won't be from me. Fix yourself before you ask anyone to go out with you, huh? Go to therapy."

"Therapy?" That's the word she picks up on as she follows me down the hall? "Sure. Let's go to therapy. Couple's therapy. We don't have to get together right away! We both have issues to work out!"

I stop in front of the frosted doors. Emily is absolutely spying on us from her desk. Raymond probably isn't too far away. Quintin? Loving every moment of this with his ear pressed against the wall. The only one I don't want to find out about this is Peter, who will chastise me for letting my personal life cross over into work. Everyone here likes Sera almost as much as I do at this point!

"*I* have issues? I sure fucking do, Sera. One of those issues is that you won't let me move the fuck on!"

She crosses her arms in a huff. God, how did I not see it over so many years? Her immaturity, that is. Did I really have blinders wrapped around my face? Was I so *besotted* with Sera Flowers, a woman who always left the kitchen a huge mess whenever she cooked? Is it possible that I, Evelyn Sharpe, couldn't see the hot shit in front of my nose?

I refuse to believe it. Surely, this was a development at the very end of our relationship. Even if she hadn't been a serial cheater, I would have dumped her for this!

"What would it take, huh?" Sera asks. "For you to take me back. Is there any hope at all in this world? Or are you going to throw away seven years of something beautiful? Remember the trips we took? The date nights in and out of the house? How often we stayed up late, naked in bed and simply listening to one another *breathe?*"

Oh, please. In the rare moment I get so sentimental, I still have my wits about me. That's why this whole ordeal is so foreign to me. Letting someone like Sera walk all over me and offend me behind my back is the exact opposite of something I'd normally do. Me. The woman who is always particular about her image and the effort she puts into her life. It's pathetic. The mere fact that Sera thinks she can pull this shit with me...

"Do you want to know what it would take? I'll give you two options." My hands cling to my hips as my voice raises. No longer do I care if someone from the office overhears me. Oscar Birch himself could come waltzing out of the elevator with Keira in tow and I would *not give a shit.* "The first is you discovering time travel and going back to the past to erase everything *you* did. Or you could have simply been a better person in the first place!"

I'm not surprised that Sera has quit the waterworks and is going straight into bitch mode. This is more like the woman I broke up with a few months ago! "You think I'm the only one responsible for our relationship ending? Why do you think I strayed to begin with? Come on, Evie. I can admit what I did was wrong, but it's not like I slept with another woman..."

"Women," I helpfully correct.

"...Out of the blue. Our relationship had been stagnant for so long! We used to look at each other like making love was the only natural conclusion! I don't know what happened. Maybe you got so wrapped up in this job of yours that..."

"Don't you dare blame my job for *you* cheating. In case you forgot, I still made plenty of time for you! I was adamant about it! I could have been more successful in my career by now if I had completely neglected you, but I didn't! I didn't *want* to do that. And, may I remind you, I was the fucking breadwinner for most of the years we were together. You sure didn't have a problem with that condo or the car. Or the annual trips abroad!" Phew. I need to tone it down a bit before I have a stroke. I bet Emily, Raymond, and the others can hear us loud and clear in the office now! "I'm sick of this, Sera. We're done. It's over. I've started moving on, but I guess I was still stupid enough to think a cheater would have no problem moving on to the next woman dumb enough to fall beneath your spell. Well, that's not me. You gave up the opportunity to 'work things out' with me when you broke my trust. You never once said *anything* about feeling neglected, so I don't want to hear it now."

Her arms drop to her sides. "Jeeeeeez Louise! Glad I came here today! Because it's giving me a harsh reminder why we never worked to begin with! I don't know if you were always such a bitch, Ev, but thanks for the cold water on my face. I'm outta here."

"Oh, *don't* let the elevator close on you." My eyes roll so hard that I'm temporarily blind. The hallway is still spinning when I pivot on my heel and watch Sera saunter toward the lift. "Be honest. The only reason you came here today was to fuck with me."

"It's not always about you!" Sera shouts over her shoulder.

"Maybe it should be! Sure would be fucking nice for once!"

A middle finger waves toward me as the doors slide close. Once Sera is gone, I heave a grunt of frustration and march back into the office of Symmetry Insurance.

Emily slams her butt into her chair and pretends to be looking through the physical address book. Raymond turns around and mindlessly scrolls through his company phone. Quintin hustles out of the waiting area and back into his office. The only person not pretending that they hadn't heard a thing is Peter, my boss.

When he puts his hands on his hips, it's with a warning glare. Nothing like Sera, who was a huffy precious princess trying to temper tantrum her way back into an easy relationship.

"What the absolute hell, Sharpe?" He only calls me by my last name when he's proving a point. This isn't buddy-buddy Peter passive-aggressively getting me to do my work. This is *my boss* prepared to ream into me like I'm a trouble-making newbie who hasn't yet learned her place. "Why the fuck is your personal life erupting outside of our office? What if one of our clients had seen that? You couldn't have at least done it in *your* office where we could do damage control?"

I figured that's what this was about. "Please, Pete," I sigh. "She knows she's not allowed in here. Emily and Raymond were already dealing with it, which was bad enough."

"So let them call security next time! Look, I know you had a bad breakup, but *don't* bring it to work. Like, literally bringing it to work. I can hardly believe it. You're usually a lot better than this."

"It won't happen again," I assure him – and myself. "I'll have a talk with security downstairs. There's no reason for her to be in this building at all." Everything here is boring ol' offices like mine and the occasional specialty doctor. Maybe some lawyers and corporate real estate firms. Sera is in those circles like I regularly go to drag races on the weekend.

"Let me do it. It will carry more gravitas coming from me."

I concede, if only because talking to the chief of building security about Sera will embarrass me more than I care to admit to Peter. It's bad enough I'm going back to my office with my tail tucked between my legs and hurt in my heart.

Why, Sera? Why the fuck do you do this shit? Don't come into my office with tears in your eyes and begging to take you back if all you're going to do is turn around and show me your true colors at the first sign of rejection. All I can imagine is that she sought to achieve humiliation if she couldn't steamroll me with her lies.

That's not how this works, Sera. You don't get to trash our relationship *and* walk all over me with your dirty, cheating boots!

"Evelyn," Peter says as I walk toward my office. "Focus on your work, all right? I'll take care of security."

With a curt nod, I shut myself up in my office and collapse into my chair. I need a moment. Tissue out of its box and held up to my eyes. It's the allergies this time of year. Emily has some daisies on her desk. Think they might be fake, but that means jack when I'm sitting here falling apart.

Right. I'm supposed to be arranging lunch with Oscar Birch of Aspen Plastics. The man who employs the sweet tart Sera brought into our bedroom – and our car, ugh – without my permission.

I dab my eyes once more and open my appointment book. I'm free for the rest of the week. At lunch, anyway. Here's hoping that Oscar Birch likes the Italian bistro not too far from his office.

Sera and I used to eat there whenever we were in the area for visits with my lawyer. Since the breakup, I've only talked to the man over the phone and email. Stepping into his office reminds me too much of the days Sera would wait for me outside or in our car.

Now I know she was probably texting other women. At the time, though, I thought she was so patient and helpful.

Oscar Birch. I need to focus on my job. It's the only way I'm purging Sera's shit out of my head.

If I really want to knock this out of the park, I'll talk to an insider at Aspen Plastics. Someone who can help give me an edge. Tell me what Oscar's favorite lunch spots are. For the love of God, tell me what kind of jokes he likes!

There's only one person I can think of who comes close to that description. Someone close enough to him that they know every bit of minutiae about his daily life and interests.

Damnit. That person is Keira, and I would be a fool to not enlist her help right now. Fine fit of irony, isn't it? The woman who will help me get back on track at work and fully move on from Sera's bullshit is the very woman she slept with at the end of our relationship.

And the one I bedded only a few nights ago as an act of petty revenge.

What are my priorities, anyway? Do I care about Sera or my job?

Sometimes, you have to bite the big, dirty bullet. Even if it means putting my pride aside and pretending to be interested in someone I had sworn to never see again.

No matter how good the sex was!

CHAPTER 11

Keira

"Have you highlighted the proposal for me yet?" Mr. Birch stops by my desk on his way to the office. "Remember, anything that looks important. You know how these salespeople are. They pad all their facts and figures with a bunch of filler to make themselves look more impressive than they are."

"Yes, Mr. Birch. I mean, no... I haven't done it yet. It's on my to-do list before I go home for the day."

"Make sure I get it before you go. Trenton Solutions is expecting a formal response from me in the next few days and these eyes aren't what they used to be."

He disappears into his office. Meanwhile, I'm contesting what he said just now. His eyes have *never* been good. I have copies of his previous assistants' transcripts going back thirty years, and even in 1990 women like "Helen McNamara" were complaining that "Mr. Birch can't read the difference between an 'i' and a 'j' – be sure to clearly transcribe such letters if you are writing longhand." That's come in handy more than once. It's also served as evidence that my own boss shouldn't be making jabs about anyone's eyesight, least of all his own.

I need a break. I haven't been on a break since I got back from lunch, and all that contained was sitting down in the lobby with my sack lunch and a bottle of Coke Zero from the vending machine. It's rarely a glamorous life when you're attempting to save money.

Never mind forgetting some of the shit you've gone through recently.

No, I'm not whining about what happened with Evelyn. I swear I'm not. It happened. She never texted or called me afterward. I can take a hint.

I'm also not about to blow up her phone with desperate messages to see her again, no matter how much I'd like that. Believe it or not, I have *some* self-respect. Enough to dump a loser who is using me for sex on the side, anyway.

I open my top drawer and sneak a potato chip from a bag I brought from home. As long as I don't get grease and crumbs everywhere, no one will care. This is Aspen Plastics. The only guests we get are the higher-ups stopping by to shoot the breeze with Mr. Birch. Most of the time I'd forget where I am if it weren't for the name ASPEN PLASTICS plastered on my pens, notebooks, phones, and the damned desk.

The moment I think of the phone, it rings.

"Aspen Plastics," I choke out as the chip goes down the wrong way. Before I say another word, I inhale some of my water from a canister. "This is Oscar Birch's office."

"How lovely to hear your voice again, Keira."

It's not my heart dropping into my stomach. That's my brain because I lose all ability to think whenever Evelyn Sharpe is speaking in my direction.

"H... hi." I purposely blink as hard as I can. You know, in case this is a dream. When it turns out I'm still sitting at my desk in the Aspen Plastics office and that, yes, the number on the company phone's screen indicates a local office, I take my chances that this is actually happening. "What's up? I mean, why are you calling the company line?"

"Because I'm calling about company business, dear." Her voice is as smooth as honey. Think she might be laying it on me thick, too. "Besides, if I texted you, do you really think you'd see it before you go home today? Say, before you turn in your curated report about Trenton Solutions?"

I look over my shoulder. Granted, that's a wall, but you can never be too sure! "How do you know about that?"

"When you're in something as niche as corporate insurance in this city, you know everyone else's business. That, and my boss told me about it. He wants me to set up a lunch with your boss sometime this week if he's free. Just the three of us."

"You, Mr. Birch, and your boss?"

"No, honey. Me, Mr. Birch, and *you*. I'm assuming he'll want you there with him. You seem to be his right-hand girl."

"I suppose." While my heart races in my chest, I pull over Mr. Birch's planner and flip to this week. "Lunch? Oh, sheesh. Right now he's booked every day but Thursday." I don't mention that Wednesday is lunch with his daughter and Friday is when he golfs with his old fraternity buddies.

"Thursdays are perfect. Tell me, is there a restaurant around your office that he favors? This is about wining and dining him. You'll be doing me a fantastic solid if you can set this up so he's as comfortable as possible."

"There's this bistro a couple of blocks from here. That's where he usually has business related lunches if I plan them for him. It's called Luigi's. Do you know it?"

"I'm mighty familiar. Pencil me in at noon on Thursday at Luigi's. "

"With the three of us, yes? Um, I mean, they're gonna ask when I call to make the reservations."

"Yes, only the three of us. This will be on my company's dime, so be sure to order whatever you and your boss like if you get there before me. I'll do my best to be there on time. Oh, and Keira?"

"Y... yes?"

"The other night was fun, wasn't it? We should do it again soon."

Evelyn hangs up before I have the chance to respond. When I finally lower the phone, it's with a heavy breath in my chest and relief heating my skin. She did it. She called me. Maybe it wasn't a one-night stand, after all. She likes me. Enough to see me again! Maybe. Okay. Don't get ahead of yourself, Keira. She knows you're DTF. That's all. She's alluding to a booty call. Stop being a desperate slut!

Oh, I wonder what it would be like for her to call me a slut...

Ah! You didn't hear that! I definitely did not say that. Or think it. You know, some thoughts really should be kept to myself. If you think I said something about wanting Evelyn Sharpe to call me a slut while she does me dirty in all the right ways, nope. It never happened. I'm a self-respecting woman who'd rather turn her down for a follow-up booty call than get trapped in her endless spiral of sex for the sake of it.

Whoooooo am I kidding! That would be so hot!

"Ms. Lawson?"

This whole time Mr. Birch has been standing in front of my desk and saying my name. Unfortunately for him, I'm still thinking about Evelyn's pussy riding my face while her scent is permanently imprinted upon my brain.

"M... Mr. Birch. I'm sorry." I almost knock over my water when I close his planner and attempt to look like a proper lady at my desk. "I was thinking about your, uh, schedule. That was Ms. Evelyn Sharpe on the phone. From Symmetry Insurance?"

"I remember her, yes."

"She would like to have lunch with you at Luigi's this week. I suppose she wants to go over her own proposal with you. I, um..." My throat is so dry. Why! "Told her that you could do Thursday. It's between lunch with your daughter and golf with Pi Kappa. Would you like for me to go ahead and make the reservations?"

Mr. Birch chuckles. "You must be thinking about that tortellini. The spinach and ricotta one! Ah, that's a good special they have going right now. You know what? Sure. Why not? I need the week to go over Trenton's proposal, anyway. Why not have lunch on Symmetry's dime? That Ms. Sharpe isn't too bad to look at, either. Work hard and you could be a lot like her one day."

He flashes me a grin and I'm compelled to smile back. As soon as Mr. Birch turns around, though, my face falls. All I can think about is the quivering between my thighs and the rush of my blood in every limb.

Evelyn does that to me, huh? God! I know what I'm doing as soon as I get home!

Me. Bed. Vibrator. Dinner can come later!

CHAPTER 12

Evelyn

L et's pretend that I'm totally fine with going to Luigi's today. That place where Sera and I used to go whenever we were in the neighborhood because we both agreed it hit the right spots when it came to flavor and ambiance. One of us tended to care about one more than the other.

It's fine. Not like I haven't been here since two months before the breakup when we came here for an early anniversary lunch. Oh, did I mention that Sera was cheating on me around our seventh anniversary? She was. So grand that I had to tell you right before I go inside.

A single step inside... and I'm shaking. A little.

Excuses to step into a shady corner of the sidewalk to check my makeup are always welcomed. So are the heavy breaths in my lungs and the sweat accumulating behind my sunglasses. This can't be *only* about Sera, right? It's not like I *only* came here to have lunch and dinner with her. It's also a convenient place for a business lunch or someone's birthday. Why, I know for a fact that one year ago, I came here two weeks in a row for a friend's birthday *and* brunch with some old college roommates. So why do I have so much trepidation walking into a bistro I used to love?

Because Keira will be here.

I saw Oscar Birch's company car in the valet parking lot. He's here fifteen minutes early, probably enjoying a drink and the garlic bread sticks, the bastard. Except that means he's definitely brought his sexy assistant, because there's no way a man that comfortable in his position is sitting here alone on such a beautiful day. To give him the benefit of a doubt, he's probably going over things with Keira as I stand out here chewing on my cheek.

Last night, I had no problem with Keira coming to today's business lunch. In fact, I insisted, *because* I wanted to see her. Remember? Peter expressly suggested that I have lunch with only Oscar so there was no outside influence on him. Instead, I went and invited his assistant, because I wanted to sit at the same table as her again.

Luigi's. Where I made so many memories with Sera. Now, I want Keira here to counteract that stale energy. Oh, and if Sera happens to walk by? Better!

That was last night, though. When I was lying in bed, remembering how absolutely pleasant it was to have sex with that woman.

Keira, I mean. Not Sera. I'd rather not reminiscence about her ever again. Makes me throw up in my throat.

Here I go. Wish me luck as I either make a giant fool of myself or become the biggest badass the business world has ever seen – at Luigi's, at least.

"I'm here to meet with Oscar Birch," I tell the maître d' as he approaches me. My sunglasses slide off my face as I beam my pearliest smile. Fake it 'til you make it, right? "The reservation is under Symmetry Insurance."

I'm taken to the back of the main seating gallery, where meetings are held under the guise of mimosas and Greek salads. Sure enough, I see the back of Oscar's gray head, his pristine gray suit stretching against his body as he raises sparkling water to his lips. Across from him is Keira, who raises a hand in greeting and prompts her boss to turn around and smile in my direction.

Although I briefly make eye contact with Oscar, my focus is entirely on the stylish redhead who looks like a million dollars – complete with compounded interest.

For a split second, I completely forget that Keira is the one partially responsible for the death of my long-term relationship. All I think about is what happens when her amazing thighs close around my face.

Oof. I need a moment.

Except I don't get a *moment*. Oscar is expecting me to sit down at the head of the table and exchange pleasantries. He wants my undivided attention. It would be utterly uncouth for me to pay more to the assistant who is merely there to take notes for her boss.

"So lovely to see you, Oscar." I wait for him to stand up and extend a hand toward him. "Grateful that you've fit me into your schedule today. I wasn't sure if you'd have the time last minute, but your assistant was a big help getting everything together."

"Keira? Oh, yes. She's quite the treasure." Oscar sits back down. "Hope you don't mind that we've already ordered. I slipped out of the office early today. Wanted to avoid the missus dropping by to talk about our daughter's college major. Again." He winks at me while I sit down. A waiter approaches with another water and offers me a menu. I don't need it. Going ahead and ordering my usual of shrimp risotto and an iced tea clears space before me.

"I've brought everything you need to know about the changes we've made to the proposal since our meeting last week." As soon as the waiter departs, I reach into my tote bag and pull out a slim binder that's dedicated to Aspen Plastics. "We started with..."

"Is that really necessary right now?" Oscar chuckles. "Let's eat first! I don't have to be back at the office until three if I don't want. Come on, I know this is on your company's dime. You can afford to hang out for a while. Having been to your office, it's not so different from ours. I'm sure you could use the break this late in the week."

Keira gives away a small smile that insinuates her boss knows the ins and outs of getting out of work. I want to smile back, but don't risk it. It's bad enough we're in the same restaurant right now – never mind at the same *table*. She's wearing some beguiling perfume. Nothing like what I smelled during our first encounter or at our date a week before. Perhaps I'm more sensitive to it now. Now that I intimately know every part of her body, it's more common to be so aware of such things, isn't it?

Damnit. While I was keen to flirt with her – maybe go out a second time for the thrill of it – Keira is bound to be a bigger distraction than I thought. Perhaps inviting her along was a mistake. I should have made it clear that this was an off-the-record meeting with Oscar *only*.

Damnit!

"Of course." My sugary words drip through my lips as I shift my focus toward Oscar. "A pleasant lunch between the three of us. I'm assuming Ms. Lawson won't mind entertaining us for the next half hour or so."

Both of my elbows are on the table. I bat my eyelashes in her direction. A hint of blush touches her full cheeks. In another life, I'd leave a nice kiss on the cheek nearest me. That might be a bit bold before her boss, though. Definitely would not help me seal this business deal if Oscar is as conservative as I'm led to believe.

"What did you order?" I ask Oscar, making light conversation. "I've been coming to this place for years. I daresay I've ordered half of what's on the menu."

"That so? I've been coming here for years as well. I don't look at the menu anymore."

"Neither do I, if you haven't noticed."

"Why would you come to Luigi's so often?" Oscar asks, curiosity dominating his tone. "If you don't mind me asking, that is. I was under the impression that you were on the other side of town. As great as this place is, there are many good eateries over where you are, too. Did you used to live or work over here?"

"It's rather nothing," I say. "My lawyer is in this area. Anyway, we used to come here after every appointment to make the experience nicer. Have something to look forward to after the unpleasantries of a lawyer's office."

"We?"

Crap. Did I say *we,* referring to Sera? I glance at Keira, who politely sits before her empty plate and sips her water. She only pretends to be invested in this conversation.

"Yes. My significant other would accompany me. It was like a nice date."

I look toward Keira again. She's completely noncommittal to any response. Either she has a fantastic poker face, or she doesn't know I'm referring to Sera.

"What stopped you from coming here?" Oscar asks.

My valiant attempts to keep my face from falling are only met with my own disappointment. "We broke up, to be quite frank. Haven't had many opportunities to come by since then. Thank you for giving me a great excuse, Oscar."

"My pleasure! Sorry to hear about your relationship, but it happens. A lovely lady like you should have no problem finding another fella to fit your life."

Another forced smile. This time, there's one coming from Keira as well. This is it, I suppose. This is what it's like to have lunch with Oscar Birch.

How in the hell does she put up with it?

Don't get me wrong. I'm pretty damn good at small talk. I know how to talk in circles with the best of them, and can avoid topics like politics, religion, and what the kids of today are doing like a *pro.* It's far from difficult if you know what you're doing.

For the next half hour, while our food arrives and we eat, it's easy enough. Oscar dominates the whole conversation with tales of his family, including his kids and their distant cousins. Every time he mentions Ireland, it's with a glint in his brown eyes and that untold hope that he gets to retire there someday. In fact, he's so besotted with the isle of green that it takes me a moment to realize he's not *from* there. Not personally. Apparently, his grandfather crossed the Atlantic to bring the Birch's here today. That's good enough for a lot of families around here. None of that nonsense is in my family, though. Like I told you, one side is connected enough to our Native roots that we find this whole whimsical "mother land" conversation to be quaint, on a good day. Ask me in another ten years how I feel about going back to "where I come from."

For the sake of the deal, though, I'll humor Oscar. I'll tell him I've never been to Ireland but "always wanted to go," which isn't necessarily a lie. There are simply more places ahead of Ireland that I'd like to visit before I die. When he laments that one of his nephews is still unmarried at thirty-six, I politely point out that men age like fine wine – or so I hear. Except Oscar wants more children in the family. According to him, it isn't Christmas unless he's buying Legos and Barbies for all the kids. Nobody tell him that plenty of adults would love Legos and some Barbies for their shelves, too.

"Our Keira here is still single herself if you can believe it."

Of all the things for Oscar to segue to, *that's* what he chooses? Wish I could say I hardly believe it, but having been around men like him a time or two, I'm not surprised. Keira, however, is aghast enough to put down her salad fork and hide behind her napkin. Either she's silently choking on her food, or she's damn good at hiding her humiliation. I'd feel sorry for her if it weren't for my feelings toward her.

"Now, don't be so modest, Keira." Hm, had she said something to warrant Oscar replying like that? Although I look between them, I see no sign that they share some telepathic connection. "There are plenty of eligible men in this city *and* in my friends' circle, but she still hasn't agreed to a date with any of them lately. Look at her, Ms. Sharpe. Isn't she one of the most beautiful women you've ever seen? If you ask me, she should have been married at least five years ago. Of course, if she wanted to keep working for me, that's fine, but it always pains me to see a beautiful young woman not yet married."

I pretend that not only was that not dripping in sexism, but that he didn't merely imply that I am somehow not as "beautiful" as Keira. Yes. We are not touching that today, especially when I'm attempting to convince this man to buy my company's corporate insurance.

"It's a new age, even compared to when I was fresh out of high school," I diplomatically say. "Perhaps her aspirations lie elsewhere." My head turns to Keira, who looks like she wants to sink into the quicksand swirling beneath our table. "How about it? If you had to choose, would you rather be a ball-busting career woman, or would be a married hausfrau with a white picket fence and a Formica table in the kitchen?"

Is this conversation above board? Of course not! I could get in big, big trouble for asking such a question at a corporate lunch. And I'm not engaging simply to make the man to my left happy. A part of me is curious, you know? What *are* Keira's dreams? What does she think about when she lies awake at night, feeling guilty about this and that? Keep in mind, she seems to have no idea who the hell I am outside of a great one-night stand. That said, she may know Sera was cheating, and you *must* know what I think of such willing women by now...

"Well, I..." The poor dear is totally caught off guard. I'd feel sorry for anyone else but her. "I really don't know why it should be a choice. I go with the flow. If I find somebody I like and get along with, good for me, but until then... well, I prefer to keep busy with work, anyway. I like the challenge."

Before Oscar can say something intellectually stupid like *"Being a housewife and mother is her own special brand of challenge that only young women like you get to engage in,"* I say, "I like challenges, too. That's why I am so intent on selling you Symmetry Insurance, Oscar." I lean toward him, elbow on the table and fingers grazing my upper lip. "Lunch is over. Let's talk business. We'll give your assistant a reason to keep her job."

A hiccup sounds on the other end of the table. Keira lowers her napkin and says, "Would it be too much trouble if I go to the ladies' room first? I promise I won't take long."

"No problem at all," Oscar says. "That will give Evelyn and me the chance to talk more off the record for now."

"Actually, the ladies' room sounds like a good call." I stand up before Keira does. "Do you know where it is? I'll take you."

Those furrowed brows could either be the source of suspicion or attraction. It's hard to tell now that we're not in a dimly lit lounge.

"I know where it is," Keira assures me as she pushes in her chair, "but the company is always welcomed."

"You ladies and your going to the bathroom in groups..." Oscar shakes his head and chuckles. "More time for myself, then!"

"Don't listen to him," Keira confides to me. "Also, I'm sorry about that strange comment he made about me being single." We round an empty table on the way to the back hallway that leads to the restrooms. "He does things like that. I try to ignore them. You have no idea how many times he's set me up on dates with men I've never met."

I open the door to the ladies' room and offer her to go first. "I take it he doesn't know about you, then?"

"Of course not," Keira hisses as if her boss will hear her out in the gallery. "I would absolutely die if he found out I'm gay. That man is *so* traditional. His own wife would probably disown me before him."

"You've met her, huh?"

Keira lingers in the doorway of the only stall in the whole restroom. I stand before the single sink and reapply my lipstick. "Unfortunately, quite a few times."

The stall door shuts with finality. I focus on my hair and makeup as Keira does her business – what, you think I want to listen in? Now *that's* perverted. As big of a pervert as I can happily be, I do draw the line at invading a poor woman's privacy. Hmm, perhaps she's not so poor. Jury's still out on that.

"Um..." I had no idea Keira was finished in the stall until she stands behind me, sheepishly looking toward the floor and giving me a nice shot of her cleavage as it blooms out of her blouse. I move out of the way, thinking she wants to wash her hands. While she does approach the sink, Keira says, "If it's all right with you, could we possibly talk about what happened the other night?"

"Hm? What happened?" I pat the corners of my mouth while Keira washes her hands. "Besides a fabulous time between two people?" I snap my compact mirror shut. As it disappears into my purse, I continue, "Do you have regrets?"

"N... no." Paper towels appear from the dispenser and wrap around Keira's wet hands. "Guess I'm wondering if the only reason we're here meeting like this is because of my boss. Or did you want to see me too?"

She's caught me in an impossible situation. If I tell her the truth, she'll feel used and forgettable. If I tell a white lie and say, "Darling, the whole reason we're here having this façade of a lunch is because I wanted an excuse to see you again," she'll get her hopes up. Either way, I'm the bad guy, aren't I?

"Going to such elaborate extremes to see somebody when I could simply call their personal line and arrange something is really not my thing." I lean one hand on the sink and face my whole body toward her. Regardless of how I may really feel about our "relationship," I at least want Keira to think I'm giving her my whole, undivided attention. "I prefer to cut right to the chase. To be frank, I *had* intended to call you soon, but I've been really busy." Closer, I inch. Let me gauge how Keira feels about me putting on a few moves. This could be good for me, you know. Or an absolute horror. "Maybe deep down I did think of this as a way to see your pretty face again. I have very fond memories of what we did a week ago."

"Do you?" Keira meekly asks.

Oh, here we go. Those puppy eyes with a hint of *"Little ol' me?"* Please. Keira must know how hot she is. Not every woman gets to run around town with hair and a body like that. One who dresses like she's about to lead a boardroom meeting but is really there to take your notes? She's her own dream come true. I admit I'm partially pissed that everything about "Keira Lawson" has been tainted by my good-for-nothing ex. Under other circumstances, I'd be more than happy to date a fine specimen like the one brooding before the bathroom mirror. I honestly wouldn't mind putting my hand on her hip and whispering something in her ear.

Yet I don't want to get too close to the woman who helped wreck my best relationship.

"Of course I do." My voice lowers. I'm an inch away from her. While Keira continues to stare into the sink, I rub up against her. Instantly, I'm reminded of the fires that burned in my body only a week ago. Fucking this woman had been a thrill in more ways than one. Would it be terrible if I indulged one last time? "Don't you think about me, Keira?"

My tongue rolls over her name and comes dangerously close to her ear. She shudders, like a wilting virgin about to have her whole world turned upside down. It's not fair how much fun she is. For every time I think that I wonder, *Is this what attracted Sera so much?*

She must sense my tension, for Keira slightly tilts her head and says, "Every day. I've thought about you every night when I go to sleep." She looks away again. "You're the first person that I've thought of in that way who doesn't make me feel bad about anything."

To anyone else, that would be such a strange comment. To me, though...

Deep down, I know what she means.

I poke my head out the bathroom door. After I confirm nobody is coming this way, let alone a woman who looks like she wants to powder her nose, I lock the door and swing my body around toward Keira.

She knows what I want. I think you do, too.

CHAPTER 13

Oooh boy. Oooh boy, oh boy, oh boy.

I should have seen something like this coming. I mean, if I had, I would have immediately disbelieved myself for thinking of something so *preposterous,* but that's how it is!

Evelyn Sharpe doesn't play games, does she? The moment she decides she wants or needs somebody, she's going into overdrive. Her desire can only be cut off by the likes of me saying no. Probably. Maybe. I might be giving the universe too much credit here because I certainly have none to give myself.

She's coming closer. Pushing me against the counter and surrounding me with her body. Doesn't this feel so familiar? Say, almost a whole week ago, when she pressed me against the hotel room wall and fingered me until I came right there?

It had felt so impossible back then. That someone as bright and unbelievable as Evelyn wanted *me.* I mean, I get a fair amount of offers. As you know, it's not ludicrous for a woman I like to come right at me with her terms. Over the years I've been told that I put out "that" energy. Lots of people can tell that I'm pliable and submissive. Good. I like it that way. Not having to tell people and instead watch one fantasy after another come true is more than enough for me.

Still, call me incredulous when she plants a big kiss on my lips, her fingers wrapped around my chin and my ass pushing against the counter.

"We wouldn't have a lot of time..." That finger lands in my blouse, undoing the top button and pressing into my skin. I'm speechless. How can I be anything else as Evelyn Sharpe kisses me again? "But we could have a fun quickie right here. Calm both of our nerves before we go out to that meeting."

"I get why you want to calm *your* nerves," I whisper, "but since when do I have any?"

"Since I felt you trembling beneath my touch, sweetheart."

That's true, but only because this woman makes my legs numb and my pussy ache. Ugh. Something to put in my diary tonight. "That's... that's not what I meant," I stutter. "I'm out there doing my job. It's nothing special to me today."

"Even though I'm there? That doesn't make it special?"

"I didn't say that!"

Evelyn chuckles. "If I make you come right here, I bet you'll focus more on your work when I tell your boss why he should buy my *boring* insurance. Otherwise, you'd spend the whole time thinking about me doing this." She hikes up my skirt. My head automatically falls back; my throat is exposed. I could let her bite it – but I can't help but think this is a mistake. We're in public, for fuck's sake. I can be pretty quiet when necessary, but what if someone tries to come in? What if they go get someone with a key? What if Mr. Birch finds out that Evelyn and I are late getting back because we're doing it in the bathroom? I could never live that down! Nor would I ever work in this town again!

Except it feels so good when she parts my legs with her hand and touches my underwear with a single finger.

"Right here." That purr is cataclysmically sexy. Just from that I'm sighing, eyes closed, thighs relaxing around her. It's like the hotel room again! Sometimes, when I think too much about that night, I chastise myself for falling into her arms so easily. That was the moment I gave up any chance to properly date her – let alone have Evelyn see me as anyone but an easy lay. "Give me two minutes. Then you can go back out there and be the good girl he hired you to be."

"I'm not that good."

Those are the magic words that welcome Evelyn's finger beneath my underwear. My skin is so hot that I barely feel her breath as it warms my chest.

Why is my chest exposed? Does she work that quickly?

"I think you're a good girl. In fact, I'm attracted to good girls. Problem with that?"

Evelyn might as well have asked me to come right now. Because I'm so close from a single touch to my slit that I'm about to burst. "No problem," I squeak. "I don't understand..."

"Stop trying to understand things and go with the flow. Life is more exciting that way."

I don't disagree. Which is why when I completely give in, it's with my legs spread wide and my ass firmly planted on the counter. As Evelyn's kisses cover my face, throat, and chest, her finger goes straight for my clit. This is how we're doing it. Hot, fast, and heavy.

Fuck me for being so wet for her, right?

Once I give in, it's with the understanding that we *really* don't have much time. I slam my mouth against hers and embrace the softness of her hair and the heft of her perfume. Much like my thighs embrace her damned arm. Now's the time to come. Not five minutes from now. Five minutes ago would have been preferable, but I wasn't *with* it then. Now I am.

It has to be now. This quick, fleeting feeling with a woman I hardly know but want in my bed by the end of the night. The few times I've met Evelyn Sharpe in the flesh have been so electric that my heart is still palpitating and my hair has not fallen back into place. I want her inside of me like this every single day. I don't care where it is. A bathroom in an Italian bistro? Her office? The back of her car or in her condo?

I'm familiar with such trysts.

I cling to her and the escape she offers. No longer do I think about my bad breakup, the string of failed relationships, or my own self-loathing. I don't have to be the girl who made someone cheat anymore. Nor am I that forgettable one-night stand that nobody comes back for after she gives it up, either on the first date or the fifth. Trust me, when you figure out that's the game, you get it over with on the first date. That way you don't waste anyone's time, least of all your own.

Yet this is the second time I've been with Evelyn. Maybe the world isn't so bad, after all. Clearly, there's something about me that draws these women into my web. Maybe I'm not good at keeping them in it, but I never claimed to be a black widow. I'm just...

I'm trying to enjoy my life!

"Ah!" Evelyn's mouth clamps over my mouth. Dare I believe this is permission to groan into it? Because her finger is so deep inside of me again that I can't help but roll back my eyes and give in to orgasm. She hits that spot so good that I might as well forget everything I said about being quiet when necessary.

"Shh," she coos to the beat of her finger plunging into me. "Let's not have this moment ruined because someone heard us."

I nod. What else can I do?

"You better come now. We don't have a lot of time before they'll wonder where we are."

That's easy. Once the C word is out of her mouth, I'm undulating against the counter and humping her hand like it really is that easy to have sex with me. The single second I have my eyes open captures Evelyn's grin of triumph as she claims me for a second time in a week.

This may not have been a date... but it was hot and damn satisfying.

I wish I could say clarity consumes me once I'm done coming and her hand has left my body, but I'm not. My eyes are still heavy and my whole body is sluggish. While Evelyn cleans herself up and politely suggests that I get my outfit back in order, I slip against the counter and pray that all of that *really* happened. This wasn't a dream, right? A really pathetic dream that traps me in my own head and forces me to face my own second-hand embarrassment?

"Let's go finish the meeting," Evelyn says, one hand on the door. By now, I've fixed up my skirt and blouse, but anyone looking at my flushed face must know that I've been up to no good in this bathroom. "How about I call you soon? We should go out again."

Did those words really come from Evelyn's mouth? Or am I losing my mind again?

"Keira." She steadies me with both hands on my shoulders. We're in the hallway now, so she's careful to keep her distance and her voice low. Just in time, too, for a woman in Jimmy Choos and wearing Chanel No. 5 hustles past us and into the bathroom. "Pull yourself together. We had sex in the restroom. We are now going to rejoin your boss at the table, push aside our dirty dishes for the waiter to collect, and focus on the meeting. What happened back there..." she lowers her hands, smoothing out her own skirt, "don't worry about it for now. We'll hash it out on our personal time later."

Evelyn winks at me before marching toward our table. Oscar looks up from several feet away, a smile on his face. Meanwhile, I'm trying to remind myself that hanky-panky in the bathroom is a thrill, not a cause for an existential crisis.

Suppose I'm worried she won't actually call me at all. Wouldn't that be a fine thing?

No point thinking about it now. Evelyn is right. I need to get back to the table. Preferably *after* I've pulled myself together.

CHAPTER 14

Keira

This is what they call one of those "impossible situations."

Here I am, lounging in my room after getting ready for bed. A terrycloth bathrobe is a bit heavy for this time of year, but my window is open, and the faint sounds of the city remind me that I'm not really alone in this world.

Of course I'm not. Because there's a voicemail from Evelyn on my phone, left there while I was in the shower.

"Hello, sweetheart." I replay it again, my phone glued to my ear because I need to hear the lust in that mature voice. *"I hope you're having a great evening. Thank you again so much for... today."* That sigh may be practiced, but it's effective on me. One minute ago, I wasn't thinking about sex at all. Now? My thighs ease open as if Evelyn is about to climb through my voice mail service and bang me again right here in my bed. *"I don't know what came over me, but I'm glad it worked out. Going forward, though, we should be more discreet, yes? I'm sure you would appreciate it if your boss wasn't so close to our sex life. Because I'd like to continue that with you. How about this Saturday? My friend bought a small yacht to celebrate a big achievement at work and wants to christen it with a party. She's told me I can bring a date. In fact, she insists. I'd love it if you would be my date that night. You and me, chilling beneath the stars on a warm spring night, complete with Champagne and some good food. I think you'll like my friends. The ones who aren't professionals like us know what it's like to have fun. Don't worry. We can save the sex for the afterparty. Let me know your answer by tomorrow night. Have sweet dreams, Keira."*

That's the third time I've listened to it. The first time, I wasn't sure I was hearing what she said. After all, why would Evelyn Sharpe ask me out again? Like this? To meet her friends? On a yacht? Down at the marina!

My instinct is to instantly accept. After all, I yearn to feel her lips on mine again. I want to get on top of her for once and ride until I can't feel my legs anymore. I already know that I'm going to spend the night with my vibrator against my clit. Maybe something more. Wouldn't be the first time I've thought about Evelyn while I whined into my own pillow.

So why am I not telling her *yes, yes, yes?* It's not like I play hard to get. After all, I went to a hotel with her only an hour into our date of drinks and not much else. There's no purity over here on my end. If anything, I've proven time and again that I'm so easy I might as well shave a landing strip onto my pelvis and install some lights while I'm at it.

I love sex, but I love hurting myself more.

Evelyn is the perfect woman to ruin me. She's someone who knows what she wants, and right now it's me. Yet for how long? How far will I fall into her embrace and make an absolute fool of myself when it inevitably ends? Is what Laura suggested about Evelyn also being a cheater true? Maybe not, if she's willing to introduce me to her friends. Although I know she's not serious about a relationship. She's looking for a hot fling to make her memories with, and if I'm not careful, I could get seriously hurt again. After the lies Sera told me, I wasn't sure I'd be dating again yet. Evelyn brought out that self-destructive side of me. The one who wants to go straight to the sex and let the aftermath blow up in my face.

That's how I get validation, after all. Right through my pussy.

Something I've known about myself for a long time, and I'm not that ashamed to admit it. That's what happens when you're used to rejection. Don't know what it is, really. Is it my generation? The bluntness in high school and college was nice, in a way, but it certainly didn't do anything for my self-esteem. People outright saying they're not into me, don't find me pretty, or that I'm "too fat," whatever that means... you get used to it, but it also cuts you deeper every time. The few people who didn't push me away and showed me some affection couldn't counteract all the instances of "You miss every shot you don't take." Take it from me. Many times you wish you hadn't taken any shots at all.

Maybe that's why I'm so submissive in my relationships. That's how I meet women like Sera, who step all over me while hurting someone else. They took one look at me and know they can rip me in two without any trouble. After all, if I don't pursue anyone, and if I don't bother with love unless it comes to me... shit. Is it any wonder that when someone *does* approach me I'm all over it like butter on toast?

I play Evelyn's message one more time. Indulging in how aroused her voice makes me feel is as dangerous as it is expected.

I'm still in no hurry to reply, though. Perhaps I *should* play a little hard to get. If this is something I seriously pursue, I better reorient my head and stop feeling so sorry for myself. I'll be thirty soon enough. It's about time I moved on from Sera and all the other people who took advantage of me. At some point, I must admit that it's my fault, too. I'm only enabling my own toxic behavior.

Harder than it sounds, though...

Bambambam.

The knocks at my door startle me upright. Who is calling at this hour? This is when I relax before bed. The only people who drop by are anyone I'm dating, or maybe a neighbor, if something was misdelivered to them. It's definitely not because I'm a noisy neighbor. Even when someone stays the night, I blast the fan and hide my moans in my pillow.

I tighten the sash of my robe as I get off my bed and shuffle to the door. Although I stand on my tip-toes to see through the peephole, there's nothing there. Either they realized they had the wrong door, or something was left at my door.

I crack it open.

What a mistake.

"Keira, wait." A hand slams dangerously close to the gap I'm attempting to close. The apartments here don't have chain locks, so all it takes is a little effort for the door to open wider. Before I know it, I'm looking up into Sera's unforgettable face. "Can we talk?"

She's already halfway through my doorway. Nevertheless, I refuse to budge from my spot. She's not big and tough enough to bowl me over unless she's looking to rob me blind, so I'll take my chances that this is a "pleasure" call and not an effort to steal my cheap TV and everyday laptop.

"What do you want?" I ask, shoulder slammed against the doorway. "I really don't have a lot to say to you."

Her exasperated airs would have beguiled me a few months ago. Hell, they had! This is a woman that was hard to shake once she was humping my leg. I'm not talking about when we were "happily" dating, either. After I dumped her, she showed up to several places and called my phone a dozen times trying to "talk things out." I kept letting her, too. I enable the people who take advantage of me as much as I enable my own insensitive actions.

"I've been thinking a lot these past few months," she says with a haughty sigh. Poor me, looking right into those sparkling hazel eyes that might as well be imprinted upon the back of my own eyelids for the rest of my life. To think, I had fallen in love with this cheating fool. "I really fucked up, babe. I should have told you about my ex. The fact that we weren't *totally* broken up yet. I just... you were so breathtaking when we met that I didn't want to wait. I didn't want to miss the opportunity to get to know you!"

"Get to know me?" I shoot back at her. "You're talking about fooling around in the bathroom, right?" God, that sounds familiar. Who else have I fucked in a bathroom lately? "That's how you wanted to introduce yourself to me?"

"I mean... that's how the mood went, babe." Sera shakes her head. "Can I come in? Please?"

She attempts to push the door in. I, to my great pride, remain firm. No help needed! For once, I'm going to say a second firm no and not let someone wear me down until they get what they want from me – no matter how good it would feel to get laid *twice* in the same day. "No. I would appreciate it if you don't come around again. It's over Sera. You don't get to use me like that and keep it up for long!"

Sputtering her words, Sera holds back what she's really thinking before she comes to a single conclusion. "Is there someone else? Already?"

"What do you mean 'already'? It's been months! Why the hell shouldn't I have moved on by now? Do you think I'm not worthy of going out with someone else by now?"

"Who the hell is it? Is it that friend of yours? Laura or something?"

"Laura's straight!" I shoot back at her. "Come on! You can do better than that! You picked the first person I was friends with!"

"For all I know, you were already messing around with her."

"Not everyone is a cheating shithead like you!"

I slam the door in her face. The very definition of sticking up for myself right now!

You bet your ass, though, that I stand on my tip-toes again and peer through the peephole. I will make damn sure that Sera evacuates my premises, and I'm not above calling the night security on her flaky ass.

Her figure looks like it wants to kick my door, but she eventually turns around and marches off. I wish I could say it's with her tail tucked between her legs, but I don't get to behold such a grand sight tonight.

Hmph.

Why did she have to do that? Come to my door, acting like a hotshot who "wants to talk?" I saw right through her shit, didn't I? Yet before I can be too proud of myself, my lip trembles, and I'm flinging my body toward my bed so I can bury my whole face in my pillow.

No, I don't cry. I have *some* self-respect left. I'm merely blocking my senses from the rest of the world.

Why? Why did Sera show up right when I'm thinking about moving on and claiming my *destiny* as someone with her own direction in life? When I'm crafting the perfect reply to Evelyn Sharpe?

I cling to my memory of this afternoon when Evelyn followed me into the ladies' room and treated me to something I haven't felt in so long. Her magnetic pull is so intense that I wouldn't mind circling her orbit for a few weeks.

Maybe a few months...

I won't get ahead of myself, though. I'm not looking for a real relationship, after all. There's no way I'm ready for love yet. Not even with Evelyn, who is the exact kind of confident woman I've always seen myself marrying. Sure, she's older than me, but so was Sera. Isn't that what makes my ex extra pathetic? That she was in her thirties and acting like a child?

Instead of texting her, I call Evelyn back.

"Hello," she breathes right into my ear. Instantly, I forget Sera's arrival and swift departure. I'm not thinking about how humiliated she left me in some stranger's apartment. Nor am I lamenting all those tears and sleepless nights wasted on someone who never deserved me in the beginning. "So lovely to hear from you. I hope my call didn't interrupt your evening."

"Not at all. Sorry I wasn't around to hear the phone ringing. I was taking a shower."

She bites my bait. "Oh? I'm sorry to have missed *that*. I bet you're absolutely succulent in the shower. Now I'm thinking about you in a bubble bath. I don't want to brag, but I have a jet tub that hits you in all the right places."

"Do you?" I squeak. "Everything comes back to the water, I suppose. You said something about your friend buying a yacht?"

"*Don't* let your imagination get away from you. I've seen the pictures. It's a little thing that doesn't go that far from the marina, but it's a slice of quiet in the city. My friend Raquel is quite the bigshot in local real estate and has won a slew of awards and made a killing this past year. That whole 'people fleeing the cities' thing. For every person who moves to the city, someone is moving from *another* city who discovers how much more cheaply they can live here. Her commissions are envious. You must meet her."

"Does she know about me?"

"I've told her that I had someone in mind. Let's play our affair by ear, angel."

"Angel?"

"Do you like that one? I've been trying some different nicknames on you. For size. Sweetheart and babe are fun and all, but they're rather generic. I don't want you feeling like there's nothing *special* or *memorable* about you."

I lay across my bed, feet kicking in the air and robe falling open. My bare stomach is soon on my soft comforter. A part of me hopes Sera comes back so she can see me flirting on the phone. *You could have still had this if you weren't who you really are.* "You can call me whatever you want. Some people call me Kiki. Coming from the right person, I like it."

"Your mother doesn't call you that, does she?"

"Goodness, no. She calls me Keira when I'm *not* in trouble. The full name comes out when she wants me to repent for my sins."

"Good. Because I'm not calling you what your own mother calls you. Kiki. That's sweet. Suits you well. Hope you don't mind if I let it fall from my tongue next time we're getting it on."

"Will that be Saturday night?"

"If you're willing. Meet us down at the marina around six. The evenings are getting longer so that will give us plenty of time to head out of the harbor and take in the sunset. I don't know how many others will be there, but I'm mostly wanting you to meet my good friend Raquel. You'll love her, and her younger girlfriend. She's closer to your age than mine, so it will be nice if you two get along. No pressure, though."

"I like meeting new people." A white lie, but who is counting them? I'm already imagining us lounging on blankets while we sip something yummy and watch the sunset explode into so many colors. Purple! Orange! Yellow! I wanna see them all in one moment. And I want to do it with Evelyn, who is absolutely not my ex-girlfriend.

Because I'm moving on, you see.

"The forecast says it will be clear, but you never know how cool it gets once the sun goes down. So be prepared. No matter what, wear something comfortable. It's a yacht. You're meant to be cozy while we bob on the waves."

"Yes, ma'am."

My flirtatious tone isn't lost on her. "I'd stay on the line and play with you a bit, Kiki, but I have some boring work calls to return before I turn in for the night. Do me a favor and think of me while you go to sleep."

"I was already planning on it. I've got some unfinished business with my clit that my vibrator is going to take care of."

"Ooh, how delicious. Then you should *definitely* think about me while you do that. I know that I'll be thinking about you later tonight. I've got some unfinished business of my own. Have a fun evening, Kiki."

She hangs up, but I don't feel abandoned. If anything, her using my nickname has put a smile on my face. Giggling over my impending date with a woman who wants me? Or crying over someone who used me in her shitty relationship games?

As soon as I take a few deep breaths, I'm opening up my nightstand and refusing to think about Sera. Not for a single second.

CHAPTER 15

Evelyn

"You are *not* going to fall overboard." Raquel stands at the rear of her yacht, hand grandly gesturing to the ramp leading down to the floating dock by the vessel. "For Pete's sake, what kind of shitty friend do you take me for?"

"One who entertains in her bathing suit."

While I hobble my heels down the ramp, grabbing onto the ropes the whole way, Raquel pulls back the linen robe covering her sapphire blue one piece. "I like to pretend I'm filming a music video every time I'm on this thing. Which is almost every night now."

Her words go in one ear and out the other as trepidation brings me to the tiny, floating luxury craft. When Raquel told me she bought "the smallest yacht" she could find, she wasn't kidding. While there is a decent table set up on the back deck, as well as an impressive bedroom and bathroom in its depths, I swear to God the two of us are going to tip the whole thing over and plunge right into dirty marina water. Never mind those seagulls floating by! They don't know what they're doing!

"Honestly, one would think you're afraid of water." Raquel takes me by the hand and steadies me once I'm on the deck. The more I think about it, the more I swear the boat is tipping back and forth. Am I seasick already? It's been years since I've been on a boat of any kind, and the last time was a speedboat that made me hurl over the edge. I'd rather not repeat that.

"I'm not afraid of water." I fix my hair as soon as I stand up straight again. "I'm afraid of getting my dress wet."

We share air kisses and she gives me a tour of the vessel, aptly dubbed "Princess Lisa" after her young and bouncy girlfriend. Sure enough, we bump into Raquel's darling in the cabin, where she's prettying up her pink toenails and letting them air dry the moment we walk in.

I've always been a bit envious of Raquel's taste in women. Even when I was with Sera, the first thing we always talked about was my friend's great, insatiable appetite for co-eds. You know how it is. She gets older, and her girlfriends stay the same age. I will say, though, that Raquel's cougar days might be over as she and Lisa have been together for over three years now. (Before you ask, yes, Sera always used to stare at those flawless thighs and perky tits as they bounced by us. To be fair, so did I. How can you *not* when you look like you're built to titillate older people?) That's not to say that Raquel isn't a looker herself. She's a few years older than me, but we've always felt like kindred souls. She was also the first to tell me that something didn't smell right with Sera whenever I griped about our relationship – back before I found out about the fresh cheating.

"So, where's the new strumpet that has you slobbering like a frat boy in a sorority house?" Raquel sashays by after filling a glass with Champagne. She offers it to me, but I decline. I prefer to not drink until we're settled, and that won't happen until you-know-who arrives. "What was her name again? Claire?"

"Keira." That's where I leave it. All Raquel knows about Sera's cheating was that it was with another woman. As soon as I learned Keira's identity, I kept it to myself. The only reason I'm daring to expose Keira to one of my closest friends is *because* nobody else knows who she is. As long as Sera's common name is kept out of everyone's mouths...

"Isn't that Irish? I have a cousin named Kieran."

I chuckle. "You're going to love the way she looks, then."

"Red hair and freckles?"

"A body you have to grab."

Lisa approaches with a tray of finger foods. Between the crackers, sliced cheeses, and small bits of peppered sausage, I'm about to get fat tonight. "Raquel told me you have a new girlfriend," she says after I take a cracker and cheese slice. "Can't wait to meet her. Don't suppose she's around my age? Believe it or not, just because she chases after young ass doesn't mean all her friends are the same age."

"She's not quite thirty, I believe. So, could be your old classmate."

Lisa grins. I get it. That big, girlish smile is infectious. So is the brown ponytail and the flowy pink top that accentuates the stringy bikini beneath it.

As soon as Lisa is back in the kitchen area slicing more cheese, I lean in toward Raquel and ask, "You've rolled that all over the bed below deck, right?"

Raquel maintains her smile while she drinks Champagne. "The bed has been adequately christened even if this is our first party. I've had this thing for a week now, you know."

"I heard that," Lisa calls over her shoulder. "You're lucky I like you, Evie."

I check my phone to see what time it is. "She should be here any minute. How about we go sit on the back of the deck to see her when she arrives?"

"You just want to show her off from a distance."

I'm already up. "Of course I do. Come on. Get that butt of yours out here. Bring the bathing suit, while you're at it."

"Do you think I have a habit of lounging on my own yacht without any clothes on?" Raquel is right behind me as we sit on the cozy couch at the rear of the yacht. The evening air tickles my skin. While it's warm, I'm inclined to grab a spare sweater. One never knows when they might catch a cold. "That's my girlfriend's thing. She's already attracted a few fake boyfriends around the marina. They love coming down to ogle her nude sunbathing. She's *so* shameless."

"You say with pride in your voice. She doesn't get in trouble for that?" Surely, there must be decency laws.

"Oh, honey. You don't know? It's legal for any adult to be topless in this city. It's just most women don't want to bother with the unwanted attention. Not Lisa, though. You know how she is. She loves to show off her body."

"Must be so *terrible* for you."

"I prefer if I don't have to chase off every twenty-something male sniffing around Princess Lisa, but I do love the view." Raquel raises her glass. "Tell me more about this Keira before I meet her. I want to imagine what she looks like naked from you painting a picture with your words."

I don't get the chance. As soon as I settle into my seat, I catch a glimpse of red hair descending the ramp from the parking lot down to the marina. Hell, that's not the only red thing coming this way. That's Keira, all right, and she's bedecked in a stylishly red shift dress that flutters as she walks. Her thick hair is wrapped into a ball against the back of her neck, which is only more apparent as she quickly finds me waving to her from the back of a yacht.

"Good evening, darling!" I call up the wobbly ramp I traversed only a few minutes ago. "Watch your step coming down! Champagne and cheese are waiting for you, though!"

Like a total pro, Keira comes down the ramp as if it doesn't wobble and she's not about to plummet into the freezing cold water. I'm envious. Yet Raquel's envious gaze rivals mine, and I'll take it – any time my friend lets out a low whistle at the women I'm dating, I take it as a good sign.

"This is really cool." Keira orients herself once we're together. After I take her hand and lure her down to the couch, she faces Raquel who is sitting on the other side of me. "You must be the friend I've heard so much about. Is this your vessel?"

"*Bienvenu* to Princess Lisa." Raquel extends her hand across me. "My name's Raquel. That there is Princess Lisa." Because her name was spoken, Lisa emerges from the cabin, bringing a small plate of snacks. "Don't let her girlish features fool you. She's old enough to rent a car."

"Am I old enough to drive your yacht yet?"

"Absolutely not. This baby's mine."

A few minutes later, Raquel is in the cockpit, taking us out of the marina and deeper into the harbor. Everything she promised when she invited me to this excursion has come true. Not only is the weather *perfect,* but the water is still and the mosquitos are less than active so far from land. We can see the outline of the city where we are, but aside from another boat zooming by, it feels like we're in our own private paradise out at sea.

It's a damn good thing I'm not afraid of the water, though, because it's all I see for miles in either direction.

"What do you think?" I ask Keira, as Raquel and Lisa prepare for our dinner. "Could you see yourself tanning on this deck? Perhaps with your top off?"

"Oh, my."

"I hear that's what Lisa there does."

Keira is nothing but giggles as Raquel asks us to get up and wait in the cabin for a few minutes. The couch we were sitting on is soon tucked inside a hidden compartment in the deck, and in its place is brought out a square table and a few chairs. Lisa places the bottle of Champagne and four glasses of ice water on the table while Raquel reveals the pasta salads, fresh fruit, and pitas she quickly heats up in the toaster oven before bringing them out to the table. Everything was thought of ahead of time. While Raquel couldn't cook us a hot meal with what she had, everything looks delicious as we sit down to dinner beneath the sunset.

"How did you two meet?" Lisa asks while breaking apart her pita. "Raquel hasn't told me much. Did you guys recently start going out?"

I answer before Keira can give too much away. "She appeared at one of my meetings last week. Usually, it's such boring shit, but there she was, wowing me with her sense of style and that pretty face of hers. I simply had to ask her out." I look toward Keira, who is blushing. "Lucky me, she said yes. What was that, a week ago?"

"Our first date was last Friday."

"That's right. We've decided to make it a regular thing. Turns out she's as pretty inside as she is on the out," I say right through my teeth. "I guess she must think the same thing about me."

Raquel slightly cocks her head. Lisa is eating it up, though. Such is youth. To be that age where you believe everything a pretty woman tells you... hmph! I could still be that person if I open my heart!

"I'm going with the flow right now," Keira says. "By the way, this pasta salad is delicious. Did you make it?"

She asks that of Raquel, who is caught off guard by such an inquisition. "No, I can't take credit for the salad. That's all Lisa's doing." A smile beams in her young girlfriend's direction. "She always was quite the adventurous cook, but ever since she moved in with me a couple years ago, she's only become a bigger wonder around the kitchen. She's been taking lessons at the culinary institute."

That leaves me somehow incredulous. "Really? Thinking of going full-time?" I ask Lisa.

"Oh, no. It's only a hobby. You watch The Food Network and *Master Chef* enough times, and you start thinking, hey, you can do that. So, I did it! Glad it's so tasty. I put in a special ingredient."

"It's oregano," Raquel drolly says. "That's her secret ingredient for everything. Oh, that reminds me. It's been a while since we got some of your bombastic oatmeal cranberry cookies." She says this while I'm in the middle of drinking ice water. Before I can respond, Raquel says to Keira, "Have you had her cookies? I don't know how she does it, but the texture is always..."

"That wasn't me," I curtly interrupt. "You know I don't bake. I rarely cook. You're thinking of someone else I used to live with who made the cookies."

"Oh. Oh!" That's right, Raquel. You've magically forgotten about Sera. Don't know how, considering she always bragged about how much people loved her baked goods. To be fair, Sera knew her way around an oven and a bag of flour. Cookies, cakes... the only thing she occasionally floundered on were pies, but she was more into the super sweet. Chocolate chips were a staple in my house until I cast that cheating liar out. I don't care how good her cookies are! "I'm so sorry. I forgot it was Se..."

I loudly clear my throat. Yes, it's obnoxious, and only serves to call more attention to myself, but the last thing I need is Keira finding out that my ex was named *Sera*. For right now, I'd like to keep that information on strictly need-to-know, and Keira does not need to know anytime soon!

"Sorry. I don't want to bring her up here. I want to let bygones be bygones and move on with friends, old and new."

Did that sound convincing? Or should I worry that Keira is looking at me like I've lost my mind?

"Forgive me. Of course we shouldn't bring her up." Raquel sits back from her empty plate and holds her glass of Champagne close to her chest. "Besides, I can already tell that Keira is in a league all of her own! Watch out for this one here." The glass lazily moves in my direction. "We've been friends for so long that I know all of her tricks. Let me guess. She took you to the Lighthouse Lounge for your first date?"

"Only because it's the best place in town to get to know a discerning lady," I explain before Keira can inadvertently call me out. "Look at her." Now all attention is on Keira, who slows her eating to ladylike bites. "Isn't this a woman you ask out the moment you see her? Of course I took her to the Lighthouse Lounge. Where was I supposed to take her? Rusty's Grotto on the edge of town?"

Lisa laughs. Raquel bites her lip with a smile. At least she's not asking if I took Keira to "the usual hotel" across the street. Please. Raquel likes to tease me, but she knows better than to make me sound like a restless slut in front of my date. Besides, if you ask me? She likes Keira. That's why she's being engaged in conversation and invited to partake in Raquel's success.

Perhaps I really shouldn't fuck this up...

"There's rice pudding for dessert," Raquel mentions when I've finished my dinner. "How does that sound, Keira? Lisa and I will put the table and chairs away so we can enjoy the sunset with our dessert."

"Oh! You mean it hasn't happened yet?"

Keira is pointing to the sun as it makes love to the horizon. Already a splash of golds, purples, and pinks splay across the sky. I admit it's a beautiful sight to behold, and not only because I'm in good company. I daresay this is some of the most relaxing fun I've had in a group since my breakup. Knowing that I can bring someone to dinner and it's *not* Sera mucking up my life... I know next to nothing about Keira's history besides her role in the end of my relationship, but I'm...

Grateful, I suppose.

Is it any wonder that I'm looking at her "weird" while we wait for Lisa and Raquel to take our dishes into the cabin, followed by the furniture that is soon replaced with the comfortable couch and a lounge chair for Raquel to claim as her queenly throne? Bowls of rice pudding make the rounds as Lisa gets out her phone and takes endless photographs of the sunset before us. Every ray of light reflecting off the city skyline is another reminder that life moves on. The *world* moves on. As for every star appearing in the sky as it grows darker and chillier?

The more stars in the sky, the more insignificant your problems become.

"You're not cold, are you?" Lisa asks Keira, who only has a light sweater to wear as the warm night encroaches upon us. "I always get so cold out here. Doesn't matter how warm the air is."

"That's because you're hardly wearing any clothes, love." Raquel doesn't have much room to talk, but at least her abdomen is covered. "I've told you to wear one of those pretty shift dresses I got you. Don't you have some stored here in the bedroom?"

Lisa shrugs. "I was asking about our guest. I have to make sure she's comfortable."

"I'm fine," Keira says with a mouthful of rice pudding. "This is really good, by the way. Did you make it, too?"

"Oh, that? No way. Bought it at the store. Glad you like it, though! It's my second favorite brand."

While the two of them talk, Raquel and I exchange a look. She's happily rolling her eyes while I shift uncomfortably on my seat. Keira is sitting in the middle of the couch, between Lisa and me, but it's Lisa who is all up in the other's face. While I know that Lisa merely likes to make friends and find validation through how many people like her, Keira might not be in the know. Should I jump in *now* and save her, or should I wait until Keira is finished with her pudding?

Neither comes to pass. In fact, I don't have to worry too much about anything. It's a lovely evening. The darker it becomes, the more comfortable I am wrapped in my sweater and enjoying the sunset with two of my closest friends and someone I've brought along for the ride. Once again, I briefly forget that I met Keira under forced pretenses. I'm not thinking about Aspen Plastics – let alone Sera – when I look at her. That red hair glows beneath the purple sky, and those pretty eyes twinkle along with the stars. I've always thought Lisa a gorgeous girl – and Raquel a lucky woman – but she's completely eclipsed by the flowy dress flirting with Keira's legs and that look of *"What is it?"* that meets me when I look at my date for too long.

After a while, Raquel stands up and motions to Lisa. "Why don't we step inside and clean up some of the dishes, sweetheart? Better to do it now than to let them jostle around when we drive back to the marina."

Lisa pulls herself away from Keira and follows her girlfriend into the cabin. It's dark enough now that you can't really see them moving beyond the barely-lit curtains that have been drawn to offer us some privacy. While I know that they'll be back soon enough, I don't doubt that Raquel is giving Keira and me some privacy on purpose.

"Your friends are really nice." Keira turns toward me, arm slung over the back of the couch and touching the white paint of the yacht. While we can't see the words "THE PRINCESS LISA" from here, I know it's proudly painted not so far away. Personally, I like the name KEIRA for a vessel. It's straight and to the lovely point. "They have a really nice boat."

"It's a lovely night, isn't it?" I'm not looking at the sky right now. I'm savoring the contours of Keira's face as my eyes adjust to the impending darkness. One light flicks on above the door leading to the cabin. There are other lights at the front of the yacht, and ambient lights we can turn on with a touch of a button, but I'm content to sit here on this pillowy couch and absorb the attentions of a woman I've brought on board.

"The view is very lovely, yes."

My fingers walk up the length of Keira's thigh. "It would be a shame to head back to shore early so we can hurry up and get to the hotel..."

"Hotel?"

That squeak in Keira's voice catches me off guard. I snatch my fingers away. "What is it? I haven't made a reservation yet. We can..."

"I was kinda hoping we could go to your place."

I redirect the nervous energy toward tucking my hair behind my ear. "My place? You mean where I live?"

"Would that be a problem?"

Oh, let me count the ways! Let's start with how Keira has already been there at least once before. It's bad enough she's making me think about buying a new car. Moving for this relationship, just to keep everything under wraps a while longer, isn't good for me. There's also the fact that remnants of Sera might still be there. I've thrown out all her shit that she left behind and there isn't a picture left on the wall, but you never know. Odds are high I've overlooked *something*.

"My place is a mess," I say, my tone so controlled that she must hear right through it. "I haven't properly cleaned it since my last breakup. Trust me, you don't wanna go there tonight. Not on such a nice night. We should go somewhere with a great view of the city and a hot tub."

"Was the person you broke up with the one who made the really good oatmeal cookies?"

"You were really paying attention, huh?"

"I'm interested in you, Evie. Is it too much to ask that you tell me more about yourself? About who you are these past few years?"

That's one way to put it. Who *am* I these days, huh? So much of my recent life has been defined by Sera and my job. I am Evelyn Sharpe, damnit, but what does that mean? That I work my ass off at a *corporate insurance* job? For what? To make a nice living. Invest a little. Retire early. See the world and pursue my hobbies, whatever they are.

Hey, some people get to do their dream jobs. The rest of us kick ass at what we can and hope for the best.

"What is there to say?" I shrug against one of the brown pillows that are now black in the shadowy night. "Until a few months ago, I was in a long-term relationship with someone who wasn't... who I thought they were." Yeah, right. I knew exactly who Sera was because she showed me more than once. All the signs were there. The only person I have to blame is myself in the end – think of all the time I could have saved by not letting her pal around behind my back. I could have totally moved on by now. Been the one actually in *charge* of that breakup instead of letting it crumble around me like a house of cards. "They hurt me. Badly. Suppose that's why I'm not in a rush to get into something serious." Here I am, wrapping my hand around her knee as if she's not the one I caught in my bedroom. My head is split in two and my heart is more confused. No, I'm not falling in love with this girl. I'm, quite simply, confused.

About what I want. About what I *need*.

"Don't get me wrong, Kiki," I continue. "I think you're intriguing and a lot of fun. I'd like to see where this goes. I'm merely in no hurry to take you to my house and show you where I lay my head most nights. It's a vulnerability thing."

"How about my place, then?" she whispers in the crevice between us. "It's really small, but I don't have any roommates. We'll have the whole place to ourselves. After my breakup, I'm ready to let some people in."

She drains her Champagne glass when she says that. "Has it been a while since someone visited your place? Sounds like it's lonely."

"A few months for me, too. My ex-girlfriend... I never told you, but her name was Sera."

That hits me right in the chest. I look away so she doesn't have to see me nearly puke. If anyone asks, I'm feeling a bit seasick.

"We met in a bar. That dive where queer girls go on the weekends. You know the one?"

"I'm aware of it," I say through gritted teeth. Like I don't know! That's the stinking place Sera used to go to with her friends whenever they had a "boys night out" as she liked to call it. While I never got along with her more tomboyish friends – nothing to do with them as they were, I just can't stand aimless individuals who care more about sharing sexual exploits than anything *meaningful* – I never held her back from hanging out with them, either. In turn, I spent a good chunk of time with my own friends without Sera around. We attended plenty of functions together. It always felt like a good balance. Apparently, I should have been bribing the bartender of her favorite dive to keep an eye on her!

"She was playing pool and I was hanging out feeling sorry for myself. You see, I'm not used to people being so interested in me. Anyone who doesn't look right past me only wants me for the novelty. I guess there aren't a lot of redheads around here."

"No natural ones, no," I sigh. Too bad I'm sitting here imagining the moment my ex decided to cheat on me.

"She made me feel so wanted. It was the closest thing to cloud nine I've ever felt." Keira looks away – her whole body is facing away from me.

"Then the most embarrassing thing happened. You won't believe it. You'll think I'm the dumbest person on the planet."

I say nothing. It's either that or agree with her.

Keira wipes something from her eye. With a sniff, she says, "She finally takes me to her place after being together for several weeks. In the middle of my visit, someone shows up, and the next thing I know, I've got a blanket over my head and she's trying to shove me into the closet like I'm some dog. Turns out she had a 'real' girlfriend the whole time she was with me. I was a dirty secret, and looking back on the 'fun' we used to have, I get it now. That wasn't fun. That was her trying not to get caught. I just thought she was kinda kinky."

My tender emotions swing between anger and despair. It's one thing for this woman to have no idea that *I'm* her. *I'm* the girlfriend she didn't know about. It's another for me, that fucking woman, to sit here with my ex's sidepiece and convince myself that I'm somehow not involved in this story.

"That's awful." A frog has entered my throat.

"Yes. It is." Keira massages a wrinkle out of her skirt. "I had fallen in love with her like an idiot. So even though that was over four months ago, it still hurts. Do you know what it's like to unintentionally be the other woman? Do you have any idea what it's like to have that on your shoul..." When she looks in my direction, Keira stops. "I'm sorry. Tonight is supposed to be a nice night with your friends. I shouldn't be unloading this shit on you. We hardly know each other outside of the bedroom."

"You're the one who said we should get to know one another."

"I guess. I don't want to know what you think of me now, though. In truth, you're one of the first people I've talked to about this. I have a close friend who knows. That's it, though. I'm so embarrassed to talk about it, usually. I don't know if Sera was that good at hiding the fact she was already living with someone else, or if I'm so stupid and blinded by love. The whole thing has left me jaded. Anyway... sorry."

"If you didn't know, you didn't know."

That's all I can say right now because quite frankly, I don't know if it's the truth. For all I know, Keira is the world's greatest liar and is taking me for a ride right now. Wouldn't that be the finest thing? Here I am, seducing my ex-girlfriend's lover. What right do I have to *not* be lied to by the same woman who was in my bedroom only a few months ago? I haven't mentioned this yet, but Keira wasn't exactly fully dressed when I came home that fateful afternoon. While I didn't see the kind of goods I've since seen, I can only imagine how embarrassing it was from her perspective. Yet how true is it that she didn't know? About me, that is?

Whether she knew my name and face doesn't matter. If she knew that Sera was in a relationship when they got together, then I'm not shedding a tear when we split up, too.

This has already gone on much longer than it should have. From the beginning, I only intended a one-night stand to satisfy my strange desires.

"I've been feeling a lot better ever since you came into my life." Keira twirls some of her red hair around a finger. Is that a hint of blush I detect on her cheek? It's so dark, I might be imagining it. "Uh, I don't say that to put any pressure on you. I know this is only for fun right now. But I *am* having fun. It's been nice to forget about that person who totally fucked up my life a few months back. I think about her sometimes, you know."

I sit back. "About who?"

Such a tentative question would alert anyone else, but Keira shrugs. "The woman my ex was really with. I know that they've broken up since. In fact..." With a sigh, Keira looks away from me. "Sera came by my place shortly after you called me Thursday night. She wanted to get back together. Can you believe it? She really thought I'd take her back after how she had humiliated me! Let alone how she cheated on the woman she lived with for years." The hair falls from Keira's finger. "I told her no, of course. She really showed her true colors after that."

I gasp.

"She didn't hit me or anything!" God, is that what Keira thought I was gasping about? No! I'm gasping because Sera is such a spineless shitnugget! Imagine, moving from my office to Keira's apartment, trying to get back with one or the other! Boy, am I glad I sent her packing from my office! Can you imagine? She didn't care about *me*! She didn't want to be alone!

I remain further convinced that she would have cheated on me the first chance she had again. No. Never worry about me taking Sera back. I have too much self-respect.

Contrary to what I might have thought a week ago, so does Keira.

"Did you love her?" My voice is hushed as if I can't bear to hear the answer. Either she loved Sera and it breaks my heart, or she didn't care at all, and it was for nothing.

Keira sags against me. "I thought I did. I was definitely falling in deep with her. That's what made dumping her after everything came to light so hard, but also so easy. I couldn't be with someone with such low character. Besides, if she was cheating on someone else, she would only cheat on me, right? I gotta love myself."

Her head rolls up the length of my arm. As the yacht gently bobs on the water, Keira's gray eyes glance up at me.

"What about your ex? I'm guessing you must have loved her."

"I..." What is there to say? The truth? "I did love her. That's what makes betrayal hurt so much. You think you know somebody, right?" Just because I see the signs now doesn't mean they were evident when things were good. Sera had never broken my trust like that before. It's not because I refused to see it, either. She was that good at hiding her infidelities, and I'm an idiot for being so shocked.

"I could never do that," Keira says. "Cheat on somebody, I mean. It's so callous. Like, if you're not happy, break up. How hard is it, really? Granted, I've never had to do something like that before, but I like to think I could. I don't want to hurt anyone." Another sigh breathes against me. "I'm sorry. You don't want to hear this. Besides, someone like me is a dime a dozen. I want a nice house with someone who loves me. Maybe we could have kids, but we don't have to. I like the idea of a couple of cats and maybe a dog."

She chuckles. That lilt to her throat throws me off guard. It's so... innocent. Naïve? I don't know which it is, but it hits me right in the heart. This is a woman who is old enough to be a cynical bitch like me but has somehow held on to her girlish wishes.

Having a house with a cat and a dog... God, it's so pedestrian, I should be cackling in mild amusement. Yet here I am, feeling sorry for her.

Because... why? Because Keira had fallen in love with a woman who was already taken? Someone who would only do to her what had already been done to me?

I'm not supposed to feel sorry for her. I'm supposed to seduce her, use her, and forget about her.

That must be why we're on my friend's yacht in the middle of the bay, the warm night enveloping us and privacy ours for the taking.

"Hey," I say. "Don't beat yourself up about it. We all go through shitty stuff like that when we're out there looking for love. Look at me. I'm a little older than you, and I was cheated on after seven years together. I'll never understand why. Like you, I'd rather end a relationship that isn't working for me anymore than betray someone who is counting on my loyalty. Maybe that doesn't sound romantic, but..."

"I think that sounds hella romantic." Keira wraps both of her arms around mine.

Is it me, or is it kinda stuffy out here?

Much to Keira's bemusement, I shake her off me and stand up. A little too quickly, based on how easily I wobble where I'm standing. I can't blame everything on the ocean beneath my feet. There's something else on my mind, and I have to corroborate with one of the only people who can call me out on my shit.

"I'll be right back." I put on a brave face before heading into the cabin. "Stay here, Kiki. Enjoy the warm air while I get something."

The door is closed on her before I hear her respond. Instead, I'm now in the present company of my friend Raquel and her partner Lisa, who were quietly squabbling over where to stash some of the trash when I popped in unannounced.

"What's up?" Raquel asks. "Need something? We'll be right back out in a few. This is taking longer than we expected."

Like the helpful friend I am, I interrupt everything they're doing to interject my own problems. "Am I crazy, or is Keira a really nice person?"

Raquel slams her hand on her hip while Lisa looks over her shoulder. She's been washing dishes in the sink ever since I walked in, and *that* is what gets her undivided attention.

"Huh?" my friend asks.

"Keira. She's impossibly nice. Like, saccharin sweet, almost. She says all the right things, is really hot and confuses the shit out of me."

"Oh, dear." That comes with a dramatic sigh as Raquel leans against the counter. "Here it is, sweetie," she says to her girlfriend. "This is what happens when you've spent your whole life either living a lie or recovering from it. You can't trust people for who they are at face value."

"That's not true." I definitely sound indignant when I say that. "Come on. Can you blame me?" Yes, backtracking. That's what I need right now. Totally doesn't make me sound like I have something to hide. "After what Sera did to me?"

"You are moving on rather quickly."

"What's that supposed to mean?"

Raquel looks as if anything she says will only be met with more of my harsh words. She may be right. "You're not the kind of woman I expected to kick out the person you've had your heart on for several years and turn around to fuck someone else. That's all."

"I had a couple rebounds, but they weren't serious."

"Keira is?"

"I brought her here to meet you, didn't I?"

"You sure did. Which is interesting." A quick gesture to Lisa sends the young woman downstairs with a cloth towel in her hands. "I know it's been a few months, but are you really the type to move on that quickly? I pegged you at least a year or two. Where did you meet this girl?"

I don't like her tone. "I told you. At work."

"You happened to flirt with a woman who came into your work and asked her out? I may have been out of the dating game a couple of years now, but I don't remember lesbian femme dating being so... seamless. What you're talking about only happens in the movies."

"What are you getting at?"

"Maybe something. Maybe nothing. Honestly, what's it to me?" Raquel shrugs again as if my predicament is completely beneath her. "Don't yank that poor girl around. She looks fragile. On that note, don't let her yank *you* around. You've got a lot to offer, Evie. And I don't mean the condo and the cushy job with the income. I know how you get when you want to spoil someone, too. I know because I'm the same way."

"Is there some reason you sent your girlfriend out of the room, by the way?"

"Before you get all worked up at me, consider something I'm offering." Raquel pushes herself off the counter and approaches me with a Cheshire grin. "It's a beautifully warm night out at sea. Trust me when I say this kind of environment makes women... you know. Handsy."

"What does this have to do with..."

"I have a feeling Lisa needs me downstairs. Now that we're all cleaned up in here, it's only right I give her some romantic attention. Maybe you should do the same with your date. Don't tell me you two aren't sleeping together."

"Sleeping? Not really."

"Whatever you're doing, have at it on my deck. I'll give you somewhere between half an hour and forty-five minutes before we come up for one last chat and I drive us back to the marina. Will that be long enough for you to pop your date's nautical cherry?"

That's bold, including for a friend of mine. "Was this your plan the whole time?"

"Hell, no. But before you barged in here, Lisa and I were getting hot and heavy and wondering how we could ditch you two on our own yacht so we could get it out of our systems. Knowing us, we'll be too tired by the time we dock."

"I see."

"Why not take advantage of it? You were going to take her to your hotel room anyway."

"As a matter of fact, we were talking about going over to her place."

"Are you really going to look a gift horse in the mouth right now?" Raquel heads toward the cramped staircase leading to the lower level, where the bathroom and bedroom lurk. "We won't rock the boat too much if you two don't."

I let her go in silence. Was anything she said supposed to be helpful? All she's done is put my thoughts back on Keira, and how sweet she felt while we enjoyed the dark, starlit night.

Damnit, Raquel!

CHAPTER 16

Keira

S itting alone on the back of a yacht wasn't high at my list of things I wanted to experience in life, but here I am, wrapping a spare blanket around myself as I stare at the darkening sky instead of hyper fixating on the fact that if I fell overboard, nobody would know!

I'm an excellent swimmer, but I somehow doubt I'll stay afloat long enough to be rescued at this point.

Luckily for me, Evelyn pops out of the cabin. She moves her hair out of her face and steadies herself on the deck before sitting next to me once more.

To be honest, she could have kept standing there in front of the door looking like my favorite dessert. While her friend Raquel is rocking the bathing suit and robe look, there's something about Evelyn's effortless style that always punches me in the chest. Or is it between the legs? Whenever I look at her on nights like these, I imagine it's both. The ol' one-two: one in the heart, one in the pussy.

"How are you friends?" I'm proud of myself for not stuttering a single word in that sentence because Evelyn has stolen most of my vocabulary away. "You'd think they'd want to be out here enjoying this beautiful night with us."

Evelyn wraps her arm around the back of the sofa, one of the wine-colored pillows digging into her dress. While she stares up at the starry sky with me, she says, "To be frank, they're hanky-pankying in the bedroom. I think I must have interrupted something. You know how it is." A wicked smile flashes in my direction. "Young love."

"Oh... oh!" Am I scandalized? Maybe. This is, after all, Raquel and Lisa's yacht, and if they wanna have a quickie in the bedroom to take the edge off, who am I to say they can't do that on their own property? Still, it's not something I would do if I were entertaining guests. At the same time, I'm relieved to know that I get to spend some more alone time with my date. Evelyn may not be my "girlfriend," but being around her friends and none of mine was making me anxious. I try not to be that way. Socially anxious, that is, but I can't help it when it happens. I'm grateful that more strangers didn't come to this party out on the water.

"The thing you have to understand about my friends," Evelyn begins, "is that Raquel was the queen cougar in this town for a long while. Before she settled down with Lisa, who has completely consumed her soul these past three years. Hmph. Guess it's sweet that they're still so obsessed with each other. Anyway, I'm rather surprised you haven't met Raquel before, let alone slept with her. There wasn't a young gay pussy in this town that slipped under her radar. You would have been the perfect age for her."

I hide my embarrassment within the depths of the blanket curled around my body. "I swear I've never met her before tonight. To be fair, though, I didn't move here until a few years ago, and I've never been a big dater. She might have gotten around to me, though, if she didn't end up with that nice girl." That's one way to put Lisa, who must be one of the most conventionally hot women I've seen up close in a long time. She's got the kind of body that either comes naturally or a girl like me spends all her free time attempting to achieve – I have a feeling it's the former, and it absolutely blows my mind that she's *gay*. I mean, that isn't to say that hot women like that don't exist in queer circles, and for all I know she doesn't ID as a lesbian but... I can't tell if I'm insecure around her or invigorated. I don't want to date her, yet here I am, comparing myself to her while in the presence of a woman who probably could have yanked her away from her friend at any time.

That's assuming Evelyn has a cheating bone in her body, though. Maybe I have some scars from Sera that still need healing. *Not everyone is a cheating bitch,* is what I must now remind myself every single day.

"It was nice of your friends to inform you that they're going to be a while, though." A frog has hopped into my throat and made things more difficult. After I croak, I continue, "Even if that kind of is TMI."

"It's only TMI if you're bothered by it. I'm used to it. Them ditching me for a few minutes to go play with each other. I mean, they made it pretty clear we could have the deck all to ourselves while they're downstairs."

More than a few seconds pass before I pick up Evelyn's meaning. "Uh, you mean like... fool around?"

"Only if you're interested."

I look around as if there's anyone who could possibly overhear our conversation. We're on a yacht, for God's sake. The only other people onboard are downstairs. It's just Evelyn and me, two people who already Biblically know each other! Yet she wants to do it here? Out here? *Exposed?*

Granted, the more I look around, the more I realize there isn't anyone for miles. If another vessel whirs by, it's too far away for them to see a damn thing, and it's so dark now that the only reason I can see Evelyn is because of the light hanging above the door a few feet away.

We're still gently bobbing on the water. The sea is calm and the wind dead.

We have as much privacy here as we do in a hotel room, where neighbors might hear us or a dedicated perv might peep through the window anyway.

So why am I nervous?

"Guess it would feel so vulnerable." Am I aware that Evelyn is coming closer, her fingers walking up my sheltered arm? Give it a few more seconds, and her tongue will be in my ear. By that point, I'll be completely putty in her hand. So before that happens, allow me to be strong enough to make my point. "I've never done it outdoors before. It's one thing to have a one-night affair with someone you've recently met..." Evelyn's hand disappears beneath the blanket. Sure enough, there are her fingers, digging into my thighs and threatening me with a good time. "I don't know how I feel about getting it on outside."

"That's your prerogative, of course." Her hand slips away. "Not like this would be our only chance to have some fun on my friend's yacht. Come on. Why don't we enjoy how beautiful this night is? When Raquel is done making a mess in her bedroom, she'll drive us back to shore and we'll head wherever we want."

"My place?"

"Sure thing. I can't wait to see what kind of place you've set up for yourself. I bet it's cute as fuck. So like you."

"I'm not *only* cute, right?" There's one of my insecurities rising from the dead. "I've had a lot of people call me cute in my life. Most of them use it as an excuse to break up with me because I'm not ticking their boxes anymore."

"Hm. Seems I've stricken a nerve. Fine." Evelyn pops up my blanket, helping herself inside. Arms wrap around me. Here we are, snuggling together on the back of a yacht while we bob beneath the twinkling stars. The moon is absent from the sky tonight, but that only makes the stars more apparent as constellations appear before my very eyes. "You don't have to be *cute*. How about sexy? Gorgeous?" Here come Evelyn's lips, buzzing against my neck. "Irresistible?"

"You really think that?"

"Of course. Do you forget that only a week ago I asked you out the first time I met you? As soon as you walked into the meeting, I knew I had to have drinks with you. Getting you into bed would be a bonus. Because as soon as I saw you, I wanted my body all over yours."

She squeezes me closer. While my skin is alit with desire for her, I can't help but wonder what would happen if somebody *saw* us having sex. On a yacht, of all places! I'd be so mortified if someone stumbled into my sex life like this. I doubt it would get back to my boss, but what if it did? Or, worse?

What if it got back to my exes, who always knew me as the queen of being careful? This is especially true since Sera, who often fooled around with me on quiet roads.

"I don't usually do it in the open." Although I know we had moved on from talking about sex out here, I can't help but bring our conversation back to it. "But I've done it before, you know. Just not out on the water."

"Tell me everything."

There's darkness in Evelyn's voice. Not sinister, but... dark, yes. I struggle to parse if she's intrigued or disgusted with me. Surely, she's intrigued. How could she not be, if she's right here, right now, rubbing against me and attempting to make love to me beneath this blanket?

"I... I've done it a car a few times. In broad daylight."

Evelyn stiffens against me. Lest I believe she's turned off by my confession, she hikes her hand beneath my skirt, fingertips meeting my underwear much quicker than I anticipated. "Go on. Did you make that car rock? What kind was it? Paint a sexy picture for me."

"A... a silver BMW." My nipples awaken beneath my dress – and the blanket – as Evelyn teases my slit. My head leans back against the back of the couch. One of the pillows digs into the bottom of my back as I adjust my posture. So, I guess we're doing this. Evelyn is lulling me into security by showing how far we can push things on a yacht in the middle of the water.

A drone could fly over us at any minute. Her friends could burst out of the cabin. I guess if she doesn't mind...

"What did you do in that car?"

I'm taken back to those dates that I always mistook as "thrilling" as opposed to us merely sneaking around someone else's back. Sera was good at selling the experience. *"I have to have you now,"* is what she would say. *"I can't wait to take you back to your place. It has to be here, on this dirt road with no one around."* Whenever I asked what would happen if someone spotted us, she told me not to worry about it. We'd be quick, but we'd make it hot.

It was always hot. It wasn't always quick.

"I was always on the bottom, you know," I whisper. "I liked it, though. I like it when someone is between my legs."

"Your thighs are very cushioned. I think any woman would want to be between them."

Evelyn is soon beneath my underwear, stroking my slit with her fingertip. I sigh, slipping further into depravity. Doesn't take much to make my legs part and my mouth open enough for her tongue to touch mine. Before I know it, Evelyn is kissing me – and I'm kissing her back, my pelvis rubbing against her finger and encouraging her to go deeper.

"I think you like the thrill," she whispers against my lips. "Maybe you don't really want to get caught, but you love the possibility that someone will see you being pleasured."

I don't respond. Not with anything but a kiss.

You know, I think I'd be content with this. Evelyn and me making out beneath the night sky as it embraces our part of the world. I'd be lying if I said it wasn't *so* romantic. I mean, I haven't been high on romance in a long time, but a part of me still screams in delight at a bouquet of roses and someone planning something special for my birthday. A date on a yacht with only our bodies to keep us company in this heated moment?

It's bliss, isn't it?

Yet in true Keira Lawson fashion, I'm succumbing to the possibility that we could do *more*. This is how Sera got me, you know. One minute I'm sitting in the front seat of a decent BMW while we go for a drive to the countryside. Next thing I know? We're parked on the side of the road, she's putting on the moves, and I'm agreeing to hop in the backseat with her already going at me like we only have five minutes.

Too true. Now I know why.

It's the same feeling, though. Evelyn suggests we do something, I turn it down because of my own insecurities, and now here we are, daring each other to take it to the next stage.

As soon as her finger slips inside of me, I pull her atop me, and I'm not letting her go. Not until I'm good and ready.

She's right. I *do* like the thrill. I like *many* thrills. I love it when someone comes on to me and wants me right there and then. It makes me feel not only attractive but wanted by the universe – like I really am the protagonist of my own universe. If someone happens to see me in the bar bathroom, the back of a car, or on the rear end of a yacht? Fuck me, let's do it! They can join in!

Is it really my fault if I dig the idea of Evelyn's friends popping out of the cabin and catching me in the middle of an orgasm? The practical part of me is mortified at the thought, but the big ol' slut who goes home with whomever and accepts dates in the middle of offices can't get enough of it!

Maybe that's why I don't stop Evelyn when she throws the blanket onto the deck and sinks down to her knees. It takes me way too long to realize that she's using the blanket and one of the pillows on the couch to cushion her knees as she pulls my legs apart and dives her face between my thighs.

Talk about *exposed!*

Every part of me is alit with an infectious fever, though. Sweat drips down my forehead and arms as gravity pulls my hands down to the sofa and my fingers into the soft upholstery. I'm bracing myself against everything. From the weight of the vessel to the aloofness of my own heart, I'm not about to fall overboard because I got excited about some tongue on my pussy.

I will, however, get excited about untying the top of my dress and letting the fabric fall down my chest. This isn't exactly the kind of dress you wear with a bra. Has anyone noticed? I'm pretty good at hiding the fact I'm not wearing a bra when fashion necessitates it, but there's no hiding it now. My breasts belong to the night. Every being in the cosmos can see me as I spread my legs and expose my chest to the warm air. Although I've liberated more of my body, I'm sweating more. It can't be nerves at this point. Is it excitement? Is it the friction of my body against the sofa? Or is it my inability to control basic things in my body?

Like how easily I respond to Evelyn's tongue as it caresses my clit and explores my depths once again?

I don't know where to put my hands. To clutch the sofa is to let my dress drop down on Evelyn's head. To hold up my dress is to awkwardly sit here while I'm pleasured on the back deck. I want to grab Evelyn's head and hump her face. I want to lie back and let her do all the work. Why can't I have the best of both worlds? If she can claim my pussy and eat it too, why can't I really get into it while also feeling like the most pampered princess in the city?

Fuck me, Evelyn. Take me and make me your captive slut on someone else's yacht. Make me feel the warm night air on my breasts and your hot tongue all over my cunt. I want everyone lucky enough to see me know that I not only belong to *you,* Evelyn, but that this moment belongs to them, too. I'm not really shy. I only think I am. Propriety and prudishness. That's what I sell in a meeting, but anyone who really knows me can see the desperation in my eyes. I want to feel like I'm *alive!* That anything is possible if I'm with the right person and I play my cards right.

Shit, I'm no good at gambling, but I can play poker. Does this count as a royal flush?

"I'm coming..." Nobody can hear me, least of all Evelyn who is deafened by my thighs, but it feels good to say. My hips gyrate in circles as Evelyn meets the rhythm of my body. Her tongue is wholly focused on my entrance while her lips only care for my clit. She's not playing any games. I don't know how much time we have, but this isn't any different than getting fingered in the back of a car.

No. It's better. For one thing, this is *way* classier! How many women get to say they've displayed themselves like this on a yacht before? Let alone one owned by another woman? Hell! When will I ever get to do something like this again?

"I'm coming!" Although my legs jerk against the couch, Evelyn slams her hands into my flesh and pins me down. This gives me free rein to move as much as I desire – which is enough to rock this boat right onto its side.

Her tongue stills against my slit. If Evelyn doesn't come up for air soon, she'll drown without ever leaving the deck.

To be honest, I'd take it as a compliment.

———————

"It's nothing much..." I giggle as I fumble for my keys in my purse, "but it's all mine."

Evelyn is fixated on my hair as I attempt to unlock my door. She's completely unperturbed by the bag of trash left outside another neighbor's door or the old woman who is always wandering the far end of the hall around this time of night. I don't know who she is, but people are always calling security, and security has told us to knock it off.

Yet Evelyn doesn't care. She only looks at me, a woman vainly attempting dominance over her own door lock.

The yacht feels so far away now, but it's only been half an hour at most. Once Raquel drove us back to the marina, Evelyn and I thanked her for her hospitality and escaped together in a cab. I gave the driver my address after asking my date if she *really* wanted to see where I lived. Her hand never left mine as she said, *"Absolutely. I've got plans."*

Now here we are. My legs are shaking in anticipation of more of what I've already had tonight, and Evelyn is acting like she's been wanting to fuck me all week. As soon as I get this door...

Unlocked! Thank goodness. I was starting to worry that I'd have to call the locksmith, and this would simply be a dire porn plot situation.

The lights flick on. Without regard for taking off my shoes, I slam the door shut and lock both the deadbolt and the chain. Evelyn takes a few steps into my small studio apartment and lets out a low whistle.

"It's adorable like I knew it would be." She doesn't have to go far to find my Ikea kitchen table and the two chairs that fit around it. Her sweater lands on the back of one chair and her large purse in the other. "You've done a lot with a little space."

Already the heat is getting to me. Normally I'd open the window, since this high up I rarely worry about people climbing inside, but I instead turn on the oscillating fan by my bed. You can feel it all the way in the kitchen, anyway – that's how small my place is!

"It's not bad for not spending a whole lot of time in it. Do you want something to drink? I've got seltzer and iced tea."

"The only thing I want to drink..." Evelyn appears in the small entryway to my kitchen, where she drapes herself against a cabinet on one side and the wall on the other, "is your body."

Normally, I'd be all a titter at a statement like that, but I know Evelyn well enough by now that I can sip some tap water without spitting it everywhere. "Didn't have enough of it back on the yacht, huh?"

Evelyn snorts, lowering her arms. "I have plans tonight, Ms. Lawson. Those plans include you on your knees while I spank your thighs and put you away wet."

"You would be the kind of woman who uses that phrase in a sexual way."

"Doesn't everyone?"

I place my glass in the sink but don't go anywhere near Evelyn. If she wants me, she can come get me. "Do I look like a horse that needs to be overworked?" I tease.

She does, in fact, come closer. "Were you ever a horse girl? You grow up with them? Because I've got a saddle for you and a riding crop with your name on it."

"So we're kinky now?"

Evelyn grabs me by the waist and pulls me into her embrace. I trip over my own feet as I cling to her shoulders and await her lips on mine. "How well did you tie this thing?" Evelyn murmurs, playing with the back of my dress. "I couldn't really see that well in the dark." With one deft movement, the front of my dress falls down again. We're so close to one another that she can't see anything, but I feel one of my nipples gently glide against the fabric of her outfit. "Looks like you wanted that to happen, Kiki."

I can't hold it in any longer. I laugh, my feet stamping lightly against the worn-out tile of my cheap kitchen. Strangest thing, isn't it? This place is so small and dark, especially with navy blue walls and only one big window overlooking a dirty alleyway. Yet with Evelyn radiating in effervescent beauty, I'm blinded. By my own apartment!

"What kind of plans did you have?"

Evelyn steps away, drawing me near her with a touch of her finger. I don't bother holding up my dress as I follow her to my bed. The comforter was made by my grandmother – that's how small my bed is, and that's how little money I spend on this place. Yet Evelyn makes it look like a sea of possibilities when she sits on the edge and tells me to bring over her purse.

When I return, she's staring straight at my naked chest. I drop her purse and finish dressing down to my underwear. I definitely feel the air from the oscillating fan now. It's hitting my back and tickling the hem of the only piece of clothing still attached to my building.

"You look like the kind of girl someone should paint." Evelyn opens her purse and sticks one hand inside. "I'd buy a copy and hang it in front of my bed."

"Not above your bed?"

"How am I supposed to see it there?" Without looking into her bag, Evelyn pulls out a box that must have added some extra heft to what she carried all day. Now that I think about it, she really didn't do much with her bag today. It sat inside the cabin on the yacht, then in her lap in the back of the cab, and now it adorns my bed.

I also know why she brought such a large bag. As Evelyn leans back on my bed and pops the lid off the box, I'm treated to a sight that tells me I picked the right woman to bring home.

"That's impressive." My bed shakes as I land beside her. I only have eyes for the strap-on lingering in the box. "Good thing you brought a new one. I don't have any condoms on me."

"You don't have anything on you at all. Nothing but the skin and hair God gave you."

"You like?" There's something powerful about being in your own space when a woman wants to have her way with you. This is my bed, after all. I'm allowed to climb around it, rearrange the pillows, and move some of the pictures on the wall if they're getting in the way. Evelyn may be here to do me hard, but she's still my guest. The first one I've had here since...

No. You know what? I'm tired of thinking about Sera. Now's the time to forget all about her and instead focus on *Evelyn.* The new woman in my life.

I should appreciate her while I have her. Being with Sera taught me that all of that can crumble at any moment.

"I like it enough that I can't stop thinking about what I want to do to it."

"Does it include this?"

That's how emboldened I've become. I slap my hand in the box, grab the toy, and raise it into the air. The straps flutter down, smacking against the cardboard box and plopping upon my bed. Evelyn looks between the strap near her hand and my bare breasts not too far from her face.

"It includes it all the way inside of you, yes."

In a grand moment of absolute frivolity, I fling myself across the length of my bed and raise one leg into the air. "Then what are you waiting for?" Excitement mounts my body. Much like I expect Evelyn to mount me in the coming minutes. "I'm still wet from what you did to me on the yacht."

The only way I could have made that cornier was if I accompanied it with a big, fat wink. Good thing Evelyn cuts me off with a kiss before I have the chance to truly ruin the mood.

CHAPTER 17

Keira

Sometimes, all you want is for the woman you like to make slow and mesmerizing love to you. The kind that solidifies *"I'm going to marry this woman,"* and the time you talk about with her for the rest of your lives. Kids, anniversaries, retirements...

Let's not forget the other times. You know the times I'm talking about.

Hard. Fast. Unrelenting.

I was totally right about my feelings on the yacht. Back when I worried that someone might see us, but I rationalized that my own neighbors could hear me fucking my date if I were loud enough. Most of my cries of pleasure and pleas for the occasional moment of mercy are muffled by my pillow. My grandmother's comforter also does a decent job keeping the squeaks of my mattress down to a minimum. But when Evelyn thrusts hard enough to send my bedframe against the wall?

My neighbor totally knows I'm fucking!

How the hell am I supposed to explain it? I *love* that everyone next door is probably listening with rapt attention right now. The possibility that I'm annoying them doesn't cross my mind. How often do I get to do this, anyway? Not even with my previous dates did we make this much noise! Then again, it's rare for me to get it like this. Usually, when a strap-on enters my bedroom, I'm the one doing the giving, or my partner is a lot more sensual with her movements. It's almost like Evelyn wants to hump me raw and impede my ability to walk to my own bathroom after this. My legs are mush already. Hair is pasted against my forehead every time I dare to raise my head and catch a breath. Evelyn's skills with a strap-on have me seeing those same stars that twinkled above us on the yacht. I may be in my dingy apartment now, but you can't tell me I'm not *really* back on that boat!

"You really love it, don't you?" Evelyn stuffs herself to the hilt as she leans over my back and tickles my skin with her hair. A tongue as wet as it is curt licks the length of my ear. Any part of me that isn't shuddering is begging for more. How long have we been going at it now? Ten minutes? Twenty? How much can my pussy take before I don't recognize how it feels anymore? How quickly can we get there? "Let me hear you say it."

"You know I fucking love it," I gasp.

"Say my name, baby."

"Eve..." I'm halfway through remembering her name when she slides a little deeper into me – enough to turn the second half of her name into a growl in the depths of my throat. All that's missing is a finger on my clit and a hand on my breasts. We can't all be superheroes in bed, though. "Evelyn!"

"Is this the best fuck you've ever had in this bed?"

God, is it! Who the hell else has been here? I can kinda see her face in my memory. Her name is on my lips. Yet all I hear, smell, and feel is Evelyn Sharpe, the successful businesswoman who strolled up to me a week ago and all but demanded I give her my panties right there.

Does it really need to be said that I come more than once? Honestly, I don't know where one thrill ends and the other begins. Evelyn was so right. I *like* almost being caught. I don't actually want someone to stumble upon us, but there's something so erotic about half the world being clued in on something as naughty as Evelyn doing me like a wild animal. I don't think anyone else could do this to me. Is she the hottest I've ever had in this bed? What kind of question is that, anyway?

I'm so out of it when she finally stops that it takes me more than a few minutes to realize she's been sitting on the end of my bed, freshening her naked body up with her fingertips and a spritz of water from a bottle in her bag. The strap-on is still attached to her waist, but one would never guess that she knew it was there. She looks like she could be sitting before her own vanity with a robe on and her hair wrapped in a towel.

Instead, she's on *my* bed. With a strap-on sticking up from her lap.

"Are you..." Why is it so difficult to get my words together? "Do you need anything?"

Her brows pick up as if I had asked if she needed a glass of water or directions to the nearest restroom. When she finally gets what I'm asking, Evelyn lowers her spritzer and says, "I feel great. You've done plenty tonight by simply being the most fuckable girl in the world."

She says it so sweetly that it feels like an honorable compliment. Is it any wonder I fall back down to my pillow and giggle? A part of me is grateful she doesn't need any more sexual stimulation, though. I'm so out of it after all that I might as well roll over and go to sleep.

"I'm popping into the bathroom and clean myself up." With a bat of her eyelashes, Evelyn stands up. She unsnaps the belt of the strap-on and carries it at her hip as she enters my bathroom, closing the door behind her. The fan pops on and lulls me into a half-baked doze.

Now, I don't want to say I'm falling in *love* with Evelyn Sharpe, but I think I've officially reached the point that I would be upset if she broke up with me. I've become attached to her. It's not only her innate confidence or how she has no problem treating a girl like me to the finer, sexier things in life. There's something *permanent* about her. She could be very ride or die, huh? Hearing her talk about her old relationship tells me she's willing to put in the time and love necessary to make something work. After all, that relationship ended because someone cheated on *her,* not that I can imagine it. How does one cheat on Evelyn Sharpe? You've seen her! She's bolder than red lipstick and a magnet for adoration. How could anyone break her heart?

Of course, I know how common cheating is. You know who you're talking to, right? Sometimes I think about that woman who completely lost her shit when she walked in on Sera and me. She had her whole world destroyed that day. I don't know who she was – and I don't want to know – but I bet she didn't deserve it, either. Does anyone?

When Evelyn emerges from the bathroom, it's with a refreshed complexion and a clean strap-on ready to pop back into its box. "What? Not gonna leave it here?" I tease. "Never know when next time might happen."

"I like to be in control of the toys."

Her bag snaps shut. Evelyn turns toward me, her naked body a godly sight to behold. Only a few minutes ago, her nipples were so hard that they were all I could look at. Now, they've softened, and I can better appreciate the balance of large pink areolas as they crown her already magnificent breasts.

Perhaps it's uncouth to focus only on *that,* but if you saw her as I do right now, you'd agree. It's the only thing to catch the eye more than the look of self-satisfaction on her face.

"Are you... leaving?" I push myself up in case I need to grab her hand in a vain attempt to win her love. "You don't have to. I was thinking you could stay a while." Maybe the whole night if I'm being truthful.

"It's a small bed," Evelyn says. "Do you really think we'd be comfortable in it?"

"Yes?"

That garners a sympathetic smile from her. "Perhaps I can stay longer. Not like I have anywhere to be in the morning. Where am I going? Church?"

She climbs in behind me because of course she must be the big spoon – not that I'm complaining. I'm simply glad that Evelyn has agreed to hang out with me after rocking my world so hard. If she kept bailing after we did the deed... honestly, it wouldn't feel that much different from my relationship with Sera. She always had an excuse for needing to leave quickly. In the beginning, I believed all her lies. Then when I began to doubt them, it was too late. I was in too deep. You know the rest...

I know better now. If my gut tells me something is off, I'm apt to believe it. Only I don't think Evelyn has someone else she's seeing, whether casually or seriously. Just because I think that, though, doesn't mean something else isn't up.

Except she's willing to spend some of tonight with me. Simply being... a couple.

In the haze of post-coital bliss, I brave asking a question that is probably best left for later. "What are we, exactly?"

Her arm tightens around me. "What do you mean?"

"Are we girlfriends? Are we fuck buddies? How exclusive is this relationship?"

My voice squeaks by the end of my question. I can't help it. This is the most vulnerable I've been because Evelyn is sure to interpret it as me *hoping* she'll say we're forever-ever. Which I don't necessarily wish right now.

Maybe one day, though...

"What would you like us to be?"

Great. She's put it all in *my* court. "I dunno. That's why I asked you." I roll over in her arms, aware that her breath is right on my nose. It smells like a breath mint she must have popped when in the bathroom. That's Evelyn. Always aware of her appearance, even when in the afterglow of sex. "I... like where this is going." I cuddle closer, my hand searching for some of her hair. I want it wrapped around my finger. "We have great sexual chemistry, don't you think?"

"Sexual chemistry can't carry a whole relationship. Ask me how I know."

"Remember who you're talking to here. We both know what it's like to be hurt by someone we cared about. I don't want only sex, anyway. I mean, if that's all we are, that's fine, but I don't want to nurture any feelings that might be growing in there."

"In there?"

"In my heart, silly."

Evelyn contemplates my words for a minute. While I wait for her response, I inhale her scent, wondering if there has ever been a woman who makes me feel so safe in her arms.

"I don't know how ready I am for a more emotional relationship."

That's what I expected to hear, yet it still crushes me. "I understand..."

"But, if I'm being honest, I don't necessarily want only sex, too."

"So we keep taking things one date a time?" I'll cling to any hope I can find. "I'm fine with that. I guess what I'm asking is if we're exclusively dating each other and no one else."

"That sounds doable to me."

I'll take what I can get. "So that settles it. For now."

"For now, yes."

As long as we're in agreement, I'll happily cling to her and simply be in this beautiful moment.

I hope she's half as happy as I am right now.

CHAPTER 18

Evelyn

E very so often I consider who I am and what I've done – and I feel like an idiot.

This isn't a feeling I'm accustomed to, although this humble pie I've been inhaling these past few months is starting to taste familiar. First, it was turning a blind eye to all the signs that my ex was cheating on me.

Now? Here I am, three months into a relationship with the woman my ex cheated with.

Why, yes, it has been a while since I've seen you. I'd ask if you're doing well, but I don't really care how voyeurs feel. Besides, I have a feeling that three months for me is a blink of an eye for you. Who am I to know?

Who am I to *care?*

Keira remains a complete anomaly to me. While I continue to work, never mind on her boss's account, she continues to both beguile and infuriate me. I shouldn't be so into her. She's the woman who indirectly ruined my relationship of seven years. When I forget about that, though, all I think about is her cute smile or how *happy* she always is to see me.

Like I told you back when this all started, Keira isn't my usual type. Happy femmes who could raid my closet and look fabulous with only minor alterations alienate me. Usually. That's how I ended up with someone like Sera and thought we would be *forever.* Yet here comes Keira, the woman *I* seduced, mind you, and I can't believe that after three months we're still going out a couple times a week and frequently texting. Sometimes about absolutely nothing at all!

I also can't believe she still hasn't figured it out. God, that's why I have bile in my throat half the time I'm around her. I keep waiting for the other shoe to drop. It would be one thing if Sera's ghost didn't hang between us. But it does. At any moment, Keira will put two and two together and... surprise! This all dies in a fiery bullshit storm.

Maybe that's why I can't really get into it. I know it's doomed from the start.

Yet I can't break up with her. Sure, when I'm alone at night or staring at my work computer during the day, I think how easy it would be to meet her for drinks and give it to her straight. *"I'm sorry. It's not working for me. I'm sure you'll find someone great."* Yet that means no more Keira. No more cute texts in the morning while she's running errands for her boss. No more kisses that go on a few seconds too long. No more thighs I can grab with all my might and all I get is a giggle.

And, if I'm being completely selfish, no more sex that should be outlawed in this country.

I'm not saying that I *love* Keira. Even if I were the type to fall in love quickly and easily – like she so clearly is – I've erected a firm force field around my heart. This is, after all, one of the enemies of my life. Yet I acknowledge that I'm no longer fucking her for some petty revenge toward the universe. I'm doing it because I like it. I get excited knowing that I'm about to kiss that clit and watch those thighs jiggle every time I thrust into her. The primal sounds Keira makes when I completely own her is addictive. On a scale of one to the '90s "Just Say No" campaign, I'm over here flagging down the dealer and buying up all the stock I can.

All for some bombastic pussy.

In another universe, Keira is an incredible rebound who gives me faith in the universe and the confidence I need to get back in the game. Maybe we'd turn into a long-term thing, maybe not. It wouldn't matter! Because all I care about is living in the moment and reminding myself that there are other women besides my shitty ex out there.

That's the thing, you know. It's not only getting caught in my lies of omission. Even if I were a total sociopath who didn't care about Keira's feelings, I'd still feel bad that I'm always thinking about Sera whenever I'm with Keira.

Do you know how bad this whole thing has become? I traded in my car. I knew that sooner or later Keira would see it and recognize it as the vehicle that would rock when I was at work. So, why not avoid the whole debacle and get a new car? Traded in my BMW for a Mercedes. Different color, too, because I *really* didn't want Keira thinking about what she used to do when I took her on a weekend trip to a cottage in the woods. I'm proud to say that we were unclothed for most of that trip. It also encouraged her to scream at the top of her lungs instead of conservatively containing every cry of pleasure into her pillow. I thought she would lose her voice that weekend.

There's one thing that's bringing me to the brink of insanity, though.

"Will I finally get to see where you live?" Keira asks me at dinner. We're in a sushi place where, much to my dismay, I've discovered that Keira is more *Japanese grill* than she is *celebrated sushi and sashimi chef.* Good thing this place is also famous for its noodles. "I've been dreaming about it since we met."

"Why in the world would you dream about where I live?" I almost drop my chopsticks when I pick up the choice piece of sushi I've had my eye on since it was brought to me. "Have you been dating me for the sole purpose of casing my joint?"

Her giggle is always worth an easy hundred dollars. "No! It's just kinda weird that we always go to my place. Or we go out of town. Not that I have a problem with it. I just assumed that it would be nice to mix it up and stop by your house once in a while." She lowers her voice. "It's been three months, Evie. I'll have to see where you live eventually."

"Uh huh." I could change the subject like I usually do when she brings this up, but I can't do that for much longer. Eventually, time will run out.

What am I going to do? *Move?* Jesus! My condo isn't my car!

"Truth be told, I'm not comfortable having people over. Besides, I'm thinking about moving. That's the condo I bought with my ex. It has a lot of memories."

"Then wouldn't you want to make some new memories in there? I mean, you've been coming over to my place, and it's not like you were the only one in my bed before."

Thank you for the reminder. It's bad enough I've spent more than one night imagining what those two must have looked like when doing it. I can't say the imagery turns me on.

"I'll be ready eventually. I'm not hiding anything from you."

"I... didn't think you were?"

"Joking." I must have said that with the ferocity in my belly. "How're the noodles?"

Keira looks at me as if she's not ready to drop the subject, but thank God, she says, "Just the right texture! It's not soaking in sauce, either, which I appreciate. There's a fine line between yakisoba noodles and yakisoba *soup*."

"You sound like an authority. Have you been to Japan?"

"No, but my dad used to be stationed there before I was born. My mom learned a lot of cooking tips and used to make Japanese noodles when I was a kid. So many restaurants think it's all about the sauce with the noodles as a garnish."

"I'll keep that in mind."

"Thinking about cooking some for me soon?"

"Me? Cook?" I laugh. "You still have a few things to learn about me."

I get off work an hour early on a Wednesday. Something has been bothering me for the past week. Enough that I text Raquel and ask where she is.

Since it's a weekday afternoon, she's working, but she shoots me an address and tells me to drop by the suburban house she's staging for a quick sale. Because when you're at her level, you can have your friends come by to chat about their problems while you vacuum beige carpets and hang pictures of innocuous flowers on gray walls.

"Don't you have someone who does this for you?" I lean against the bare kitchen counter, recently remodeled to match the current trends. A piece of loose plaster gets stuck on my shoe. When Raquel isn't looking, I scrape it off on the barstool an interior designer propped up the day before. "A cleaning crew, for example?"

"I like doing the finishing touches myself. Open house starts tomorrow." Raquel steps back and determines that the picture is not centered enough. We'll be here all night. "That way I know it was done right."

"I guess you haven't reached your level without being a micromanager."

"Used to be I did all of it myself. It's only recently my boss springs for a professional cleaning crew instead of sending over Joe from accounting because he messed up again."

I chuckle, but only because I remember when my friend was a scrappy realtor working sixty hours a week. Not because she had to, but because the crazy woman *wanted* to! She was hustling before it was trendy. "At least you're thriving."

"What's wrong with you, huh? Is your boss criticizing your performance again?"

"Please. I've scored two more accounts in the past month alone. He has nothing to complain about." Watch him, though. Just to "keep me on my toes" or whatever his inane excuse is this time. "Actually, I wanted to ask your advice about a real estate matter."

"Hm? Didn't realize you were in the market."

"I'm thinking about selling my condo and moving. Maybe away from the city center. I don't know." I step back and look around the spacious kitchen that is waiting for some perfectionist to whip through and make it their own. "How much is a place like this going for these days?"

"A house this size and in a gentrified neighborhood close to the city center without all the city problems?" Raquel laughs. "Almost nine hundred. The only reason we don't list it for a full mill is because it would take that much longer to sell. It's all marketing psychology."

"How much is my place worth again?"

"Your place is nice, but I'd be surprised if you got more than five hundred for it. Unless you're sitting on some serious savings..."

"Yeah, I get it. Not like I need a place this big, anyway."

"Since when are you abandoning condo life for a house in the 'burbs? You've never struck me as the type."

"You know I recently traded in my car. Maybe I need a new place to live, too. Purge Sera's name from my life forever. I can still smell her in every nook and cranny."

"Hmm." Raquel joins me at the counter, but it's not to hang out with me. Not when she's on *her* time. She busies herself with the wax fruit, rearranging every piece until the apples rest primly atop the bananas. "Now, I'm no psychologist, but I have a feeling this is more urgent than you wanting to forget about your ex. That's a bigger change than trading in your car. You didn't like your car, anyway. You love that condo."

"*Loved.*"

"Even four months ago you were saying that at least the condo was in your name because you'd be damned if your good-for-nothing ex got to keep it."

"Principle of the thing. I paid for it, after all."

"Which makes me realize that you haven't brought this up until you started dating someone new. Keira, was it?" Raquel looks up from a wax pear in her hand. "The irresistible redhead with thighs worthy of a Grecian goddess?"

"Maybe I want to start over."

"Granted, I didn't know you before you were in your last relationship, but you don't strike me as the type to completely change your life for a girl you're into."

"Hey, I'm possibly offering you work here. Why would you turn it down?"

"If you weren't someone I'm invested in on a personal level, I'd have no problem taking advantage of your mid-life crisis. But you're my friend, so I feel compelled to point out it might not be the right time. Unless you've got a lot of cash to play with or the market goes back to favoring downtown condos instead of suburban single-family homes."

For that, the moment she turns around, I turn the apple askew in its basket. So, there.

"Something tells me there's other shit afoot." Raquel rips a square of paper towel from its roll and wipes down the stove. "Actually, this whole relationship of yours has been kinda weird. She let slip the last time we had a double date that she's never been to your place." Raquel looks me square in the eye. "In three months."

"Is that weird?"

"Considering you have a nice, convenient place with no roommates... yes, that's bizarre. I'd think you'd have her tied up to your bed whenever you're not home."

"That's *your* fantasy."

"It's yours too, I'm sure. So, are you going to come clean about what's going through that rattled brain of yours? Or should I tell you to get out of here and stop wasting my time? I want this place locked up by six. I need a good night's sleep before the open house tomorrow."

Telling Raquel the full truth is out of the question. As things currently stand, I'm still the only one who knows what's going on with Keira. Our background, at least. If Raquel knew I was pursuing my ex's girlfriend, she would have been concerned, but not stand in my way. That's if I only intended to keep it an intense one-night-stand to satisfy my depraved curiosity and thirst for cosmic revenge. If it continued from there? I would never dodge the judgment this woman can hurl at another.

"I don't like the idea of having her over while so much of Sera remains."

"So I'll buy some sage and we'll cast the demons out of your place. Come on. We'll make a party out of it. I'll have Lisa bring this craft beer her friend makes."

"That's not enough. She's infected the walls. You got sage for that?" Hell, is there sage to completely wipe Keira's memory of what my place looks like?

"I love you," Raquel says with a sigh, "but you're damned difficult."

She enlists my help with the house, and it's the least I can do since I've taken up so much of her time. After I take over the paper towel duty in the kitchen, I help her gather the garbage she's created and carry it out to the street. Raquel snaps a few pictures before locking up the house. While I stand out on the sidewalk by my new Mercedes, I look up and down the street, attempting to imagine myself living there.

I've never been a "suburban" woman. That's only confirmed when I shudder to imagine life with sprinklers going off at eight in the morning and kids riding their bikes up and down the streets. Give me honking cabs and planes flying too close any day.

That seals it. Now is not the time to sell my condo. I'll have to come up with another plan. God help me.

CHAPTER 19

Evelyn

I'm running out of ideas for date night. Not for a lack of imagination, but because I'm hindered in how many places I can take my so-called girlfriend.

Yes, that's part of the problem. Technically, I suppose Keira is my girlfriend. We go out. Exclusively. We have sex and sleep whole nights together. I've learned some of her more unsavory habits that only come to light when you spend enough time with a person, and she's unfortunately learned that "First Thing in the Morning Evie" spends a lot of time in the bathroom if she took her probiotic too late at night. Because I am now old enough that I need to take a probiotic every day if I don't want to suffer.

It doesn't feel real, though. Mostly because this is a woman I have to be careful about when going out. Damn me if Sera accidentally stumbles upon us, and that is absolutely a possibility if we go to any of the usual lesbian haunts in the city. While she favors one more than the others, I don't want to take my chances.

Do I like her enough to keep seeing her? Apparently. Do I think this relationship can continue if I don't tell her the truth?

That's the rub. I'll have to tell her. Maybe it's for the best that she dumps me afterward. I wouldn't blame her.

I'm simply not ready yet.

I don't know why! You'd think this would be easier than telling Sera to pack up her shit and get the hell out of *my* condo. I loved that woman for seven years and pictured us growing old together, yet breaking up with her is easier than ending it with Keira. Suppose I wasn't intending to like her as much as I do. For fuck's sake, I call her Kiki without thinking about it. I have a pet name for her. I spend more time in bed than I should because I like her warmth. I go to sleep thinking about the faces she makes first thing in the morning. Sure, I could possibly be falling in love with her – but how can I imagine it when such a bald-faced lie lurks between us?

It's all my fault. That's what makes me feel shittiest.

Things continue to grow more reckless with every date. Now, if I told you I actually *wanted* to take Keira to one of Sera's favorite haunts, you might think I was doing it on purpose. Hoping it would blow up in my face and do the dirty work for me. You might be partially right. After all, I can't tell you what's going on in my subconscious brain.

There's dominance to it, though. I get hot thinking about taking her to the place where she met my ex. The fact they first did it in the bathroom? I'd like to imagine it. Call it me taking control over an unfortunate situation. No, no, I have no intention of doing her in the same place. Simply a drink, maybe a game of pool, and nothing more.

It's enough for me to know that I achieved it.

Don't judge me. You've had plenty of time to click your tongue and shake your head at me, yet here you are, always the voyeur. You were there when I told you my first plan to seduce the woman who had beguiled the love of my life. Then you stuck around to witness me doing the deed. Who should judge who here? That's what I thought. I'm not the only devil here. Let's agree that I'm a hot mess who needs to get her shit together. Even I can attest to that.

"How about we head over to the queer bar?" I ask my date when she meets me outside of her office building after work. "It's not too far from here. Could be a nice change of pace."

Any other woman and I wouldn't notice her missing a breath. "Which queer bar? The one on...?"

"The southern one. About seven blocks from here. It's a bit of a dive, but the drinks are cheap for what you get. Besides, I don't mind if they water them down a bit on a work night."

"Oh. Uh, sure. I haven't been there in..." Keira rubs a lock of hair between her fingers. "That's the one where I met my ex. She's a regular there."

"Does she tend to go there during the week?" I already know the answer to this. Wednesdays? No, that's not a big day for Sera at the bar. Thursdays are one of the few days of the week she has to be up early for an appointment. I'm assuming it hasn't changed. Her cheating ass was always in bed by nine on Wednesday nights.

"I don't think so, but you never know. I... I guess we could go. I definitely feel better if you're there."

She takes my hand. Although we're not the kind to walk down the street holding hands, I'm moved. After squeezing her palm, I drop it and lead the way.

The bar is far from busy on a Wednesday evening, but it's *just* patronized enough that we don't feel like the center of attention. That's my favorite balance, and why I love places like the Lighthouse Lounge. I don't want to be packed in like sardines while God knows what goes on, but there's nothing worse than trying to mind your own business at a bar and it's only you and some lonely Schmoe who keeps putting their sights on you.

There's enough room to move around, enough privacy to sit at the end of the bar and gossip, but enough life behind and around us that Keira forgets about seeing Sera and instead focuses her attention on me. As God intended.

"I'll have a lemon drop," Keira tells the bartender. "She'll have..." She bites her lip as she looks me up and down, anticipating what I'll want tonight. I know this game. Hell, I *love* this game to the point I've convinced myself I invented it. "A gin and tonic."

I shake my head. "Whiskey sour, please."

"Damnit." Keira lightly pounds her fist on the bar as our drinks are prepared. "How could I be so far off after all this time? How many times have I seen you order drinks? Did you know what I was going to order?"

"I was close. Thought you'd get a straight martini."

"Still vodka, though."

"Because I know you like vodka by now."

"Yet I can't pinpoint that you like whiskey enough to order a sour at the bar." Her lemon drop appears before her, but she's in no hurry to sample it. All of Keira's attentions remain fixated upon me. "What do I really know about you, anyway? Besides the superficial."

I thank the bartender when my sour comes promptly. The drinks here may not be the best in town, but they're quick, and I'll tip well for that. "To be fair, it's not like I'm an open book."

"No shit! You still won't let me see your place."

Although Keira's laughter uplifts her words, I can't help but feel that's a direct dig at me. Because of course it is. For good reason, she won't let that go. Nor will the cosmos allow me to forget that this relationship is bound to give me an ulcer.

"Fine. What do you still want to know about me?" I ask. "I reserve the right to forego an answer I don't feel like giving, but hey, you might learn something new about me today."

"Okay. Why the hell are you so secretive?"

I should have seen that one coming. "I've never been one to air myself out. As I've gotten older, that becomes truer when you're in my line of work. You learn to keep most of yourself... to yourself. Besides, when you've been burned by people enough times, you don't feel like sharing anymore."

"Even with the women you've been dating for three months?"

"Suppose so." There is truth to my words, though. It wouldn't matter if she were someone completely independent from my breakup – I would be almost as cagey with someone named Gidgette Gadot as I am with Keira

Lawson. Look, *mystique* makes up a lot of my appeal. When you're an otherwise average woman whose only claim to fame is that you're pretty hot and fairly successful (with those qualifiers in place – very important) you've gotta have something else to lure the few ladies around into your web. Keira wouldn't have been half as interested in me if I told her my life story from the word *hello*. Some women can score like that, but they have to offer something else, like suave and pizazz. Like... Sera.

Sera can introduce herself, talk all about her year in third grade, and you're sitting there thinking about how you can't wait to sleep with her. I need another technique. Mystery it is.

"It's not that I don't want people knowing me. My friends know me. My ex knew me." I sigh, wishing I had a bigger drink. "I've always been guarded, though, so don't take it personally. Why? Want me to tell you all about my parents and my hot takes on college life?"

"Come to think of it, you've never told me much about your parents. You said something about your dad being Jewish, but that's it."

"Calling my dad Jewish is stretching it. I mean, technically we are, but he didn't practice, and thus I wasn't raised with any of that culture. My grandma, though, if she had lived longer I might've had a *bat mitzvah*. I don't think my mom wanted to deal with that. You ask me, she was relieved when her mother-in-law died when I was eight. The pressure was on to send me to Hebrew lessons. Now I'm kinda bummed I never learned any Hebrew. No idea if it would've come in handy, but I've always believed being a polyglot is a huge advantage in this world. Do you speak any other languages besides English?"

"N... no. I took French in school, but I scarcely remember any of it. So, your mom wasn't Jewish, I'm guessing."

"Nope. If you can believe it, she was a quarter Onondaga. Which carried enough weight in her life that I actually attended some events when I was little. My mom had an Onondagan name. I don't go around telling people that, though. Most people will tell you they're an eighth this or a sixteenth that as if it's supposed to mean something. I'm told this is very American of us."

"Trust me, I know all about that. My parents can *both* trace their Irish roots, but the most recent immigration happened over a hundred years ago. That's like, a million years in American history. Yet my boss makes such a big deal about it. I'm pretty sure he hired me because I remind him of a place he's never actually lived. He's always trying to hook me up with some distant cousin's nephew or a family friend's boy. Blech."

"So you've told me. I don't know how you put up with it."

"I need the job. Besides, that's the worst I deal with."

"Except he doesn't know you're gay."

"Does he actually have to know?"

"It's rare that I meet someone who doesn't mind staying in the closet sometimes. That always feels like something from more than ten years ago."

"Yeah, well... I take the path of least resistance if I think it saves me some grief. Guess that comes from me being such an introvert at times. Or I guess it has nothing to do with it at all. What do you think?"

"I think we need more to drink if we're going to get into that."

I'm saved from having to talk about such frivolous things thanks to the grace of alcohol. Like I said earlier, this place waters down their drinks, but it wasn't my plan to get drunk on a worknight, anyway. Not that I want to get drunk most nights now. Never been my style. If you haven't figured it out, I like to be in control of myself, my situations, and my *life*.

Like I'm in control of this situation right now. I swear.

"You know..." Keira drops her smile an hour into our visit, her shoulders sagging and her elbow landing on the bar counter. "I really have to go to the bathroom, but I don't want to."

"Why? This place is safe enough."

It's not until the words are out of my mouth that I realize the reason Keira is apprehensive about a simple tinkle. Even so, I let her tell me herself.

"Because it's bad enough this is the very bar where I met my ex. That bathroom is where we..." She burps something back, her dainty hand briefly covering her lips before landing in her lap. "Could you come with me? I mean, you don't have to come inside, but I'll feel better if you're outside the door. It's a single-stall restroom."

"Must be if you were banging in there." Who am I kidding? It's not like I forgot the Italian bistro! "You really have a thing for restrooms, huh?"

"This isn't a joke, Evie." Keira slips off the stool and grabs her bag. "Please?"

I regather my cool. "Sure. I'll stand guard outside the bathroom door." I don't let her see the small roll of my eyes as she leads the way to the restroom. I don't doubt remembering our mutual ex is difficult in a place like this, but I'd be damned if I let some superstition ruin what has been a run-of-the-mill date. Hell, I have barely remembered why I asked Keira to come here. Something about me wanting to stick it to Sera one more time before I decide what to do about this new relationship. One that was built on a giant lie.

Ugh. A problem for tomorrow's Evelyn.

Keira pops into the empty bathroom, saying, "This might be a few minutes. Sorry." The lock clicks. I lean against the wall, taking in the sights of a quiet weekday night in a bar that caters to women of a certain persuasion. Occasionally a guy comes in, but he's almost always accompanied by a girl who knows exactly whose ass to kick at pool. I can respect that.

But I can't respect everyone. Nor can the universe respect me. Which is why I'm soon "blessed" with the presence of a woman whose purpose is to keep fucking up my life.

"Hey, Archie." I hear that familiar voice before I see Sera's head bob up before the bar. She's directly referring to the bartender, who high-fives her over the counter. Hmph. Before tonight, I've never seen that bartender before. Would explain why she didn't know I was Sera's ex, not that I think anyone would try anything funny here. Nobody except Sera, though, who sees me the moment she grabs a bottled beer and heads back to the pool tables.

We lock eyes as soon as she's within ten feet of me.

"Evie." Although her face pales and she loses grip of her bottle, she recovers nicely. Complete with lazy swagger and a penchant for almost ignoring me. "Why the hell are you here? Hanging out by the bathroom? You know people basically die in there, right? You're going to be waiting a while."

My smirk is a lot more casual than I anticipated. With my back firmly against the doorway in case Keira gets the idea to come out *now,* I say, "I should be asking you why you're here on a Wednesday night. Don't see Dr. Johnson at eight in the morning anymore?"

"Appointment changed to Tuesdays. Not that it's any of your business anymore."

"You're right. It's none of my business." My back leaves the wall and I step two feet closer to my ex. I can practically *smell* her. Don't know what I expected. To be totally fine with it? Because I'm not. It's taking everything in me to not shake before her. So many memories. So many promises broken by one woman. "Which is why I don't have to tell you why I'm here."

She places her bottle on a table and picks up a cue stick. "It's a free country."

Should I be glad or sad that she's not hitting on me? Begging me to take her back? I suppose it's been a couple months since that episode at my office. Sera really did take the hint. All I can hope is that she gets her act together before she breaks another woman's heart.

All that aside, I can't linger here. I need to step out before Keira pops out and the inevitable reveal happens. Hell, it still might happen, but I need to come up with a story before it does. After all, I want it done on my terms.

"I'm sure I'll see you around." I brush past Sera.

"Not going to wait for the bathroom?"

"As you said... things die in there. Like our relationship."

Her face falls. That's right. I know the details, asshole.

Without looking back, I head out of the bar. As soon as I'm outside, I'll text Keira and let her know where I am. She doesn't yet need to know why I couldn't wait for her as I promised.

CHAPTER 20

Keira

I don't care how many people make fun of me for looking at the phone while I'm on the toilet. It's because of that I discover Evelyn must step outside and will be waiting for me around the corner. Isn't that better than leaving the bathroom and discovering she's not there like she promised she would be?

After washing up, I wiggle into my sweater and check my hair to prepare for a trip back to my place – alone, with Evelyn, it doesn't matter. I have a feeling that's where I'm going next.

The door swings open without much prompting on my behalf. A woman is standing beside it, but it's not Evelyn. Good thing she told me she was leaving because a woman with short blond hair and a leather jacket would *probably* startle me under the alternate scenario.

"Excuse me. Sorry." I push past her as she slips into the bathroom and latches the door shut. My intentions to head straight outside are fumbled when I see a familiar face at the tables.

Sera looks up at me the same moment I lose my breath.

I should have known it was a bad idea to come here.

What should I do? Oh. Of course. I should haul ass out of here. Pretend I didn't see her. Fling myself into Evelyn's arms when I get outside and tell her to take me home with her. It's about damn time.

"Keira?"

Why on God's green Earth does she sound so surprised to see me here? Did she think I would never bother her again? I mean, this is the woman who practically lives here, not me!

"H... hi." As if I'm trying to look cute for her, I tuck some of my hair behind my ear. I still refuse to make any eye contact, though. "Looks like I picked a good time to leave."

She doesn't try to stop me from leaving, but I feel those incredulous eyes on my ass as I hustle out of the dive bar. My attempts to quickly swing my purse strap over my shoulder ends with me dropping my bag in front of the door. Nobody gets up to help, but it gives Sera a few seconds to chase after me like this is the first night we met.

If she thinks I was in the bathroom reliving old times, she can think again! The whole reason I didn't spend my time in there crying my eyes out is because I knew Evelyn was waiting!

"Wait!" Sera bars the door with her body. I shouldn't be shocked. What I should be doing, though, is hailing the bouncer to kick her ass to the curb. "What are you doing here?"

My ears burn with disbelief. "What business is it of yours?" I hiss. While I don't want to create a scene, I *will* enlist the bartender's help, now that I realize that I don't see an actual bouncer anywhere. Jesus, do they need one here most nights? They're probably used to regulars like Sera simply going home with everyone, not fighting with them! "Maybe I'm spending my time freely as I please."

"Are you seeing someone else already?"

"I...!" She must be kidding! That's what she asks me? If her goal was to get me to gape at her like a wet fish, she gets what she wants! "It has been over half a year since I last had anything to do with you! What, do you think I'm incapable of dating anyone else, let alone after so long? I bet you think you were my first, too."

Damn, I'm proud of myself for that one. Especially since Sera backs away a few inches. "No. That's not what I think. It's..." She glances outside when someone comes into the bar, pushing her out of the way. Fake apologies fall from her lips. Is she apologizing to me, or the person who is giving her the stink eye? Shit, I don't care! "You know what? I'm seeing things tonight." Her whole back turns toward me. Am I satisfied? Disappointed?

Honestly, sick to my stomach.

"Bye." She doesn't deserve a farewell, but some old habits can't be overcome when I'm flustered and trying to get away. So enjoy that *bye,* Sera, because it's the last one from me.

Or so I think as I scrunch up my shoulders and bravely march down the sidewalk.

"Evie!" I crash into her the moment I see her. Arms wrap around hers. Fingers cling to her shoulder. I won't ever let go of her hand, no matter how much she attempts to shrug me off with the excuse that I'm hurting her.

"Did you not get my message right away?" she gently chastises me. Is she... shaken? Sweaty? While it's a warm spring night, it's not hot enough that she should be perspiring in the shade of the evening. "I told you I had to step out. It was so stuffy. I wanted some fresh air."

That would explain the sweating, I guess. "I got it. I'm glad to see you. That all right?"

She snorts. "Glad to hear it. I felt bad after you asked me to wait for you, but I thought you might understand."

"I wish you were there, though." I give her hand one last squeeze before granting her some personal space. "You won't believe who came into the bar after you left."

Are her cheeks redder? She must have really needed some air. "Who?" she chokes, before popping a mint into her mouth.

"My ex."

Her head perks up. "Is that so? She might have been in there before I stepped out, then. I waited a good five minutes. What did she look like, again?"

"Tall. Boyish. Short hair and the kind of face you can't trust." After I'm done spitting on Sera's image, I sigh. "I told you that was her favorite hangout. I haven't seen her since she showed up on my doorstep when we started dating."

"I'm so sorry. Are you all right?"

"Yes, surprisingly enough. Must be because I have you now." A semblance of relief washes over me as we walk down the sidewalk hand in hand. Evelyn's is rather clammy, though. I hope she's all right. "Maybe I'm finally moving on. How about you? Moving on from your relationship yet?" I flash her a smile. "Don't suppose I'd have anything to do with it."

She squeezes my hand; I squeeze hers back, giggling. "Every day is a little stranger and a little easier than the last."

I let the weirdness of her words wash over me. "She said the weirdest thing to me when I tried to leave, though."

"Who?" Evelyn squeaks.

"My ex. She asked me if I was *already* seeing someone else. Why would she ask such a stupid question? It's been seven months since she humiliated me and put me in that awful situation. Makes it sound like I'm the crypt keeper or something. What, did she think she was the only one in the whole world who would want to date me?"

"I highly doubt that, Kiki."

My smile returns. "She never called me that, for the record."

"You're the one who told me to call you that."

"For some reason, it sounds nice coming from you. It would have been silly coming from her. She's the type of person to call me *baby,* and there's no shaking it from her."

"She does seem the type, yes."

"So you saw her in there?"

"Suppose I did, as I said."

Her curt, faraway words continue to flummox me, but I chalk it up to me being on edge. "You know," I begin again, "she was so surprised to see me there, although that's where we met. I used to go there before meeting her. Why would it be weird for me to see her there?"

Evelyn stops at the end of the sidewalk. It takes me a moment to realize we're waiting for a light.

"Perhaps she saw a ghost from her past."

I remain speechless while trying to parse her meaning. Am I the ghost? Is Evelyn suggesting that Sera has moved on as well, and can hardly believe that I existed? I don't know if that makes me feel better or worse. Does that mean I can move forward without looking back, though?

That's exactly what I do when the light turns and we're free to step into the crosswalk. With my hand still in Evelyn's, I walk forward, never once glancing over my shoulder.

Yet I can't help but feel like someone's watching me.

CHAPTER 21

Keira

Nothing would make me happier than knowing that Evelyn loves me. Or, at least, she is falling for me in ways she did not anticipate.

This is where I am now. Almost four months into my relationship with Evelyn, I think it's fine to admit that *I'm* falling in love with her. It's not like the passion-pumping lust I felt for Sera, who would never love me the way I deserve. Evelyn dotes on me. Takes care of me. Makes incredible love to me. Why wouldn't I fall for someone like that? Someone who at least has her shit together!

I simply don't know how to tell her.

"What do you think?" I ask my friend Laura, after spilling my guts over a summer's meetup on a patio. This café is famous for its iced coffee one can sip by a fountain surrounded by gorgeous red geraniums. So that's where we are now because heaven forbid we not be as trendy as social media implores us to be. "I'm not crazy, right? It's totally normal to be falling in love with a woman like her by now. I mean, like, real love. Not infatuation."

Laura puts her phone away after snapping some pictures of her iced mocha in front of the geraniums. "Four months is a good chunk of time of regularly dating someone. Don't see why you shouldn't know how you feel about her by now. I think your real question is... how does she feel about *you?* Am I right?"

Leave it to Laura to always go straight to the heart of the matter. "God. You're right. I have no idea how she feels about me. Sometimes she's hot, sometimes she's cold. The other night she cuddled me for hours and I swear we had this cosmic *moment*. Like, genuine affection that I've never had with anyone else. Then in the morning she kinda blew me off to go to work. I mean, she had to be there in fifteen minutes and my apartment is farther away from her office than hers is, but..."

"But?"

"I still haven't seen her place!"

Laura sagely nods. "Serial killer."

"She is not."

"Why else would she keep you out of her place? That's where she does all her killing." Laura says this so matter-of-factly like she's a YouTuber who's pieced together a puzzle only they see! "She's waiting for the perfect moment to slaughter you, girl. Once she's done playing around with your hot bod..." Laura snaps her fingers. Stupid, superstitious me jerks back. "You're dead. Hanging upside down from her shower rod."

"Why am I upside down?"

"To drain the blood! You never dealt with hunters before?"

"No!"

"Huh. Thought you grew up rural."

"Nobody in my family hunts! I don't know about these things."

Laura shrugs. "It was nice knowing you. You're toast."

With a sigh, I fling myself back in my chair. "Could you be serious for a few minutes? I'm trying to figure out how to tell Evelyn that I'm sort of in love with her. In a way that won't send her running."

"Suppose that depends what reaction you want her to have. Would you be okay with her saying *'I need more time to figure out how I feel?'* Because I have a lot of advice in that case."

"Obviously I want her to say that she's obsessed with me and wants to marry me this time next year." Keira was only half-serious. "You know how it is. I want to rent a U-Haul and hitch my shit to her place."

"I wasn't going to spout off any stereotypes until you did."

"Can I help it? I haven't felt this good in... years."

Laura traces the lid of her drink with her finger. "You really mean that? You like Evelyn more than the other shithead you were seeing a few months back?"

"Yeah. I mean that." I won't tell her all the reasons Evelyn makes me feel safer and more wanted than Sera ever did. While my ex made me feel things I hadn't in a long time, Evelyn has a maturity to her that I desperately need. She's stable *and* fun. I don't have to worry much about my bills, not that I plan on quitting my job anytime soon. Yet when I imagine a future with Evie, it's the two of us sharing some nice, bright, spacious condo in the middle of the city. She's let slip that she lives in such a thing.

So did Sera, but really, anyone who lives in the actual city either inhabits a run-down apartment or a nice condo. Someone making money like Evelyn? She lives in a condo, and I wanna see it!

"Next time you're in bed with her," Laura says, "which is every other night..."

"No, it's not. Come on. Give me some credit here. I *wish* it was."

"Anyway, next time you're snuggling and whispering sweet nothings in each other's ears, mention that you had a dream you woke up in her place and it was the best sleep of your life. Something totally innocuous that will stick in her head for a long time. I bet you it will work."

"This isn't *only* about seeing her place, you know."

"How are you going to reach the next stage of your relationship with Ms. Businesswoman if you're not scoping out her digs? You need to at least confirm that she doesn't secretly live with a roommate or, worse, her mom." Laura leaps back in her seat, gasping. It's enough to startle the crap out of me! "What if she's been hiding a kid this whole time!"

That's it? That's what she's making into such a dramatic spiel? I might as well take my drink and go. "She doesn't have a kid. Nor is Evelyn a serial killer."

"Why aren't you letting me have any fun? It's not like I'm getting laid right now. Especially by some hot, busty lady who wields a dildo like a sword." Laura mimics jabbing a strap-on at my arm. Groaning from how *embarrassing* this is, I regret ever telling her about my girlfriend's prowess in the bedroom. Then again, Laura always gets it out of me. She knows the right questions to ask and doesn't think twice about saying something inappropriate in response. Which I enable, of course.

"I'm supposed to meet her tomorrow night," I muse. "Maybe I could drop your hot advice then."

"Drop it like a hit record."

All right, that made me laugh.

CHAPTER 22

Evelyn

The things we do for so-called *love*.

My home has never been cleaner. Between the weekly maid's work and my own upkeep, the kitchen legitimately sparkles and my ability to fold hospital corners on my bed is unprecedented. Personally, I'm enjoying walking up to my living room's windows and beholding how clean and crisp the view is. Thanks to some WikiHow articles, I've discovered the secret to efficiently cleaning my windows.

Company is coming over. I bet you'll never guess who it is.

The time has come. I can't hold the secret back for much longer, and the more dates I go on with Keira, the "more real" this farce of a relationship feels. I've sunk so low that I would only be insulting myself if I kept pretending nothing was amiss and this was *totally normal*.

I don't know what sent me over the edge. Something Keira said the last time we were together. There I was, enjoying the last flickering moments of post-orgasmic bliss, and Miss Cuddle Bunny snuggles up to me with these heavy eyes that suggest she's about to fall asleep. Yet instead of feeling drowsy, she says something about a dream that she woke up in my place and it was actually Heaven.

Jesus, woman. Make it any clearer that you want to see my home, would you? God only knows what she's been assuming about where I live.

Tonight will be the night. I will tell her who I really am. After that, it will be up to her if she wants to stay with me. I won't blame her if she leaves. I might get over it soon enough, but I don't pretend to be a prognosticator.

I spritz my favorite perfume onto the back of my neck and analyze the face looking back at me in my vanity. Have I gained weight? My cheeks are heftier than they were a few months ago. I'm used to having the occasional line on my face or a spray of gray hair on my head. Nothing a trip to the clinic or salon can't solve. I'm not *that* old yet, but both sides of my family grayed early. My mother was the type to dye her hair until I graduated college. As soon as I was handed my diploma, she declared she could finally "drop all pretense" that she wasn't old enough to be my grandmother. Today, she definitely looks it.

When I analyze my diet for the past few months... I suppose I've been eating out a lot more. Most of my exercise comes from walking around with Keira and having sex. A far cry from the personal trainers I used to visit with Sera. No wonder my clothes are tight.

Suppose this ends tonight... guess that means I'm hitting the gym and hiring a dietician before convincing someone else to go out with me.

Dinner is on the stove. Once it's safe enough to take the pot off its burner and let it simmer, I head downstairs to meet Keira in the lobby. I must bring her here myself.

She's not here. Not yet.

"Running behind?" I text her. The sun is still plenty bright outside, but I sit in one of the chairs by the front window and wait for Keira's reply. She was supposed to be here fifteen minutes ago. Anything could have happened, but what if she took one look at my building and ran away?

She doesn't text me back. Instead, Keira enters my building with her head held high and her sunglasses whipping off her face. She turns toward me by the window and offers an apologetic smile. "Sorry it took me so long," she says. "My map had me going backward around the block." Only now that she's closer do I realize her laugh is more nervous than I initially heard. "Couldn't quite believe this was where you lived."

"Why's that?" I stand from my seat and invite her to the elevator.

"Believe it or not, I've been here before. It's kinda giving me deja-vu."

The elevator doors close before us. We're alone in the car, but only because it's past the returning hour for the common dayworkers that make up most of my neighbors. Small families, retirees, and work-from-homers call this place theirs. You have to reach a certain level of success before they'll rent to you, but don't get any ideas that it's all about flaunting middle-class success. There's a reason this whole building looks like a box from the outside.

"Not surprised you've been here before," I say. "There are a deceptive number of units here. Oh, could you hit the number nine for me?"

Keira presses the button before we shoot upward. "Ninth floor, huh? Wow. That's a helluva coincidence."

My fingers toy with the pendant around my neck. "I've made spaghetti for dinner. Something simple. Hope you don't mind."

"Huh? Oh, yeah, that's fine."

"Something on your mind, sweetheart?"

Keira shakes her head. "No."

"You know," the doors open, and I take Keira by the hand to lead her down the hallway to my place, "I've got a great view of the river from where I live. By 'great' I mean I pay extra to see a sliver of barge on a clear day. Ninth floor doesn't help you see much around here." I squeeze her hand when we reach my door. "Sorry, need to get my key."

It's dangling from my other hand, but I take my time, gauging Keira's reaction. Her shoulders tense as she looks up at the number on my door and at the fake plant propped up at the end of the hallway. If she already knows where she is, then she's not saying anything. I have to admit, I don't know what to make of it.

We head inside. Before I can check on Keira, I realize that I actually *didn't* take the noodles off the burner and they're still cooking on the stove. Sure enough, when I dash into the kitchen, I discover water boiling over and sizzling against the burner.

"Shit! Sorry about the mess!" I call over my shoulder as I attempt to mitigate this unfortunate situation. The pot of noodles slams into the sink. Some hot, boiling water splashes out and misses my hand by an inch. The steam warming my face makes me wipe my forehead with the back of my hand. At least I remembered to turn off the oven before heading downstairs. The garlic bread I was toasting hasn't burned!

I open one of the cabinets and pull out a bottle of Sauvignon blanc. "Want some wine?" I hold the bottle above my head. Flashes of Keira's red hair appear in the corner of my eye as she helps herself to one of the stools at my island counter. She spins around, staring out at my living room. I go ahead and pour her a glass before bringing it over. "I told you my place was fairly cozy. I pay a pretty penny for the HOA, but at least I don't have to maintain a yard." The glass lands behind her on the counter. I lean my elbow against it, sipping my white wine and studying the back of Keira's head.

When she slowly spins around again, it's with eyes so wide that she probably drank in every detail of my home.

"What's going on here?" she softly asks.

I shrug. "What do you mean?"

Keira props her arms on the edge of my counter. My heart skips a beat. Is it from the captivating way her hair slips past her cheek and scrapes my counter? Or is it the feeling of impending doom weighing heavily on me?

"This is the same apartment I've been in before." Keira's eyes are glued to a picture on the wall. Don't worry. I've removed all traces of Sera. Anything of hers she didn't take with her was thrown into the trash, but some of my own tastes are on huge display in this condo. Like the black and white photo of a rose that hangs on the wall between the living room and my kitchen. Keira is still staring at it. Perhaps she's remembering that life-defining moment when it was all she saw from beneath the blanket Sera had thrown over her head. "When did you move here?"

I've already vowed that I won't lie tonight. "A few years ago. You've been here before?"

"Yes." When Keira looks at me, it's with a self-preserving fury behind her otherwise sweet eyes. "My ex brought me here on the day I found out I was the other woman. Trust me. You don't forget a place like this." Her orangish brows knit across her forehead. Is she studying me? Criticizing me? Questioning my very existence? Perhaps she's dreaming. Or this is a nightmare she's suffered every night since that unfortunate day we met.

You know. The *real* day we met.

"What's going on?" This time when Keira asks that, it's with a snap to her voice and a hitch in her throat. I must remain calm. While I'm not surprised that she recognizes my condo – isn't that the whole reason I didn't want her here for so long? – I am rather shocked that it has happened so soon. Because that's an accusation on her lips. I only need to stand here a few seconds longer. "Is this really your place, Evie? Are you really the woman who lives here?"

Desperation lines her words. She doesn't want to believe that it's true – that I could be who I say I am, no vocabulary required.

"Yes. I live here. Why? What's gotten into you?"

"You're... you're her!" Keira stumbles off the stool. She hasn't taken off her sweater yet, but I soon find a button left behind on the seat. When I offer it to her, Keira bats it away. Somewhere in the corner of my kitchen, a plastic button clatters to the floor. "You're the other woman! The... the one Sera was..." She gasps. "You're Sera's girlfriend!"

"Keira." I forego pet names to focus on what's going on here. "Let's talk about this."

"You know who I am. How could you not? I've talked about her. You know all about me and Se... oh my *God,* I've told you things like the car! Is that why you have a new car? Is that why you didn't want me here for so long?"

I have no choice but to stand up and attempt to calm her down. "Let's go to the living room and talk this through before we have dinner."

She shrugs me off her. "Why? You never brought it up. You never said, *'Huh, ain't it funny that my ex is named the same thing? Wouldn't that be some great coincidence?'* Because it's not a coincidence, is it, Evelyn?"

"I don't know what you want from me."

"I want the truth."

The truth. That thing that's hung above my neck like the Sword of Damocles ever since I brought Keira to my friend's yacht. That was the first time I seduced her for my own desire, not because I thought it brought balance back to the universe or for some petty revenge. Sera still doesn't know this. Did you know that was part of my original plan? To tell Sera the next time I saw her? *"I fucked your sidepiece. I can see why you cheated on me with her. She's much better in bed than you ever were."*

Petty. Cruel. That's me, Evelyn Sharpe.

"Yes." For some reason, I can't bring myself to look her in the eye. "I've known for some time now that you're the woman my ex cheated with. It was easy to put two and two together."

"Yet I didn't." Keira clutches her chest and looks for her escape. The door is right there, yet she doesn't run. Instead, she swings toward me, the fiery fury of a woman who has been humiliated raining down upon me. "I was so stupid I never realized that you were the woman I heard and saw that day. No, I guess I didn't see you well enough, but I heard you. When I... when I was in the hallway..."

Her arms lift. A finger points. Sure enough, she's referencing the hallway that leads to my bedroom. That's where I saw the first real glimpse of her bewitching red hair and the innocently freckled face that didn't know what the hell was going on.

I hated her at that moment. She had ruined my relationship. Taken the only person who had ever truly mattered to me in my adult life.

Yet here I am, desperately hoping she won't run out that door.

"Kiki," I softly say. "I don't hold any of it against you. You didn't know."

"But you did."

What can I say? I dangerously tread into waters that will lead to me lying so I can save this farce of a relationship. One I never saw myself clinging to all those months ago.

"Let me start from the beginning," I say. "This isn't what you think."

"What is there for me to think or not think? This whole time, you've been linked to one of the most embarrassing moments of my life. You're a part of the reason I couldn't look myself in the mirror for *months*. To think, I was falling in *love* with you!"

Could her words sting more? Even if she told me that she hated me now and never wanted to see me again, knowing that she had been falling in love with me makes it worse.

She's so beautiful. So hurt.

"Won't you sit down on the couch?" This whole time, I've been operating on borrowed sanity. The closer Keira gets to that door, the more I know I'm in too deep, too. Only two weeks into knowing her I could have let her go and not felt a thing. No pain. No loss. Nothing like what I felt when Sera proved to be too untrustworthy – and unworthy of my love. "We need to figure out what's going on here. You're clearly in shock. See, Kiki, this is why I didn't want you coming here. Once I figured out who you were..."

"How long?"

"Huh?"

She shakes her head as if she's attempting to knock the hurtful memories from her head. "How long have you known about this? That I'm the one your ex was with?"

I respond without thinking. "It didn't take me long to figure it out."

With a gasp that's raspier than the voice chiding me in my head, Keira lunges for my front door. Her sweater clings to her arms as she wrestles the door open and grabs the archway like we're experiencing an earthquake.

"Keira!"

Crazed eyes look over her shoulder. I'm frozen where I stand, afraid to go to her, and afraid to look too soft. If I want her, then I should grab her. Pull her into my apartment and lock the door behind her. I've already lost one woman from this place. I can't possibly lose another.

She flees into the hallway, the door swinging open behind her.

Just like that, I've lost another. Perhaps this place is cursed, after all.

CHAPTER 23

Keira

G o on and laugh at me. It's what you've been wanting to do since this charade began.

I'm used to people laughing at me. Most that I come into contact with do to some extent.

Is it the way I look? The whole *laugh at the ginger!* spectacle is something I associate with relationships across the pond, not so much in my corner of America. I shouldn't be surprised, though. We're always looking for ways to tear our fellow humans down and make our lives absolute hell. Because if someone else is suffering more than you, that means you win.

Or maybe it has nothing to do with my freckles and red hair and everything to do with not having the perfect figure. Maybe I'm easy to laugh at because I'm naturally reserved and introverted. Is it because I get sentimental and cry over the lamest shit? I can still remember my parents chastising me for making a scene at my grandma's funeral. It was over ten years ago. I was barely out of high school when the only person in my family I ever really got along with passed into the great beyond. There I was, bellowing like a beluga whale at her graveside and refusing to get back in the car to attend the wake. Never heard the end of it for months. Wasn't invited to my uncle's funeral because everyone was afraid I'd have a meltdown again.

You ever wonder if you might be the universe's punching bag? That you have to be wary about every good thing that happens to you because it might be a prank in disguise?

When everything around you turns into a trojan horse, people shouldn't be shocked when you push them away and lock out the world.

That's what I've been doing for the past few days. At first, I took two sick days, telling Mr. Birch that I have the flu. Then I had to dip into my vacation days. Since I don't have a doctor's note on hand, it meant coming up with all sorts of excuses as to why I won't see the inside of a clinic. I don't need a GP. What I need is a good therapist who can unpack why women like Sera and Evelyn treat me as their toy.

For all I know, that was the plan the whole time. They might still be together to this day.

The safest place is beneath my covers, where I wear the same pajamas every day and subsist off nothing but water and crackers. You'd think I really do have the flu and not a broken heart that has been stomped upon by someone who thought I'd be a fun game to play.

I don't know what else it could be. Evelyn *knew* me for who I really was. This whole time! The woman who came on so strongly when we met in her office must have known who I was. That's why she was quick to ask me out, and when we made it to the bar, she wanted to sleep with me before the night was over. Was everything a lie on her side? Did she fuck me for four months because it turned out she liked the thrill it gave her? She was the one who told me *I* liked thrills. Was that nothing but projection?

What is the truth? Could I bear to know?

"Hey!" Laura knocks at my door on the third day. My laptop plays endless reruns of a show I used to love as a kid. Yet all I hear are the fake promises Evelyn left behind in my ears. When Laura finally breaks into my apartment using nothing but a hairclip and her wiles, it's with a threat to call 911 if I don't sit up in my bed right now. "What's going on, girl? You haven't answered my texts in almost four days! Are you dying? Are you already dead?"

Sighing, I roll over in my bed. Why do I have to live in a studio? It's way too easy for Laura to slam my door shut and chase me down from only a few feet away.

"Leave me alone," I mutter.

She climbs into bed behind me. Has she bothered to take off her nasty shoes? "What happened, huh? You and Evelyn break up? Last I heard, you were finally having dinner at her place." Laura leans back on my pillow and snorts. I stay facing my wall, wishing that this wasn't the same spot I've gazed at whenever Evelyn was with me. How many times did I count the blotches on the wall when Evelyn cuddled me – like she *loved* me?

I want to throw up.

"Did you find her stash of dead bodies? I knew it. Serial killer."

"This isn't funny," I mutter into my blanket. "She really fucked up."

"Hm?" Laura drops the sarcasm from her voice. "What happened, hon? You were over the moon with her a week ago. Talking about having her babies. What's up?"

"She..."

"Did she hurt you? 'Cause I know a guy who could fuck her up really good."

I don't know what that means, and I don't want to know. "You'll never believe it if I told you. I feel like I belong on an episode of *Maury*."

"Would you tell me already? Otherwise, everything I think up will probably be worse than what you're actually dealing with."

"She's Sera's ex-girlfriend."

"Huh? Your crappy ex? She's her... what? Like before you?"

I push myself up. I've moved so little these past few days that it actually hurts to lift my chest. "You know how I told you about that day? When Sera took me to her place and I found out she had a girlfriend she lived with that whole time?"

"Yeah."

"What if I told you that Evelyn lives in that apartment, and she was the one who had been screaming her head off the whole time I had some blanket thrown over my head."

I shouldn't be so surprised that it takes Laura a few more minutes and multiple explanations to figure out what I'm saying. When the truth finally sinks in, she jerks against my bed so hard that the whole thing shakes against the wall. My neighbors probably think I'm having sex again.

They couldn't be farther from the truth this time!

"So Evelyn was the other woman from your last relationship? Did she have any idea?"

I nod against my best friend's shoulder. "She said she figured out who I was a long time ago. I don't know what that means exactly. Did she figure it out after the first time we were together and that's why I didn't hear back from her for a while? Or did she know from the very beginning?" That's what's giving me the biggest headache. There's something about the whole situation that smells like shit, and I'm too chicken to say it out loud.

Apparently, I'm counting on Laura to say it for me.

"Do you think that's why she asked you out?" Laura asks. "Because she wanted to purposely break your heart to get back at you for making her ex cheat?"

"I didn't make Sera do anything!"

"No, no, I get that. What I mean is from her point of view she might have been pulling a big ol' power move over you. Because fuck you, that's why."

"I hate you for saying that." The covers are soon over my head again. My grandmother's blanket. The same one that has kept me safe and warm all these years is the same one Evelyn made such intense love to me on so many times. It got to the point I thought about getting a new blanket under the excuse of it being summer and needing something lighter. More like I didn't think my dead grandma would appreciate how much gay sex I was having all over it. Can't exactly conceive some new little Lawsons in my womb with someone like Evelyn, no matter how good she fucks.

Great. Tears in my eyes!

"Sorry for saying what's on my mind." Laura is sitting up now. Glad to report that she is *not,* in fact, wearing shoes on my bed. "Doesn't that sound plausible, though? You say she was so nonchalant the other night when you were at her place. Either that was all part of her plan, or she really did want you to stay calm and talk to her about it."

"Pft! Which do you think?" I know which way *my* heart leans!

"Oh, I think she's a fucking bitch who knew exactly what she was doing. She had a plan, and it included your O face."

I feel so used. From head to toe, I was Evelyn Sharpe's used washrag that she used to clean up her scorned and broken heart. She never cared about *me.* It was never about my ass or my hair, or the freckles she claimed to count more than once. It was about Sera having been here first. Maybe she believed me when I said that I had no idea Sera was cheating until that fateful day, but she made me pay for my involvement, anyway.

Did she actually care for me at all? Why did it drag on for so long? Was the sex good for her? God, how could it be? I was the one who wrecked her home! How could she compartmentalize that when we were together?

These are questions I'll never know the answers to because I'll never talk to Evelyn again. I have nothing to say to her, and she has nothing but venom to say to me. I can't trust a single thing she says or does. I hate her. I loathe what has happened because of her.

Yet I can't stop thinking about her. Every time I close my eyes, there she is, and she's so happy to see me that my heart sings with joy. That's the part of me still falling in love with her.

How do I recover from this? All that's left is my tattered heart that won't know how to love again.

CHAPTER 24

Evelyn

"**G**uess who I got off the phone with." Peter waltzes into the office after lightly knocking on my opened door. "If you're thinking *Lyle Pennington* from Everlasting Getaways, then you are correct."

He raises his coffee mug at me in a toast. It takes me way too long to remember who the hell Lyle Pennington is. Not my fault. My head has been a messy fog for the past week. It's a wonder I can get *any* work done at all.

"Congratulations on landing your third account of the week, Sharpe. Pennington was absolutely thrilled with the proposal. I should have Quintin shadow you during your next meeting because you are on fire right now."

"You want him to drop by with a bucket of water in case the blaze is out of control?"

That garners a wink from my boss. "You are definitely burning up this summer. Whatever you're doing, keep at it. Keep going to church, dating your current girl, putting a lucky penny in your heels... whatever. Because you're looking at a nice Christmas bonus this year."

"I'm not seeing anyone at all right now."

"Good! Keep that up, then!" Peter leaves my office as swiftly as he entered it. The only reason I get up is to close the door and give myself some privacy.

It's no secret around here that I've been working overtime this past week. At first, Quintin made fun of me, assuming that I must be behind my work because I've been off "playing." Little did he know that I have no one to play with now. Not only is Keira refusing to answer my calls, but

I'm also pretty sure she's blocked my number. I've long stopped begging her to talk to me. Instead, I've dedicated my waking hours this past week to nothing but work. Researching, touching base with assistants, drafting and redrafting proposals... the works. Suffice to say, the hard work is paying off. Not only have my last three pitches landed without any follow-up, but my current accounts couldn't be happier with my performance. I also stayed two hours late three days ago to talk one of my clients out of shopping around for corporate insurance. They're small-time, too. We wouldn't hurt to see them go. If anything, they're probably taking up too much manpower and would be better served by a smaller agency.

But I needed the distraction. Every time I'm left with my own thoughts, I spiral. Things haven't been this bad since this past winter when my whole seven-year relationship collapsed before me. All because my ex was a cheater who couldn't keep her pussy in her pants.

Yet that probably wasn't how Keira saw it. I wish she would talk to me.

When this all began, I didn't think I would care so much. If Keira discovered my ulterior motive for seducing her... oh, well! I would have had every right to tell her to piss off for the part she played. It didn't matter what the truth was. I was a righteous bitch who had her heart broken and her whole perception of reality torn asunder. The difference between a girl who was as innocent as a spring doe and a woman who sank her claws into my partner meant nothing to me. The end was the same.

This feels so different from Sera, though. With her, I consumed nothing but holy anger. *I* was wronged. *I* was stomped on by the heavy foot of a cheater. *I* lost everything dear to me. This time?

I was the offender. I went after Keira with ill-intent. It's because of me she's probably crying into a tub of ice cream as we speak.

God, I really am a bitch.

Is this what they call growth? Looking back on the people you hurt and realizing that you had no right to do that? It didn't matter that someone else had hurt me. Passing that pain along only dragged me down to their level. Then again, I don't think I cared about that, either. The Evelyn of four months ago thirsted for vengeance. I was curious what it would be like to make love to the woman Sera *had* to have instead of me. The original plan to one-night stand her and never speak to her again could have happened. If, you know, I didn't convince myself that I needed Keira to nail Aspen Plastics to my wall.

I have them now. Our first report came in from Oscar Birch, and he simply said, "Everything seems satisfactory." That means we'll keep them for at least another year. I should be sighing in relief.

Instead, I'm thinking of those beautiful bedroom eyes and that luscious ass as Keira falls asleep after we've made love.

I really didn't appreciate what I had. With her, or with Sera.

Someone knocks on my door. I can tell from the cadence of that hand that it's Raymond, and he has some urgent news for me.

"Come in!" I call.

He pops his head in, that aftershave he favors filling my small office. "I made a reservation at Luigi's for tonight. I had to pull some strings since it's Friday, but when I told the host who you were meeting, he agreed to make something happen. I may have slipped that you were planning to tip handsomely."

"How much am I tipping?"

"At least forty percent to the house."

"Good thing I'm made out of money, huh, Raymond?"

"Hey, you told me to make a reservation happen no matter what, and that's what I did. Don't shoot the messenger. Shoot the maître d'."

I wave him off with a flick of my hand. Raymond lingers for a few more seconds, testing my ability to put up with his bullshit.

The last thing I need is him looking at me like *that*. As if he has something on me and is about to tell the whole office. The real bullshit? He might as well! Right now, Raymond is the only one in this place who knows what I'm up to tonight. One of the downsides of relying on the office assistant to make your reservations because you're too busy doing actual work. Under any other circumstance, I wouldn't think twice about it. Except this is Raymond. Mr. *I-Know-What's-Going-On-And-One-Wrong-Move-Means-Everyone-Else-Knows.*

Ass.

As five creeps closer, more butterflies dance in my stomach. I don't have time to go home and change, not that I have anything *nice* I want to wear to dinner tonight. It's bad enough Raymond called my dinner date and told her to meet me at Luigi's.

"Any big plans this weekend?" Quintin asks me in the break room, half an hour before I'm due out of here. Although that question was doubtlessly uttered for the sake of small talk, my inability to keep a coffee cup in my hand means Quintin is double-taking at my floundering. "Are you still seeing that cute redhead from Aspen Plastics?"

"I... no. Not at the moment." More flustered than a plastic bag in a windstorm, I show myself to the door. "You weren't supposed to know about that, anyway."

"You date a girl long enough, everyone finds out about it. Kinda jealous!"

"Why? Thinking about trading in your wife already?" I won't mention that Keira is *gay,* so stop getting ideas in your head, Quint.

"Very funny!"

Peter stops me on my way back to my office because *everyone* needs a piece of my gossip tonight. "What's this about you and the cute redhead from Aspen Plastics."

"Please, Pete, like you remember her."

"I vaguely remember Oscar Birch coming in here with someone who fits that description. Good to hear you're moving on from that ex of yours. I never liked her, you know. Way too rough around the edges for someone as put-together as you, Sharpe."

I catch Raymond's nosy gaze too close to me. While he hastily gets back to his work, I tell Peter that I need to finish up my own work for the afternoon so I can leave on time. I am having dinner with someone tonight, after all.

My breath is far from caught when I toss my keys to the valet outside of Luigi's. The maître d' recognizes me immediately and motions me to a table that looks like it's been thrown together at the last minute. Now, don't think I always get this kind of treatment. I sure as shit did not order a red rose on the table and unscented tealight candles to illuminate the dark corner that barely overlooks the choicest parts of the city.

Even so, I thank my host and toss my coat over the back of the chair facing the entrance. I want to know the exact moment my guest walks back into my life.

Is it a shame that I'm rather surprised it takes so long for Sera to appear?

Honestly, I thought she was about to stand me up. Wouldn't be the first time she stuck it to me after begging for forgiveness for so long. *Also* would not be the first time she came to Luigi's wearing work clothes. Which, for Sera, means stained blue jeans and a wrinkled shirt. Tonight, though, she's rather fetching in the kind of slacks and blouse that always lit up a room when I was happy to see her.

Can't say I'm happy tonight. More like relieved. Nervous.

Now, I don't know what you're thinking, but I can assure you that I am *not* getting back with my cheating ex. Even if I were stupid enough to fall into my feelings after what happened with Keira, I'm not about to believe that Sera has changed her no-good cheating ways. My love for her will always be there, but it's tainted now. We'll never go on adventures or make the kind of love that we once took so much for granted. Because I'll always know what she's capable of. I know what kind of monster really lurks beneath those humble smiles and heavy, seductive eyes.

At the same time, many months have passed, and being with Keira has taught me that I *can* move on. I can date the woman who was at the center of my whirlwind breakup and not be consumed with petty rage and jealousy. Perhaps that's why I'm so conflicted right now. I look at Sera and see the woman who used to be my everything. I also see someone severely flawed and human. I don't need to know why she did what she did. That's beside the point now. We've moved on!

Even she has, based on the exasperated look she gives me when we sit down.

"Wine, huh?" She suspiciously eyes the waiter pouring us two glasses of red. "It's the cheap stuff, though, so you must not be here to tell me how much you love me again."

The waiter pretends he didn't hear that before leaving us with our menus. "It's not my fault they thought this was a romantic dinner date." Most of my attention is on the seasonal specials, not the woman who has put on some makeup for me. She must not have had work today if she had so much time to do herself up for *me*. "I'm pretty sure the wine is complimentary. I'm not paying for it." This wine is the same thing they serve every dinner date that comes through here. Based on our history, the man who took our reservation must have thought a proposal was happening tonight. Sweet, isn't it? Think I'll go throw up now.

"What's this about, Evie?" Sera doesn't bother to look at her menu. She always orders the same thing, and lucky me, it's *not* one of the most expensive things available. I really scored when I started going out with a woman who isn't into hefty steaks and truffle-stuffed ravioli. Quite the opposite. Sera always gets the most basic pasta and soup set, because she doesn't understand half of the menu. "I don't get the call from *you*. I get it from Raymond, whom I'm pretty sure was snickering through his teeth when I picked up. Not to mention you happen to be in the same place as…"

"Stop right there." Lest Sera believe that I'm about to apologize to *her,* the waiter drops by, informing my ex that this is about appearances. I order the seasonal tortellini with minestrone and wait for Sera to lower her guard enough to tell the nice waiter what she wants, too.

Her voice cracks no fewer than three times when she stumbles over the Italian on the menu. Once the waiter takes away our menus and heads to the POS system, I lean forward, my smug demeanor the only thing powering me through confronting my ex.

"I forgive you."

Sera is a frozen block of ice in her seat. That embroidered blouse she's wearing must be new. I'm pretty sure I haven't seen it before, and I used to have her whole wardrobe memorized. Drove her *nuts* whenever I suggested she wear this or that to whatever function we were hitting back in the day. This is a woman who doesn't like it when her friends find out she has a dress or two in the back of her closet. Never know when they come in handy for weddings!

"You... forgive me."

"Yes." I sip the wine. You know, I assumed they gave this away for free to couples they liked because the owner has a stake in the company and considers it *marketing.* Now that I try it again, it's rather good, isn't it? Here. Take a whiff. The aroma is subtle, and the flavor complex. A hint more cherry than usual. I take another sip. That will be the last one for a while – don't need to be drunk while telling Sera what's on my mind. "I forgive you for cheating on me."

"That's something, huh?"

With a happy sigh, I flatten my palms on the table and smile. Already Sera is more unnerved than I've ever seen her before. "I've been doing a lot of thinking these past few months. I was quite pissed off when that all came to light. Was pretty mad for a while after, too. I'm not going to beat myself up over it, though. I had every right to want to flay you alive."

Sera knows me well enough that me sounding so sweet while I say these things isn't *good* news for her. If there's anyone on this planet who is aware that I can go from docile to claws out in five minutes, it's the ex who brought another woman into our home.

"Oh, don't worry. I didn't invite you here to ask you back, Sera." I unfold my cloth napkin and drape it across my nap. Getting sauce all over my favorite work skirt? I don't think so. "If anything, I'd like to put everything behind us and move forward as... well, not friends. I'd rather not hang out. Even in our relationship, we didn't have a whole lot in common, did we? It's amazing we lasted so long." Come to think of it, why *were* we together for so long? Sex isn't enough to keep a couple together. We went on some fun adventures, but in the day-to-day, the only thing we *enjoyed* was watching some TV before bed. That doesn't mean I didn't love her, but I do think she cared more about the thrill of a new relationship than sticking it out with me.

A few months ago, that would have devastated me. Think about it. Someone loves you, but not enough to overcome the malaise that's settled into your relationship. I don't fault Sera for that. Where I judge her is how she went about sabotaging our relationship. This was the woman who was still regularly sleeping with me while fooling around with Keira behind my back, after all. I reserve all right to judge that!

But I'm okay now. Does it sting? Yes. Does it leave lasting pain in my heart, though? Only when I look at her, the woman I fell asleep next to for almost seven years. Those were seven years of unfettered loyalty on my behalf. Even when we were in the midst of a "disagreement," even when we were apart because of work or family emergencies, I thought of no one else but the woman I swore myself to.

Yet here we are. Fallen apart.

"We can at least be acquaintances," I say to her. "Should we ever cross paths in the future, be it at a party or on the street, we can be cordial. Say

hello. Ask how the other is doing. Invite me to your wedding for all I care."
There! Feels so much better!

"What the hell has gotten into you?" Sera asks, keeping her distance on the other side of the table. "Are you on drugs? Like, brain drugs?"

"No. Just some perspective in life. Things have been weird on my side of the break-up."

"Yeah, I'd say so." Sera licks her lip while I admire the view from our corner of the room. "You were seeing her, weren't you?"

Although she's cut through the crux of why we're both here, I can't let her catch me off guard. "Seeing who?"

"Keira."

The way she says that name is the first thing to kill my mood since Sera sat down. "Quite the coincidence, isn't it?"

"You're trying to tell me you *happened* to go out with her a few months after breaking up with me? Come on, Eve. I know you better than that. When you're pissed off, you can be quite the vindictive bitch. Wouldn't surprise me at all if you pursued her on purpose. To get back at me? To fuck with her? Could see it going either way. I don't pretend to know you all the way down to your bones, but if you could hit two birds with one stone, why wouldn't you? You get some hot ass, and you get to hurt some people along the way."

"Hurting people was never on the agenda." That's it. I shall need more of this wine, after all. "Like I'm sure you weren't out to fuck me in the heart when you seduced her in that bar."

"I knew it. I *knew* that wasn't a coincidence."

"Hm?"

"A month or so ago, when you saw me at the bar. The moment you left, I saw Keira. First time I'd seen her since she broke it off with me, too. You'll be *happy* to know that she was pissed as fuck when she discovered she was the other woman. Been single ever since, Evie."

"Honestly, it's probably good for you to be genuinely single for a while. Have some wild one-night stands, get some girls with no strings attached... isn't that the way it's supposed to go? Rebounds out your ass? Besides, I know for a fact that wasn't the first time you saw her since the breakup. She told me you showed up at her place crying for her to take your sorry ass back. Right after you showed up at my office and made a fucking fool of us both."

"That was a rough time, all right?" Sera unfolds her cloth napkin, but it's to toss it between her hands instead of putting it in her lap like an adult. "I was going through some shit."

"Three months after the fact?"

"Yeah, well, those first three months I was purely fueled by anger and convincing myself I didn't give a shit about what had happened. My therapist pissed me off when she called me out for my crap and I cut her off for a while. That's when things got a little... I don't want to get into it. I just didn't want to be alone. If one of you wouldn't take me back, then it meant I really was terrible, and I couldn't face that."

"Since then?"

Sera gazes out the window. "Took some time for me. Moved out of my friend's place where I was crashing and got my own apartment. It ain't much. Definitely a step down from the place we shared. I'm guessing you still live there."

"Of course. Even if I wanted to sell it, that can take a few months in the current market."

"Anyway, color me shocked when I realized that you and Keira were going out."

I weigh my options. Should I come out and say that she's right? That might only inflate her ego and prevent her from hearing what I really want to say tonight. But if I deny it, she'll catch me in the lie, and then what? It's not like I want Sera's trust. She lost mine, so why should I care about hers?

What I want is for all of this to be done on *my* terms. That's what it's always been about. The power that was taken away from me must be mine again.

"You might be right." I wait to catch Sera's attention before sighing into my hand. As my elbow threatens to slip off the small table, I continue, "Wasn't difficult to figure out who your girlfriend was. I got a good look at her that night. Was easier to discover her name and where she works. Not that I'm saying I *stalked* her, but the opportunity presented itself soon enough. We would have met anyway. Maybe I wasn't in my right mind when I asked her out, but she said yes. The rest was a bit of history."

"You and Keira." Sera brushes her nails against her thumb before sitting back in her seat. Her lips smack together in disbelief. "I definitely did not see that coming. Too bad you didn't stick around in the bar. You could have seen my shock. Must have been what you wanted."

"At that point, I was a bit invested. Better for everyone if she didn't figure it out."

"Wait... you were still seeing her because you *wanted* to?"

"Of course. Why is that so weird?"

"But she's..."

"She didn't know me. She didn't know that you were in a relationship. So, if she's nice and I like her in bed, why shouldn't I have kept dating her?"

"My brain has exploded. Congratulations on that accomplishment."

"I didn't invite you here because I wanted to hold it over your head, believe it or not. I have other reasons for talking to you tonight."

"Oh, not *just* to tell me about you going out with Keira. Got it."

"Thing is, there's quite the sticky situation with us right now. See, I had to decide the best time to tell her about who I really am. You'll be happy to hear it completely blew up in my face."

Sera chortles. "I bet! She must have really loved the part where you revealed yourself as the woman who was screaming at me that night. You know, I half expected you to kick her ass before you kicked mine. It was a real crapshoot. Should've bet myself you'd go after me first. I know you well enough." She wipes something from her eye. The waiter brings us our soups. "When she broke up with me, she told me the worst part was the humiliation of that night. Like I could have made it better. Sheesh. How did she feel when she realized that you were the woman who could have absolutely destroyed her? Don't suppose she kicked *your* ass."

"Not quite." I'm glad she finds the humor in this. She might as well. What else does she have to lose? "But I didn't like hurting her. She's a nice person and I liked her. In another life, I would have kept dating her."

"Me too."

"Really?" It's my turn to laugh because what Sera said almost goes over my head it really is *that* preposterous. "You and her. I can't imagine it."

"I can't imagine you two together, either!"

"No, I can't imagine *you* two because you would have smothered the poor dear." I can see it now. A honeymoon phase that would have Keira seeing the moon and the stars swarming around her – until Sera lost interest in her. Until she really figures her shit out, that will be the fate of every relationship Sera enters for the next few years. Possibly her whole life. "No offense. It takes a strong personality to be with someone like you."

"You saying Keira doesn't have what it takes?"

"I'm saying she's a fragile kitten who needs someone who understands that about her. She wants to put her whole trust in a person and not have to worry about them screwing her over. I think part of the reason you and I lasted as long as we did was because I knew how to keep you in line."

"I always liked that about you," Sera says with a sigh. "You weren't afraid to tell me when I was being a shit. You liked me on top, but you were always the one calling the shots. Which means I can't be mad at you now." Her spoon splashes into her soup. "You've given me some great images to play in my head tonight. You and Keira. You were definitely on top."

No sense letting her words get to me. Besides, I knew that she would pull a stupid stunt like this. Of *course* she only cares about imagining Keira and me in bed together. How did I put up with Sera for so long, again?

"I want to get her back." My spoon swirls through the minestrone, picking out the choicest beans and the pieces of carrots that are sure to get lodged behind my teeth. "The more I think about it, the more this past year was probably the best thing that could have happened to me. I dumped the dead weight and was introduced to someone more compatible with me."

"We're still talking about Keira, right?"

"Of course."

"Man..." Sera shakes her head. "When your assistant called me this afternoon, this was *not* what I expected to hear. I mean, all of it together. Bits and pieces, sure... but you and Keira. To think, me fucking up might be the reason you found true love."

"Don't go declaring yourself my matchmaker. This is weird enough as it is."

My ex looks me right in the eye when she says, "I didn't expect to get back with you tonight. Not sure I would have agreed to it, honestly, but hearing that you have fallen in love with *Keira,* of all people?"

"When did I say I fell in love with her?"

"Evie." Sera sounds like she's about to keep it totally real with me. Exactly what I need right now! "The way you talk about her. The way you gaze up at the ceiling whenever you think about her. I know that sound and that look. It's the way I used to think about you when we first got together."

My ears perk up at that. "You used to think about me that way?"

"Of course. You think I didn't actually love you? Come on. We spent seven years together! Sure, things were rocky and boring in the end, but I really did love you those first few years. I think we simply outgrew each other."

I purse my lips. "Sure would have been nice if you had said that to me before you cheated. Could have saved us a lot of drama."

She nods. "I'm sorry. I can't ever make up for the hurt I caused you, but I really am sorry. I shouldn't have been so immature."

"It's nice to hear that."

"Yeah? You wanna get back with Keira, right? Because I have a feeling the real reason you asked me to dinner is so I can give you ideas."

"It's not the *only* reason. My own therapist appreciates it when I deliver my forgiveness in person."

"Damn therapists. They're almost always right."

I can't fully explain what has happened between her and me, but I like it. The tension is gone. The food tastes good and the wine is deliciously sweet. We can talk about the old times without me wanting to throttle her. Everything is laid out on the table – all I have to do is hold up what is most precious and admire it for the simplistic beauty it harbors.

This moment is pretty precious. It's like a door closing on one ugly part of my life and another, more hopeful one has cracked open only a few feet away.

All I have to do is step through.

CHAPTER 25

Keira

Sometimes, you have no one to blame but yourself for the shit you find yourself in.

"The whole thing is a ruckus." Caleb O'Connor, one of Mr. Birch's great-grand-nephews or what have yous, sits across from me at a café near my apartment. This is what I'm doing with my Sunday. Because deep down, I hate myself.

That's the only explanation for being on a *date* with a man. How long has it been, anyway? I don't think I've gone out with a guy in literal years. Definitely nothing interesting happened the last few times. So why am I here? Why are we suffering together on one of the most unnecessary dates to ever slap me across the face?

Because I'm weak. That's why.

Mr. Birch has been pressuring me to go out with one of his kin for so long that it's background noise. Yet after I broke things off with Evelyn, I must have looked moodier than usual around my boss. He would *not* let up. Kept telling me that I was too pretty to look so down and lonely. The only reason I'm here is because I didn't have the spine to tell him to piss off or I would tell HR. Instead, yours truly took the path of least resistance once again. Hearing that Caleb was in town, I agreed to a single coffee date on Sunday afternoon. After Mass, of course.

Caleb assures me it's all for show, though.

"What's a ruckus?" I ask, having zoned out what he said a few minutes before.

"The Blarney Stone." For a man who has spent half of his life in Kilkenny, he doesn't have much of an accent. Kinda kills the fantasy of going out with an Irish guy, doesn't it? Not that I purport to have such fantasies, but if I'm going to sit through a fake date with someone I have no interest in, the least that could happen is a good story for Laura! "Biggest tourist trap you've ever seen. Bigger than Time's Square." He loudly sips his coffee. Normally I don't notice these things about other people, but I guess when I don't want to be here, everything is like a pickaxe chipping away at my skull. "Have you ever been?"

"To Cork County?" Sheesh, hope he can't hear the disdain dripping from my fangs. "No. I've never been to Ireland. Thought I mentioned that earlier."

"Really? Huh. It's so normal to me now."

"Time's Square is normal to me."

For some reason, that makes Caleb grin like I've told the funniest joke he's heard all day. "If you ever go," he says, and I keep drinking my iced mocha like I'm super dehydrated, "you will be amazed."

"By Ireland?"

"By Blarney Castle."

"Ah."

"There's a man whose whole job is to sit there and tip the tourist under the stone so you can kiss the specific one. Gave me mad vertigo the first and only time I went. One of these days those stones are going to give way, and that will be it."

"I'll keep that in mind if I ever go."

"You should absolutely go! Kinda amazed you haven't been already. I'd thought Uncle Oscar would have sent you by now."

"Send me? What kind of job do you think I have? I take his notes and field his calls."

"Oh, I mean..." Sure enough, Caleb's blushing. "My mother let slip that Uncle Oscar is always trying to set you up with kin like me. She said I shouldn't come because you must be really picky and it's a waste of time."

"I *am* pretty picky, but I'm also busy. Besides, I don't know what you're used to, but it's not exactly good form for one's boss to set them up on dates. HR rather frowns on that."

"I get where you're coming from. Besides, a pretty girl like you must have a lot of suitors. Well, it was nice of you to entertain me today while I'm in town, anyway. This way I can tell my mother that I at least did something that she would consider worth my time."

"I thought you said your mother considered this a waste of your time."

"Uh, well, she wants me to date, of course. I will be thirty soon, and she wants grandkids." His awkward laughter doesn't inspire me to be the next Mrs. O'Connor, expert of Kilkenny and the owner of an apron with four kids tugging on it. "I don't think she was interested in me dating you, though."

"Let me guess. That made you want to date me harder?"

"Don't know if I would put it that way."

"So we're clear, Caleb, I'm not going back to your hotel room with you."

"I... I didn't think..."

Do you hear that? It's his brain breaking and my soul splintering. "It's fine. I want to lay both of our expectations out. I'm only doing this because I'm tired of Mr. Birch always riding my ass about being single. So what if I'm single?" My voice raises high enough to catch the attention of the people sitting at the table next to us. "Maybe I like being single! Who says I have to be partnered up? There's lots to do in this world that doesn't require having somebody in my bed half the time! Hell, maybe I want to go to a conference and hook up with a total stranger for once." What Caleb's blushing face does not get, though, is that I'm fantasizing about a woman in a hotel bar. Preferably one that isn't anything like the Lighthouse Lounge. I don't need to imagine that it's Evelyn in my bed again. It's bad enough she fulfilled the fantasy of asking me out the moment she met me and taking me to bed in a hotel room later that week. I'm good for the rest of my life. Don't need any more of that!

Caleb must have picked up on the look I'm espousing, for he glances over his shoulder before warily facing me once more. "Is there someone you hate behind me?"

"Huh?" I snap out of my strange reverie. "Sorry! Don't mind me. I just got out of a relationship. So I'm bitter about the whole thing."

"Oh. I see."

Should I be unloading on this guy? He didn't ask for this. Hell, I doubt he asked to go on a date with a lesbian, not that I'm about to reveal that to him.

Caleb sits in awkward silence while I drum my fingers on the table. How should this be ended? Do I get up and thank him for his time? Pay the bill to make it feel better? Or do I risk making my boss angry by doing that? Maybe I should sit here and wait for Caleb to end it. It's not like I have anything else to do today. Without Evelyn to take up a lot of my free time, I'm ... floundering. Sitting home alone or hoping Laura can spare some time for me. This is my least favorite part of a breakup. I can get over the hurt and such, but the loneliness as I readjust to doing everything by myself again *sucks*.

I'm also inclined to hallucinate, apparently. Because someone has stepped out onto the patio wearing the kind of outfit that makes me look twice.

Sera. It had to be *her*.

"Uh, everything okay?" Caleb asks. "Is there a bee or something out here?"

"Thought I saw someone I know." No, that's definitely Sera. She's here, right now, casually looking for a place to sit. As far as I can tell, she's alone. Just her and an iced coffee that soon sits on an empty bistro table by a tall potted plant. She doesn't look my way. As soon as she sits, her phone is out, and she's scrolling through social media while sipping her coffee.

What the fuck do I do? I shield my face, but one strategic look, and she'll recognize me! It's not like I can hide my hair or my thighs spilling out of this skirt! What? It's eighty degrees out here! A girl gets hot! *Hot,* fuck you!

Caleb glances over his shoulder. "You know that woman?"

"Don't look!"

His head snaps back around. "Uh, is there something I should know? She's not going to start something, is she?"

"Let's say that if anyone on this whole patio has kissed the Blarney Stone, it's *that* woman," I hiss.

"Right. Must be an old friend of yours."

That's one way to put it! Because of Sera, I'm in this whole mess to begin with! Fuck!

I need to make an exit plan. Now. Before she sees me and does something incredibly stupid that will only humiliate me more.

Chapter 26

Evelyn

Y ou know what I love to do with my Sunday afternoons? Chores. Absolutely love it.

Did you hear that sarcasm dripping from my lips? Good. Because I'd rather be six feet under, buried alive in a coffin than clean up my kitchen on a perfectly sunny Sunday afternoon.

I don't have anything to do outside of this house, though. No friends are available for brunch. All of my shopping is caught up. I might take a book out to dinner tonight. Maybe the Thai place on the end of my street has decent outdoor dining. I *should* be doing research for work, but I'm on such a roll professionally speaking that I don't have to sweat it too much. But I sure would like something to take my mind off things. Which is probably why the extended edition of *Lord of the Rings* is playing on my TV while I scrub my counters and do my laundry.

I'm so domestic right now I could barf.

God, it really would be too much to ask for a girlfriend right now. At least when I was with Sera there was someone to hang out with all the time. We could go to museums. Hiking! Shit, we used to go on some seriously great hikes back in the day.

Look at me. So desperate for companionship that I'm romanticizing a relationship that ended because she didn't want me as her girlfriend anymore.

Apparently, I've sent some weird psychic waves out into the universe, because my phone buzzes the moment I grab my bath towels from the dryer.

"Do u still want her?" It's from an unlisted number. Must be Sera's new digits she told me about at dinner the other night. Something about her fresh start as a non-douchebag who is going to stay single for a while. Naturally, I don't have this one blocked. Yet. *"Come down 2 the Pier Café and hear me out. I'll be here a while. Plz reply."*

Dare I answer?

"Who is this? Sera?"

"Duh."

"What are you talking about?"

"Keira. U want her? I have a plan. Come 2 Pier Café."

"Yes, I got that the first time."

"What u waitin 4 then? U got other plans?"

Her inability to type out whole words has always grated me, but it's particularly annoying now. Why, Sera? What the hell is so hard about spelling out words like *you* and *to?* You have a smartphone. I know that the predictive text is right there!

"What the hell do you have planned?" I shoot back.

"Not a lot of time. She's here with some guy. Looks like a date. Get your ass over here and I'll tell you the plan."

My heart skips a beat hearing that Keira is out with some guy. I hope to God it's not a date! She told me she was a lesbian. I know people can change in many ways, but knowing her, that sounds like a recipe for self-harm.

"You coming or what?"

This is all so sudden. Why in the world does Sera know where Keira is right now? Is she stalking her? Is she going to make a move if I don't go after her? Right now? In my current state of sweats and greasy hair? I haven't showered today!

There's no time. If I'm going, I have to decide now. Keira is out there. If I want her, I have to go to her and plead my case.

Christ! I can't decide this right now! Not like this! It's so sudden!

Yet when I close my eyes to collect my breath, I imagine her sitting there on that patio, soaking in the sun and looking more radiant than the flowers that bloom this time of year. I bet her hair is especially bright and besotting on a day like today.

Those freckles... she must have so many! More than I ever saw in the drearier days of the year.

This is my chance, huh? Guess I better throw something on and fix my hair!

CHAPTER 27

Keira

I 've done my best to avoid Sera's gaze the whole time I've been here. It helped that she swapped seats as soon as the sun moved. She has fair skin, like me. While she doesn't burn as quickly as I do, Sera moving chairs so she's back in the shade tells me she has no idea I'm here.

Except I can't exactly get up and leave without her seeing me. Besides, Caleb has struck up another conversation about his work, and it would be incredibly rude to bail on him. I've tried. Lord knows I've attempted to run off to the bathroom and hide while I come up with an excuse for leaving. Maybe my mom called. Maybe I suddenly remembered I have a doctor's appointment – yes, on a Sunday. Ugh. This is like my own personal hell. A man in front of me, and my ex only a few yards away.

Could this get any worse?

Yes, I know. I said those magic words that basically invite God to laugh at me. I hear He has a sense of humor. I mean, I never heard that at *Mass* when I was a kid, but I've heard it enough times by now to know to not try the Big Man. If there's something cosmically hilarious on the horizon, dreading it will only guarantee it's coming for my stupid face.

Because while Caleb tells me about his super exciting career in finance, I notice someone waltzing out of the café, sashay attracting my super-gay attention.

It's Evelyn. Holy shit, *it's Evelyn!*

To be fair, I almost don't recognize her at first. I've rarely seen her with hair bunched at the nape of her neck and a giant clasp holding it all together. Her summery blue dress would look average on anyone else, but this is Evelyn Sharpe, the woman always so meticulously put together that a weekend date to a café usually includes heels, blouses, and a full face of makeup. Yet this is an Evelyn who quickly put this outfit together and ran out of her den of lies and deceit. She might have been crying!

All right. That's wishful thinking on my part, but let me have it.

Caleb hasn't noticed my inability to listen to him. Meanwhile, I peer between my fingers to witness one ex-girlfriend meeting the other.

They're sitting together!

My heart completely collapses into my gut. I don't know what to make of this. Evelyn sitting in the full sunlight across from Sera? Looking gruff while she relaxes in her seat? An iced tea appears before her. She roots through her bag and adjusts her sunglasses, but her gaze is permanently set on Sera. I can't hear them, nor can I read lips, but I swear they're having a cordial conversation between friends.

This makes no damn sense. Why would Evelyn, who made it clear that her breakup was an absolute bomb of a mess, meet with the woman who ruined both of our lives? Are they getting back together? *Have* they gotten back together? Was this the first thing Evelyn did after I walked out on her? Was this the plan all along?

Did they... never break up after all?

I can't believe I'm considering this. I've thought a lot of shit about Evelyn since I discovered the truth, but the possibility that she was still with Sera all along? The woman who attempted to get back with me, too?

This is hurting my brain almost as much as it's punching me in the heart. I think I'm going to be sick. What if Evelyn seducing me and going out with me *for four months* was all some cruel prank?

What the fuck even!

"Are you okay?" This isn't the first time Caleb has asked me this question, and I doubt it will be the last. Not with the way he's looking at me like I'm about to vomit all over this table at any moment! "Seriously, you haven't looked that good for a while. Are you sure your drink is okay? Maybe you should stop..."

He threatens to take my iced mocha away. My hands snatch it back, seeking comfort in the slight chill that remains in my cold beverage.

"I'm. Fine."

"Is it that woman behind us?" Caleb looks over his shoulder and notes Evelyn's arrival. "Oh, there's two now." He looks back at me. "I have no idea what's going on, but it's pretty clear that someone over there is bothering you. Should I go have a talk with them?"

Holy shit, is he serious? I'd rather die! "No. Noooo." Am I holding back a cough because my last slurp went down the wrong way, or because I'm suppressing insane laughter? "Absolutely, whatever you do, *don't* talk to either of those women back there."

I happen to look over the moment Evelyn turns her head in my direction.

Shit. Shit! She totally saw me!

Evelyn is too far away for me to have an accurate reading of her demeanor. Is she shocked to see me? Pleased? Uncomfortable? I don't know, but I need to know.

I get up from my seat. Caleb cuts himself off mid-sentence and sighs.

What am I doing? Oh, I don't care about leaving Caleb at this table. I don't care what he tells his mother, let alone my boss. None of that matters as I use my newfound courage to approach the table where both of my lying exes lurk.

It's like stepping over a precarious threshold. The Keira of a few months ago would have rather died than do something so *bold*. Crawling into my bed and suffering from my eternal misery that only baked deeper into my chronic singledom sounded way better than, I don't know, confronting one of the people who had hurt me so much. I once told Evelyn that I was the type to take the path of least resistance. Still that way, but there are times when you have to kick some ass and raise some ire if you're going to let the universe know that you do *not* accept its bullshit!

Sera is the only one who doesn't move when I approach. Evelyn leans back with a start, air hissing through her nostrils and a lump dumping down her throat.

"What the hell is this?" Already I've started a scene. A few people are looking at me from their nearby tables. Caleb is more than mortified as he takes out his cell phone. Not to film me, but to possibly call the cops. What a guy! Exactly what I look for on a first date! Ugh! "Are you two all buddy-buddy again, or was this how it was the whole time? Hm? Are either of you going to answer me?"

"Well, well." Sera taps her phone against the table, that smarmy smile liable to paint my eyes red. "Look who it is, Evie. The bangin' bombshell you keep telling me you miss so much."

Evelyn slowly removes her sunglasses. She refuses to look at me. Good. She should be consumed with shame for what she's done. I didn't endure so much humiliation and a renewed self-hatred for who I am so she could be *cool* with it!

"Keira," she says.

That's it, huh? That's her greeting. She's acting like she had no idea I was here. Sera, meanwhile, insinuates that she actually did know I was sitting a few yards behind her. When I look between them, attempting to read the vibrations still connecting them, I chomp down on my bottom lip and contain a curdled scream.

"Are you guys back together?" I demand. "Or were you always together the whole time? Was I some fun joke to you two? What was it? Sera seduced me, you pretended to find out and break up, then you came and got some for yourself? That your kink or something? Because I didn't find it very sexy."

One of the baristas pokes her face out of the café. I send her such a stinky look that she's compelled to rush back inside. The meek and mild side of me says that I need to cool it and leave before the cops tackle me and Evelyn plays the weeping maiden who has been wronged by her crazy ex. Nothing to see here, folks! Just some lesbian drama for your Sunday brunch!

"Don't worry." Sera's laughter shouldn't be so unnerving, but based on how blasé she is about my confrontation and how Evelyn is curling into a ball in her chair, I'm wondering if my first ex was the mastermind behind everything. "Evelyn dumped my sorry ass that day we got caught. She's made it crystal clear that we're never ever getting back together."

Now really isn't the time to start quoting Taylor Swift titles, Sera. Not that I think she's ever listened to Taylor, but that's because she used to make fun of my Spotify playlists for being so "basic." Why isn't it fall yet? I'd like to throw a pumpkin spiced latte into her sorry face.

"I don't know what you've been thinking after I did what I did," Evelyn says, "but Sera and I are absolutely not together."

"So what the fuck is this, then?"

If I slam my hands on my hips hard enough and scowl at them like they've disappointed me, maybe they'll take me seriously. I simply cannot waver. With Evelyn about to shit her pants and Sera on the verge of cracking up, anything could happen.

Like the manager coming out of the café to toss me on my ass. That would be something.

"If you must know," Evelyn folds her arms on the table. The thing I hate the most? How breathtaking she is when dressed so casually. I've never seen her like this before. Hair imperfect, face bare, and a simple, wrinkled dress on her beautiful body. Those flip-flops on her feet are bedazzled but don't match the fabric on Evelyn's form. Truly, she put this all together at the last minute on her way out the door. Dare I believe Sera told her to get her ass down here? This isn't that close to Evelyn's place. Granted, I don't know where Sera is living now but is it near her as well? "Sera and I have come to an understanding. I'm forever pissed at what she did with you, but I'm getting over it. I've forgiven her, and she's... working on herself."

Yeah, she sounds really sure when she says that.

"We are not back together, though," Sera reiterates.

"Then why the hell are you both here while I am?"

"Yeah, what's the about?" Sera asks with a chuckle. "You're here with a guy, huh? Guess your boss finally got through to you. Or is he your long-lost brother?"

"That is *none* of your business. I'm the one asking questions here."

Evelyn slams one hand on the table to catch my attention. "What is there for you to know? Sera asked me to meet her so we could figure out a few of our lingering matters. Perhaps we should have mentioned that you might be one of them. Because *you're* the one causing a scene here, Kiki."

Her use of my pet name is like a breath-stealing punch to the gut.

"Should we go?" Evelyn grabs her tea and gestures to Sera, who is startled enough by her words to almost choke on her iced coffee. "We could go somewhere else to talk."

"But I thought that you..."

Evelyn throws me a calculating glare. "It's clear her anger outweighs any other feelings toward us. I doubt apologies would penetrate her ear. Why would I waste my breath? Just because I am sorry about what happened and how I made her feel? Hmph."

She stands up. Sera doesn't move from her seat. I daresay she's as shocked as I am by Evelyn's sudden change in attitude.

She's not going to try to get me back? Or tell Sera that I was way better than her? She won't pretend to use me to get back at her ex anymore? What is this about apologies and forgiveness? The Evelyn Sharpe I know doesn't leave threads hanging or words left unsaid. She may plot, conspire, and intentionally hold back her cryptic meaning, but she finishes what she starts. You were there when she first asked me out! Now I know it was part of some diabolical plan to get back at Sera and me for ruining that relationship, but Evelyn didn't half-ass it. From the moment she looked at me in her office, she made me hers.

Isn't that... what hurts the most?

"If you don't want her," Sera says beside me, "guess I'll have to figure out a way to win her back."

"What?"

"Evelyn is the greatest woman I've ever known." With a sigh, Sera slumps against the table. "No offense. You were good, too, but Evelyn is a once-in-a-lifetime woman. You've seen how passionate she is. I was a fool to ever screw that up. I'll regret it until I figure out how to win her back as my girlfriend. Possibly my wife."

I have half a mind to slap Sera right across her smug face. She's sitting there, acting like *she's* getting back with Evelyn and not me?

Silence hits me harder than any of their verbal gut punches have today. Did I say what I think I said?

....She's getting back with Evelyn and not me?

Somebody pass me a paper bag. I need something to breathe in as I parse these thoughts in my stupid, dense head!

"I can tell by the look on your face that you've thought about it too, huh?" Sera's chuckles once had the power to kick me in the teeth – and between the legs. These days? I'm lucky if memories of her laughter don't make me want to punch a hole in the wall. Because she knows what she's doing. She's goading me on as if this were her master plan all along.

Except with Sera, you can't quite ever tell. Maybe she's manipulating you into doing something you shouldn't. Or maybe she means every word she says.

"Like she would take you back," I hiss at her.

Sera shrugs. "I'll never know unless I put some real effort into it. Of course, if someone else got to her before me, I might back off. The universe would be telling me something important. Like how I don't get to be with my ex again because we have history. You know me, Kiki. I like my signs from the universe!"

"Don't call me that. You lost the right to call me that when you *humiliated* me that day."

"Oh? You didn't have a problem when Evelyn called you that."

"That's..." This whole time, my head swerves toward the doors leading back into the café. Evelyn is speaking with the manager, her casual demeanor winning over the man who is probably willing to kick me out of this place. Although he keeps looking back at me, his relaxing shoulders and the way he scratches his head suggest that he's not going to bother me unless I cause another scene.

God, do I want to create a scene! I want to paint this whole patio with my righteous, frustrated rage. These are the women who thought it would be hot to play with my heart and my body. They saw my weaknesses and insecurities and exploited them for their own sadistic gain. Look at Sera! She can hardly contain her smile behind that skinny straw. Sucking up iced coffee like she's better than me... like she didn't string me along for weeks, allowing me to think that I'm her girlfriend and not...

And not...

Evelyn.

She's going to leave. Her whole body turns toward the main entrance.

There's someone behind me. Waiting for me to return to our charade of a date. If Caleb hasn't figured out by now that I'm a crazy bitch to *not* get involved with, I don't know what to say. Maybe he's a bigger idiot than I thought.

"You gonna go get her?" Sera asks. "Or should I do it? Either way, our Evie isn't going anywhere without someone calling her girlfriend. That's a woman who is never on the market for long, but she's more loyal than I'll ever be."

"You're a monster," I snap.

"Better a monster than boring."

With her words nipping at my heels, I burst into the café and catch Evelyn as she's about to reach the parking lot.

"Evelyn!" My voice startles half the people in the café. The other half couldn't be assed with my drama. "Evie!"

She stops short of the door, fingers on the handle and intent burning behind her movements.

I'm out of breath by the time I reach her. She doesn't push me away, but boy am I aware of all the people watching us. That includes the baristas, who probably can't believe they have to deal with this shit again.

"Yes?" Evelyn asks.

She's so close again, yet I don't dare touch her. This is the woman who has tried to reach out to me multiple times this past week, yet here she is, on the verge of rejecting me right here. I barely know what to do. What to say! All I can think about is how Sera swore she would go after Evelyn herself if I didn't do it first.

This is my chance to do things my way. With *my* control exerted over the situation.

For the first time in my life, I can make something happen. I don't have to sit back and wait for someone else to act.

I'd be amazed, but I'm speechless. This is it. My big chance! Yet as Evelyn waits for me to say something, I see someone getting out of their car in the parking lot and ambling with a bag full of textbooks and their laptop. Right. It's Sunday. Other people come here besides sorry dates and besties meeting up for the first time in forever.

This is my only chance. If I don't grab it with both hands, I'm doomed to keep repeating the same mistakes for the rest of my life.

"I'm ready." I smooth out my skirt, square my shoulders, and tip up my chin. Evelyn cocks her head and looks like she doesn't know what to make of me. Meanwhile, that girl with half of her college education in her bag is getting closer to the door. "I'm ready to hear your explanation and your apology."

Although Evelyn would never expose her heart so readily in public, she allows the smallest smile to grace her makeup-less face. God. She really is beautiful, no matter how she presents herself. I so rarely saw those dark circles beneath her eyes or her naturally pale lips when we were together for four months. This is probably the most vulnerable I've ever seen her.

Such a far cry from the woman who asked me out and proceeded to seduce me in the Lighthouse Lounge.

"I'd ask you to sit with me in the corner," she says with that sardonic tone of hers, "but I thought you were already meeting with someone today."

"He can take a hint." Caleb is already wandering off with a look of *"Whatever,"* emanating from him. My only concern is this co-ed standing on the other side of the door and looking like a lost puppy who simply wants to pop inside for a few minutes. "I can't."

"Hints are what get us into trouble." Evelyn opens the door for the young woman, who thanks her as she ambles inside. "There's an empty table in the corner over there. Don't worry. The manager likes me enough to let your outburst slide."

Every question of *is this what I should be doing?* haunts me as I follow Evelyn to the table in question. Her iced tea plops onto the polished wood before she sits down, her whole body like liquid as it settles into her seat. She looks like she's ready to hear a pitch, yet I'm the one asking *her* to explain herself.

"What about Sera?" I ask before sitting down across from Evelyn.

"What about her? She belongs in that special class of 'that one acquaintance I see around sometimes.' As I said, I've forgiven her for her transgressions. That doesn't mean I've forgotten. Like dust in the wind. That's what our relationship is now."

"She was saying... well, never mind." No sense embarrassing myself any further. It's bad enough Caleb gives me an exasperated look as he finally leaves the café.

"Friend of yours?" Evelyn asks.

"That's something my boss set up."

"Oh, how helpful of him." With a delicate sigh that makes me swoon, Evelyn stirs her straw around her cup full of ice. "So. You're ready to hear my explanation of what happened and why I asked you out. Are you sure? It doesn't paint me in the best light."

"Considering how pissed I already was with you, I think I'll live."

"Right. To be honest, to start with, I've known who you were since the beginning. In fact, I wasn't the one originally assigned to Aspen Plastics' account when they came knocking. I had to pull a few strings to convince my coworkers to let me have it. Because I wanted to meet you."

"Wait. How did you know it was *me?*"

"Oh, sweetheart. I saw your bare ass loud and clear several months ago. Besides, I hired a private investigator when I suspected she had been cheating on me. He told me everything he could dig up about you. I guess you two never noticed that you were being tailed."

"I... see." How the hell else am I supposed to take that?

"Maybe I would have left well enough alone, but then I found out that Aspen Plastics was looking for new corporate insurance. I was in that sordid mental space that begged me to face you. I wasn't out to fuck you over or to punish you for your involvement. Guess you could say I was morbidly curious about you. For fuck's sake, you're not my usual type. Sera is."

My lips are dry, although not as dry as my throat. Speaking is impossible as she lays this before me.

"I seduced you knowing full-well who you were. It's why I seduced you. I wanted to know what it would be like to sleep with the other woman. See if you were really the bag of chips to end a long-term relationship."

"Well," I croak. "Was I?"

Before Evelyn can say anything, Sera slides by our table, what's left of my iced mocha in her hand. "You forgot this." She *winks* at me when she places my cup down on the table. "Go easy on her, huh? I'm the one you should be fucking up – not each other."

I don't know who she is referring to, and I don't care. I get the impression that such a thing was a message to both Evelyn and me.

Evelyn rubs her forehead until Sera has vacated the café. "Even after everything she's done," she says, "it still kills me when she's so suave like that."

"How do you think I felt in that bar?" I grab my mocha and hide behind my cup so Evelyn won't see my flushed cheeks. "There's a reason I didn't say no to her, and it's not like I knew she was seeing somebody else already."

I hate – and love – that Evelyn smiles when I say that. We have camaraderie, you know. We've both suffered through a relationship with a woman who didn't respect us. Not as much as she should have, anyway. The fact she was such a player will define how Evelyn and I look at each other for the rest of our lives.

"Yes."

Slowly, I lower my cup. "Huh?"

"Yes," Evelyn repeats. "You were a bag of chips and a half. That's why I couldn't resist you at Luigi's." She chuckles, but it's nothing like Sera's manipulative snicker. "So appropriate to compare it to eating chips. You can never stop at one. The taste, texture, and experience keep sucking you in for more."

"Are you seriously comparing me to a can of Pringles?"

"To be fair, once you popped that first time in bed." Evelyn's wink is almost as devastating as Sera's. Did they learn from one another, or did one encourage the other to be this fucking suave? "I couldn't stop."

I hate how hot that is!

"Y... you could have told me at any time," I stutter in a terrible ploy to change the subject. "The moment you decided to go out with me would have been a perfect time. For fuck's sake, Evie, you played me too! All that shit I told you about Sera, *my* ex, and how she humiliated me..." This is the crux of it, isn't it? I can't believe I told her some of the shit I did! How much of it did she use against me? To get at me? "I know it couldn't have been easy, but it was the right thing to do. You should have come clean and given me the choice. But you took that choice away from me, Evie. That's why I'm still so pissed about the whole thing. I was endlessly vulnerable, but you? You shelled yourself up and played the mysterious, sexy girlfriend. I thought I couldn't see your place because you were somehow ashamed of it or because you were *cautious* after your own breakup. You know what? I feel so stupid for not putting two and two together. I should have known. Your cagey answers and the timing of it all... the only reason I didn't allow myself to see the truth is because I was falling in love with you. You were like this dreamy goddess who came into my life at the perfect time. I was so deep in my own self-pity and misery that I couldn't believe someone like you wanted *me*. I had always been a plaything before you. Or that's how it felt. For the first time in my life, I thought I had found someone I could actually fall in love with. Even if it didn't last forever, at least I had *that*. It felt like starting over. Now I know where it all went wrong."

That gets Evelyn's full attention. "Oh?"

"Yes. Once again, I had put it all on the shoulders of the universe. Instead of putting myself out there, bettering myself, or at the very least vetting the person I was dating, I was... lazy!" My God, this is like an epiphany right here. How have I never realized it before? Did it really take watching Sera hit on Evelyn for me to realize that my problem wasn't so much *Evelyn* and what she did, but how I allowed it to happen? Again? Twice in the same year?

"You okay?" Evelyn asks. "You look like you've swallowed a spider."

"Tell me that those nice moments we had were real. Because I don't believe for two seconds that they were ever real with Sera, but I think they might have been with you." I squeeze my eyes shut, refusing to watch Evelyn's reaction. "Don't lie to me, either. I just want to know. Was what we had ever real?"

Evelyn takes a long time to answer. I hope it's because she wants to tell the truth and simply doesn't know how.

CHAPTER 28

Evelyn

"**Y**es."

The most heartbreaking thing? Not the way Keira stiffens when I say that word, but the breath of relief easing those pursed lips. It's the answer she wants to hear, but I don't blame her for disbelieving me.

"The only reason I kept going out with you, despite what you might believe," I continue, "is because I liked you. I adored being with you. Like you, I was distraught about my breakup with Sera. Yet the thing you have to understand is that she was *my* girlfriend for seven years, *and* she cheated on me. I didn't find out until that day I came home early and saw you two in *my* bedroom. It was traumatizing, to say the least. Every decision I made after that was a mix of super logical and highly emotional. She had betrayed me, so she had to go. I didn't care about her excuses or her apologies. She begged me to take her back more than once, but every time I showed a bit of a spine, she showed me her true colors. Even today, I saw a lot of that in her. She'll never be mine again, and I sure as hell won't be hers. I don't doubt that what you went through with her was traumatizing in its own right, but count yourself lucky that you didn't spend another day with her. She would have grown tired of you, too, and done the same thing to someone else. At least now it's none of our business."

Keira twiddles her thumbs. "You mean that?"

"What? All of it? Yes. I kept going out with you and spending the night with you because, against my best interests, I liked it. Hell, the only reason I told you the truth eventually was because, like you, I was falling in love. It sounds crazy, and you and I have no business being together, but I was falling in love with you, Keira. I swear it."

"You *really* mean that?" She cuts me off before I can answer. "No. I suppose no matter how many times I ask that you'll keep saying the same thing."

"I'm so sorry for hurting you and dragging you through my mud. I asked you out intending to use you, it's true, but it was only supposed to be one night. I was supposed to satisfy my curiosity and say goodbye to both you and Sera forever. I didn't care if our ex never found out about it."

No way to tell if she believes me or not. If I were her, would I believe me? Probably not. This is *me* we're talking about here. I'm about as believable as a vampire promising to not sink her fangs into your throat. At some point, I have to feed. No matter what I might mean right now, I may change my mind later.

Keira has every right to throw her drink in my face and walk away. I wouldn't hold it against her. I'd move on from it like I try to move on from everything else.

"You were falling in love with me," she repeats back to me. "That's why you led me to the truth. By inviting me to your apartment and assuming I'd recognize it?"

"I should have been forthright. Not only from the beginning but then, too. Back then, though, I was in too deep with you. I didn't want to lose you as my girlfriend, but I knew that's probably what would happen. So instead of telling you the damned truth, I passive-aggressively allowed your own mind to reveal everything. I was a coward. Because of that, I hurt you. I'm so sorry."

These apologies are coming around full circle, aren't they? First, Sera apologizes to me. Then I pour my sorrow out to Keira, who may or may not accept it. Then again, Sera had no idea if I would accept her apology. That's the whimsy of the cosmos, isn't it? We never know what's really going to happen. Some might say that's the true thrill of life. Me? I relate to Keira so much. I, too, need to have control over the few things that remain in my purview. Where we differ is that I've never had much trouble exerting control over my life and situations. She does.

I took all knowledge, and therefore her control, away from our relationship. The ball was always in my court. No matter how many points she scored, the refs were in my pocket and the whole thing was a sham, anyway.

She would have never won. If you really think about it, though, I wouldn't have, either. We were both doomed to fail from the moment I set my sights on her.

Yet I won't lie to myself. That first sight of her? Destroyed me in ways I could not have anticipated.

"So, this is where we are now." I lay my hands palm up on the table. "I don't expect you to trust me. You have no reason to. There were many things I didn't lie about when we were together, but I lied about one thing that was so big you..."

"Take me home with you."

Her words catch me off guard. "Huh?" That's it. My brilliant response.

When Keira is confident, you realize how she's been faking it all along. Anyone can posture like a peacock. It takes real poise to embrace the circumstances around you and still voice what you *really* feel inside.

"I want to go home with you, Evie." Keira drains the last of her drink without breaking eye contact with me. "To your apartment. I want to see it. With my own two eyes and the knowledge that nothing terrible will happen to me for it."

I still don't quite believe what she's saying. Yet as my tongue tosses in my mouth and excitement welcomes itself to my heart, I grin so broadly she must think that I've assumed we're getting back together, all the crap left behind us.

Except I'm not as big of an idiot as I may purport myself to be at times. I know this isn't about me as much as it is about her.

She's taking back control by asking to go to the scene of every crime she's suffered this past year. Believe it or not, I love her all the more for it.

"This is..." Keira stops before a black and white photograph I purchased from an artist many years ago. "All your taste, is it?"

I lean against my kitchen counter, a much-needed glass of wine in my hand. "That's one of my favorite prints. Bought it in Tucson when I traveled through for business. I only had half a day off to play tourist and it was 110 degrees outside. Spent the whole time wandering into air-conditioned galleries until I found this Navajo woman who photographs everyday life on and off the reservation. We bonded when I told her some of my grandmother's stories. Showed me this picture of an elderly woman sitting on her stoop and it reminded me so much of a woman I scarcely knew that I had to have it."

I don't know why I've treated those words like wine spilling from my glass. For all I know, none of them land where they belong. I'll have to clean them up later.

"You have good taste," Keira says. "So, I'm guessing nothing left here is Sera's."

"She didn't have much up on the walls to begin with. I take that back. I let her decorate the guest room, much to my own chagrin. Sera's idea of hot décor was a hodgepodge of music posters and that kitschy shit you find in the bargain bin at the stores. You know, *Live, Laugh, Chardonnay?* She claimed she *ironically* liked them. Sad thing was, I believed her, but I doubted any of my guests did. They definitely thought that was my touch."

"You don't strike me as the type to cover your home in kitsch."

"Not at all. Those were the first things to go when I kicked her out. Can't say I've replaced any of the art in the guest room, though. Not that I've had anyone come to visit since then. Breaking up with her made me realize that most of my social life centered around her friends and our mutuals. Since she's the more charismatic one, she got most of the friends in the breakup. I've got Raquel, though. That's good enough for me right now."

Keira nods. "You have a fantastic view, too." She approaches my living room windows. "You own this place?"

"Yes. I bought it with Sera when we moved in together... oh, must be about six years ago now. Since it was in my name and I basically paid for it, though, it was a no-brainer that I got to keep it after the breakup."

"Back in the café, you said that you had traded in your car. Was it the white BMW that Sera used to..."

I don't blame her for not finishing that sentence. "Yes. That was my car, for the record. She'd use it while I was at work since I often walk. Of course, I knew she used it so I never questioned why the gas was gone or the added mileage, but I had no idea she was doing... well, you... in the backseat."

Keira slumps against the back of my couch. "You traded it in so I wouldn't recognize it."

"A bit harder to trade in my whole condo. My friend Raquel highly discouraged it. The market is shit for condos right now."

"Did she know about me?"

"Who you really were? No. I never divulged that to anyone, you have my word. Sera is the only one who knows now, and she's the only one that 'needs' to know. I'm not going to tell Raquel."

Keira hovers near me but refuses to close the infuriating gap that we've both created. "I have trouble figuring out what was real and what was a concoction for your game."

"I didn't play any game with you, darling." I have a feeling that I could say this a hundred times and she still won't believe me. Not that I blame her. She's been through a lot. Both by my hand and Sera's.

I'm not sure who I resent the most. Myself? Or my ex who brought this down upon both of us? Whether I forgive Sera doesn't matter in the grand scheme of the world. She still did what she did, and here I am, struggling to keep it together.

"If I were the other woman," Keira muses, "then what were you?"

"The jilted ex who didn't know what she really wanted." I put the bottle of wine back on its shelf. Instead, I fire up the coffee pot. Out of everything I could drink in this place, caffeine sounds like what I really need right now. "I thought I wanted petty revenge, or to sate my curiosity. Turns out, what I *really* wanted was... someone. Someone like you."

"You didn't know me before that day, though."

"No, and I didn't know what you were really like until we started dating. But I liked what I saw and heard. You reminded me of the type of person I actually need in my life. Someone loyal, honest, and kind. The sex was a big bonus."

While I fiddle with the coffee pot, Keira rounds the island counter and clutches her hands in trepidation. "You were everything I wanted from someone, too. You were so strong and confidant, but without making me feel like a weak idiot next to you. You lifted me up. Unlike Sera, who sometimes felt like she was about to punch down on me at any moment."

"She can have that effect on people, yes." I'll leave it at that. I've already talked to a therapist about some of the bigger red flags in my relationship with my ex. Even if she hadn't cheated on me, the odds that we would be together more than a few years were slim to none – and that was with love on the table.

"I loved you for that," Keira whispers, "and I loved how natural that relationship felt. I just don't know how we could ever get that back."

"Does it have to be exactly like that? You know more about me now than most people in my life. Knowing those things about me would have always changed things. Didn't matter if Sera was a common denominator between us. There is... a lot I keep hidden under the surface. My whole life has been building up a character who gets what she wants and isn't bothered by criticism. It works well in my career. Not so much in my relationship. I daresay I was more open with you than I ever was with our ex."

"Is that supposed to convince me to be with you?"

"Oh, honey," I snort. Behind me, the coffee maker comes to life. "I'm not trying to convince you of anything. That's all up to you. What do you want?"

"What do *I* want?"

"Yes. What do you want, Keira?"

You should see the look on her face. This is a woman who has seldom been asked what she *wants*. Maybe someone has asked her about her needs. Maybe, somewhere out there, someone has entertained her fleeting fantasies for a mere night. Except they've never asked her to express her innermost desires. Nobody has ever asked Keira Lawson to gaze deep into her own soul and extrapolate her own fate.

"I want..." Although I wish her voice were stronger with conviction, I'll take whatever words pass those kissable lips. "I want you, Evie."

Those are the words I longed to hear but didn't believe for two seconds I deserved. Somewhere behind me the coffee is brewing and somewhere before me the sun is glinting through my windows, but none of it matters. All I see and hear is this woman standing before me, with her hopeful countenance and a thirst to prove to me that there is some hope in this world, after all.

"Want and need are such different things." I hold myself back. As much as I want to go to her, to kiss her, and to put everything behind us, how can I assert such things when I'm the source of our mutual misery? "Just because you want me, doesn't mean you need me."

Keira leaps the length between us. She's so close that I could run my fingers through her hair and nuzzle my nose into the depths of her perfume. "You don't truly know what I want and need yet. Because I haven't told you."

"You just said that you want me."

"Yes, and as far as I'm concerned, it means I need you, too."

She takes my hand. My feet are frozen to this spot. All of this has to be her doing. That's the only way I'll know that this is what *she* desires, and I haven't once again exerted my influence over her.

Although I want to. God knows that if it were up to me, my arms would be locked around Keira, protecting her from all the heartbreak in the world.

"You've hurt me, but... I can forgive that, Evie. You have shown your forgiveness to someone who hurt you so much, and I can do the same. The only difference is that I think you're redeemable. I think *this* is redeemable."

I don't ask what she means by that. All I do is allow my arms to fall around her, holding her close as she embraces me with all the strength in her body.

"You're not a bad person." Her arms tighten around my body. Finally, I give in, digging my face deep into the nape of her neck and swaying where I stand. "Nor am I weak."

I don't believe any of this is happening until Keira pulls back her head and kisses me.

Her forgiveness feels like a hundred pounds lifted off my chest. Her love? That's more than enough warm, unrefuted weight on my heart.

For the first time in my life, I finally feel like I'm moving on – into being a better person, and into truly being myself.

CHAPTER 29

Keira

I am a fool. There is no denying it now, as I follow Evelyn into the bedroom and cast aside all of my aspersions to be with her once again.

In this place. In *this* bed.

I am a fool, because it could mean the end of my sanity. To misjudge or misstep at this point in my life could absolutely kill me. I don't know if I could take another cataclysmic heartbreak like the one Evelyn served me a week ago.

Yet I can't deny the burning fury within me. No, it's not anger. Nor is it righteous harmony creeping through my body. It's fury for Evelyn. The woman who both stole my heart and taught me, once and for all, what it would mean to take complete control of my life.

She didn't beg for me to forgive her. She didn't silence me with a kiss that forever buried my precious words. The chasm between us remained wide because of her – yet she stood on the other side, waiting for me to jump.

It had to be my decision. If I am a fool, then so be it. A fool I am.

Better to be a happy fool than a loveless wise woman.

You'd think there would be tears in my eyes the moment Evelyn brings me into the bedroom – at my request, no less. No tears, though. I know where I am, and I know what happened the last time I was in here. I'm not surprised that she's shocked at my adamant desires, but please trust me, Evelyn. I know what I'm doing. I chose to be here.

I *need* to be here. I must put everything that happened seven months ago behind me. I won't bury the memories, but I'll learn from them. With your help, Evie, I'll be stronger than I ever was before. I'll have the courage and the experience to face my discomforts head-on. No delay. No hesitation. No regrets!

This isn't the room you once shared with Sera for several years. Nor is this the place she brought me, only for the most humiliating moment to commence when you came home a few hours early, Evie. This is just a room. Just a bed.

Just two women falling into love all over again.

Maybe we can do it quickly this time. Give it our all and never forget the feelings that brought us together. *All* of the feelings, from unsavory anger and guilt to heart-pumping excitement and lust. You say that you never meant to go on more than one date with me. That I was meant to be a one-night stand to sate your curiosity. What if I told you, Evie, that I felt the same way about you? You were that enigma that swept into my life when I was down. You made me feel like a billion bucks with your come-ons and endless thirst for my body. Remember that night in the historic hotel? I didn't know a woman could *do* me like that. Remember that night on your friend's yacht? I had never been so free, so vulnerable to the elements. I felt like one of our ancient ancestors, stealing a moment with her lover away from the others so we could pay homage to the gods with the bodies they gave us. There wasn't a night in bed or an afternoon in the world where we didn't make the most of our time. Your laughter had to be genuine. The way you looked at me as if you both undressed me and revered me for who I am... I'll never forget it. You best believe I want you to look at me like that every day for the rest of our lives.

This will be forever, right? Maybe not in this room. But, somewhere. You and I, learning each other's quirks and getting upset when one isn't pulling their weight with the chores. Feeling the thrill of seeing the world together and crying in the airport because we're stressed and running late. Touring a house that we might call our own one day, but we can't agree on if a south-facing garden is more important than a well-lit home office for you. Will I drag you to a concert that only reminds you of Sera? Will you take me to dinner with your stuffy older friends whom I have nothing in common with?

I want to know. I want the boring, the frustrating, and the unbelievably unsexy. I want to be doubled over with menstrual cramps while you make me soup and draw me a hot bath. I want you sick with the flu while I nurse you in bed and call your work to inform them you won't be coming in for the next few days. Every time there's a birthday or vacation worthy of documenting on social media, there will be those hard nights where our respective existential crises will get the better of us. Acquaintances will think we have the perfect relationship while our closest friends will know that we work as hard as they do to stay in love. I believe this is true because it's what I've always wanted. Deep down, I've forever known that what I really need in life is someone who can be as ugly with me as they are beautiful. I'm not talking about toxic love, either. I'm talking about the real shit. The crying on the floor and mourning our mothers kind of real. Emotion – passion, really – isn't about what we do in bed or how we declare love in public. It's those moments where you show me your glorious humanity, Evie. You have made mistakes. Maybe one day I'll decide there is one mistake too many, but for now?

I look into your wide, clear eyes and see our eternity.

That's why I'm not afraid to make love to you in this bed. As you strip away my clothes, I bare myself to you. As I kiss your lips and hear you sigh, you show me your sweetest side. You're worried, too, I can tell. You don't know how this can be sane. Here we are, at the scene of the crime. The worst day of our lives. Yet don't you see, Evie? We can take it back. We can take back the power that was ripped from us. There's no one here to tell us to stop. It's just us. You. Me. The energy coursing between us.

Isn't it what you've always wanted, too?

I know we've made incredible love before, but there's something about *today* that really spins me out into the universe. Maybe it's the delicate way Evelyn covers my body in kisses, as if every touch of her lips is another careful apology. When she holds me close, one leg between mine and our bodies doing their natural work, I swear that's her breath whispering, *"I've never felt so free before."*

She doesn't have to hide who she is from me anymore. I've seen her at her worst. It hurt, but I recovered. Moving on with the truth no longer lurking in the shadows changes everything.

We are one. Two separate beings who share one love.

I am a fool. A blissful fool.

"Do you know how long I've wanted you here?" Evelyn caresses the bridge of my nose with one gentle finger. "From the moment I saw you, I wanted to bring you home and eradicate all the bad energy in this place. The only reason I didn't was because…"

"Don't bring it up," I say. "That's in the past. We don't have to think about it tonight."

"Except I think about it every night. Even after you stopped taking my calls or responding to my texts, I thought about having you in this very spot. I still amaze myself. I fell in love with the woman my ex cheated with. I did it knowing that it could ruin everything I knew about myself. Yet here we are."

"Yeah. Here we are."

We can stay here forever for all I care. Gazing upon Evelyn's sweaty face and the way her hair plasters against her cheeks is like looking into a mirror. I know I don't look much better than her. Yet I know how beautiful she is, and that's all that matters.

Her. Me. The other woman.

That's me. That's her. That's no one that matters anymore. We are no longer the other. We're two women who happened to find love with one another.

The past will always be there, but the future is what waits for us.

Six Months Later Evelyn

This winter has been uncharacteristically dry and warm. For the first time that I can remember, there was no snow on Christmas, not even at the lodge Keira and I returned to after enjoying it so much last year. I'm sure global warming is the culprit – isn't it always? Yet I selfishly enjoy these cold but sunny days that welcome the new year. Nothing like the sunshine kissing the same skin that is windburned alive. No matter how much I hide in my scarf, I can't beat back the chapped lips that plague me as I get out of my car and huff it down the sidewalk. At least it's not covered in ice, I guess.

Beyond the naked maple trees is a two-story house that I've had my eye on for the past few months. Recently, the price has come down another hundred grand, and when I balance the current value of my condo with what I could swing at the bank, I think I can do it. Helps that the place is move-in ready, with a new roof and pipes in the wall. Sure, the wallpaper in the living room is heinous and I'd rather die than bathe in a bright red bathroom, but those superfluous updates can come when I've nailed another account at work and next year's bonus rivals the one I received. Raquel has informed me that making an offer, closing, and actually moving into this house could take weeks or months, anyway. I've got time to go over my finances.

What I don't have time for, though, is to lollygag out on the sidewalk when I see Raquel standing on the porch with my deliriously adorable girlfriend.

Seriously, what gives Keira the right to be so grabbable and squeezable in her fat winter coat and heavy scarf? Those boots are fuzzy enough to require a damn yak to make. When she heads toward the front door, it's with a penguin-like waddle that makes me want to paw at my own cheeks and groan because I can't handle how cute she is. During these cold winter months that require a few more layers, she is actually more likely to wear her long red hair up in a loose bun that allows more room around her neck. Today's clasp is a giant snowflake that contrasts brilliantly with hair that hasn't properly seen the sun in days.

Raquel sees me right before they go inside. "Hey!" She flags me down as I hustle up the cobbled walkway. Around me are plants that will either return in the spring or need to be uprooted by a competent gardener. Keira tells me she loves plants and isn't too bad at keeping them alive, but she's already lamented that this is a western-facing house and there may not be enough sunlight for the flowers she fancies. Except I can tell from the way she happily waddles inside that she likes it already. Puts an extra pep in my step as I jog up the stairs and hug Raquel on the covered porch.

"Sorry I'm late. Took me forever to find a place to park on the street." I place a kiss on my girlfriend's cheek. "Did I miss the tour?"

"We were about to start without you." Raquel opens the door wide for Keira and me to enter together. Although this is my fourth time touring this house, it's Keira's first, and her squeal of excitement echoes across the original wood floors and into the living room built-ins. "Keep in mind that this is about as much lighting as this house gets. Most of your sunlight will come in the late afternoon and evening. The exception being the master bedroom, which is on the top floor in the back. Hope you like waking up to the sun and going to bed with it cooking in your kitchen."

"Works for me." I squeeze the bottom post attached to the staircase leading up to the second floor. "I come home in the evenings. Would be nice to see some sun in the summer months." Of course, it's already nearing sunset now in the middle of a wintery afternoon, so the first thing I saw when I walked in was the sun strewn across the living room floor. It's quaint. What I really care about, though, is if Keira likes it. "What do you think of this kitchen, Kiki?"

The next hour is a whirlwind. Not only for her, but for me, too. For the first time since I dumped Sera, I'm considering buying a home with my current girlfriend. This decision didn't come lightly, though. I mean, I had to move. That's all there was to it. Even after we rekindled our love sixteen months ago, Keira still didn't come by my condo all that often. She sure as hell did not want to move in there when we talked about taking things to the next stage. Honestly, we would have moved in together a year ago except the market still wasn't right for selling my condo. Instead of buying another, I figured I was at a point in my life where it was time to move into an actual house.

Me. Buying a house. That's how you know it's love.

Keira and I have spent many dates and nights in bed discussing what we want for the future. Me, I'm quickly heading toward forty. It'll be here before I know it. She's in her thirties now, too, so it's natural for us to think about a more permanent situation. Do we want kids? How about her future job, since she's finally talking about switching careers? Keira claims this is the longest relationship she's ever been in, and I believe it, but it's also been so natural. Nothing hangs between us any longer. She's seen every ugly skeleton in my closet, and I've seen her at her most insecure. When she says she wants to move in together before talking about kids, I'm inclined to agree. One step at a time. It's treated us well so far.

Still, am I crazy for thinking she'd make a terrific housewife in this place? If that's what she wants, of course. Maybe in a year or two. The extra income would be great for paying some bills around here. This is assuming, of course, we go for it. There are no guarantees that my offer will be accepted since Raquel has convinced me to come in at twenty under asking. We've got time on the market on our side, but other offers have been rejected before.

"You thinking of going for it?" Raquel asks me while we look at the master bathroom one last time. Keira is in the walk-in closet, doubtlessly sizing up how many of her clothes she could fit in there. "You've already had two offers on your condo. Depending on if anyone goes over, you might only be out fifty grand to the bank. Your credit is great and, well..." She glances at Keira, who stands before the window in the master bedroom and scrutinizes the neighbor's fence. "You've already got someone to fill it with some smiles."

"It's what we've been needing for our relationship. I can't bring another woman into that condo." Raquel still doesn't know the truth about Keira, although I think she's suspected some things here and there. She's a smart, perceptive woman, after all. Yet as long as she doesn't know the whole truth, she won't say a damn thing. I intend to keep it that way – for Keira's sake. "Too many bad memories. Too much bad energy."

"I totally understand. As we've already discussed, I don't think you're going to find a better deal for what you're looking for and this close to your place of work. Hope you're okay with commuting in your car in nice weather too. You can't walk to your office from here."

"You'll be happy to know that I've negotiated some work from home hours with my boss. I mean, we're only talking once or twice a week, but it will be huge. That's why the home office is so important."

"Downstairs, too. So you won't be tempted to, ah, take a nap in your bed when she's around." Raquel jerks her thumb at Keira, who is none the wiser as she gestures to where she wants to put her dresser. "I think she's already mentally moved in. Shall I go ahead and hire a contractor for the sex bench and hammock?"

"You're soooo funny." Can I roll my eyes any harder?

Eventually, we step outside into the yard, where Keira gets an idea of how much sun will shine on her future rose bushes. While she babbles about hybrids and fertilizer, I gaze toward the downtown core that looms in the distance. It's true that I'll be looking at a decent commute some days. Certainly, that will be a sacrifice I make to move into the nearest 'burbs with my new beloved. Yet there's a reason I've looked at this house four times now and suggested that Keira see it for herself. I think it's the one.

Knowing that she will be here almost every day, pruning her roses and cooking that world-famous stew that slays my tastebuds every time, will be more than worth it.

It will be nice having someone to come home to again.

That's what I want this to be, you know. A home. A place where I can rest my head and giggle in the kitchen while drinking my wine of the week. Somewhere with a crackling fire in the winter and fruit punch on the deck in the summer. I want rose bushes in my yard and quiet walks to the corner restaurant where the loudest patron is some person's baby instead of a soused office worker. God, I really am growing old!

"You know that if this takes a while to go through, you'll be putting most of your stuff into storage and sleeping in my condo every night."

That's what I tell Keira when we're left alone on the porch. Her heart eyes for this house slightly lower. "That's fine. I need to get rid of most of that stuff, anyway, but it's still better than signing a shitty month-to-month lease on my current place. I wanna get out of there and live with you, babe. It's time. Besides! I can handle sleeping at your place if it's only temporary."

"Nothing about us is temporary."

That adds a touch of color to her cheeks. "You always sound so sure of everything."

"Because I am. That's what makes me Evelyn Sharpe."

I mean it, too. Like I mean it when I tell her I love her and she is so effing adorable in this wintery outfit that I could roll her across the floor and smother her with kisses.

Instead, we go down to the corner restaurant to test out date night in the neighborhood. It's a perfect end to a perfect day. And, hopefully, the new chapter in our life together.

God, I love her. I love the woman who single-handedly wrecked my world. When she laughs like this, with her mouth wide open and her voice singing above the mediocre music, I wonder how I've never met her before. I think of all the years I wasted with other people.

Maybe it was meant to be. Maybe she was never the other woman. Maybe Keira was the one the universe sent to right everything in our lives.

There could never be another woman, anyway. She's as perfect as imperfection gets.

About the Author

Hildred Billings is a Japanese and Religious Studies graduate who has spent her entire life knowing she would write for a living someday. She has lived in Japan a total of three times in three different locations, from the heights of the Japanese alps to the hectic Tokyo suburbs, with a life in Shikoku somewhere in there too. When she's not writing, however, she spends most of her time talking about Asian pop music, cats, and bad 80's fantasy movies with anyone who will listen...or not.

Her writing centers around themes of redemption, sexuality, and death, sometimes all at once. Although she enjoys writing in the genre of fantasy the most, she strives to show as much reality as possible through her characters and situations, since she's a furious realist herself.

Currently, Hildred lives in Oregon with her girlfriend, with dreams of maybe having a cat around someday.

Connect with Hildred on any of the following:

Website: http://www.hildred-billings.com

Twitter: http://twitter.com/hildred

Facebook: http://facebook.com/authorhildredbillings

Printed in Great Britain
by Amazon

36980568R10142